Banner's Bounty

Banner's Series Book Four

Carole Ann Lee

Published by Rogue Phoenix Press, LLP

ISBN: 978-1-62420-763-1

Editor: Sherry Derr-Wille

Dedication

To Rod, my very own gentle warrior. Thank you for all of your support and patience. I love you, simply for being YOU.

In Memory of Vicki Adolf

Who, many years ago, helped me with the plot for this story

Acknowledgements

Holly Smith

My best and dearest friend. Thank you for always, always being there whenever I've needed you, and once again...thank you for knowing when I could do better, and not letting me get by with less.

William C. Dietz

One of the finest authors in the science fiction genre. Thank you, Bill, for helping me to know what a spaceport might smell like, and especially for Sam McCade (the very inspiration for Nick Banner and the entire Banner Series).

PROLOGUE

Nine-year-old Jenelle Byers pressed her face against the viewport and stared out into the star-studded blackness beyond. How many days, she wondered, before they'd reach home?

It was then that suddenly, the enormous bow of a foreign freighter drifted up from beneath the porthole of their commercial passenger liner. Gradually it began sidling up next to their ship to completely fill the view with its fearsome mass.

"Look!" Jenelle cried; her eyes wide with excitement as she turned to her parents. "Papa said I might see another ship along the way."

Just then, an odd vibration traversed their ship, sending Thomas Byers to his feet and rushing to the viewport. "Jenny honey, I want you to go back and sit with Momma."

"Why, Papa?"

"Please," he said, as a second tremor vibrated through their ship, this one not so subtle.

A third tremor hit, and this time came the sound of klaxons screaming out their warning throughout the ship.

Byers turned away from the viewport and faced his wife. "I fear that vessel is not friendly, Karissa," he whispered. "Unless I miss my guess, we're under attack."

Karissa reached for her daughter, drawing her into the circle of her arms. Tom, this is a commercial liner. What would they want with a passenger ship?"

"I don't know, but that's an Adenian symbol flaunted on their starboard side. Maybe they're after something we're carrying in the hold. Who knows?"

Klaxons continued pulsing. Sounds drifted inside their cabin—staff members barking orders, pounding footfalls rushing down the passageway. Someone beat on their door and shouted, "Pirates. Stay inside and secure the locks."

Tom rushed to double check the lock, then turned to his wife and daughter. "I need the two of you to get down and hide beneath the bunk."

"Tom..."

"Honey, we haven't got the time to explain. Please. I doubt that lock's going to hold anyone back for long, and I want you two hidden."

He turned to Jenelle and patted her arm, "Don't you worry, sweetie. Everything's going to be all right," he said as he watched his wife and daughter scoot beneath the oversized bunk.

At last, he slid a travel pack—the one with Jenelle's dolls and playthings, under the bunk directly in front of her terrified face. "Shhh..." he whispered, placing a finger to his mouth. "Remember, stay hidden. Not one peep. Okay?"

When she nodded, he straightened, then silently sat down on the edge of the bunk above them, positioning his legs and feet in such a way as to add even more concealment.

Karissa pressed Jenelle's head against her shoulder, and there they quietly remained hidden. Time passed, klaxons pulsed, men shouted, above all the madness and pandemonium, computer-generated emergency warnings echoed throughout the ship.

"Momma, I'm scared," Jenelle, whispered.

"I know, darling. Shhh, let's just stay quiet and hidden as Papa asked. You'll be okay."

With her father sitting above them, his legs hiding their whereabouts, Jenelle heard her mother quietly issuing a breathy prayer for their protection.

It wasn't long before their locked entry crashed open. Peering through a small opening between her father's legs, Jenelle watched in absolute terror as three badmen surged inside brandishing weapons and issuing curt orders in a language she didn't understand.

Suddenly, her father was knocked to the floor, where he lay unconscious. Stifling a cry, Jenelle continued watching in open-mouthed horror as the men began ransacking their cabin, grabbing travel packs, rifling through them, taking what they wanted. When they reached for

Jenelle's pack—the one with her toys that her father stashed in front of her—she couldn't help crying out and made a grab for it. Although she hung-on for dear life, it was a pitiful tug-o'war that ended up wrenching Jenelle from her mother's arms and dragging her out into the open. Releasing her, the pirate stood there for a moment, studying her through narrowed eyes before uttering something in a menacing tone.

She tried ducking out of his reach, but he caught hold of her with one rough hand and shoved her screaming and kicking into the rough hands of yet another pirate waiting in the corridor. With Jenelle slung over his shoulder, they passed a man lying silent on the floor, blood oozing from the side of his head.

"Jenelle!" She heard her mother frantically call while her captor single-mindedly made his way down the passage.

Two more men lay unmoving in their path as she was carried through yet another access leading into the ship's hold. From there she was transported through a tube-like tunnel that coupled the two ships. She tried biting the hand that held her in place, but it did little good. Through tears, she watched over the man's shoulder as more bad men followed them, herding a few captives, hauling containers, and shouldering crates of valuables through the tunnel and onto their own ship. The men were moving fast and before long the airlock was secured and a grinding sound of the connecting tunnel was heard being retracted.

"Momma..."

CHAPTER ONE

The Starcruiser
Port Ireland, Terra Four

His face impassive, Marc Banner leaned negligently back in his chair and regarded the cards in his hand. Three moons, two blue planets, one silver comet and a black star. BOUNTY, it was one game he was generally lucky at, and tonight Lady Luck was smiling on him. Laying his cards face down on the table, he tossed ten credits into the pot, and calmly glanced about while waiting for the others to decide what they were doing.

As always, the Starcruiser was noisy and crowded. Blue-gray tobacco smoke hung heavy in the air, rank with the smell of spilled beer and whiskey. Laughter and loud voices mingled with musicians playing strange music with even stranger instruments. Barmaids drifted between tables, taking orders, and serving drinks—basically, it was no different than any other port dive.

With lazy regard Marc returned his attention to the game and the three men sharing the table with him. Chad Brown sat to his right—a tall, lanky man in his mid-forties. Brown was a freelance cargo pilot just in off a six-month run and anxious for a little R & R. Marc also knew Sam Williams who sat directly across from him. In his late fifties, gray-haired and stocky, Sam was the general manager at Port Ireland's spaceport headquarters. Marc didn't know the other man, Mike Baker.

As if trying to see beyond Marc's laid-back manner, Baker regarded him through narrowed eyes before tossing his credits into the pot.

"Don't see much of your brothers or Zeke anymore," Williams

said as he tossed his credits into the pot and arranged the cards in his hand. "How are they doing anyhow?"

"They're doing good. Busy." Marc replied without looking up.

Chad Brown studied his cards, laid one down, then drew another from the deck. "Yeah, married life can sure make a man out of a boy really quick," Brown remarked with a hoarse laugh. "For a while there, I was beginning to think Nick wouldn't find anyone who could tame him, yet he was the first one to get married, wasn't he?"

Ten minutes passed with cards being drawn and discarded as the men shared small talk and laughter. All the while, Marc's hand was looking better and better.

"Okay Banner, let's see whatcha got," Baker said when the game finally ended.

One by one, Marc slowly turned his cards over.

With a muttered oath, Baker tossed his losing hand down and signaled for another drink.

Oh yeah, Lady Luck was smiling on him and having raked in his winnings, Marc sat back while Williams dealt out a fresh hand. His combined spoils, so far, put him at about two hundred credits ahead of when he first arrived.

He was just picking up his newly dealt cards, when an odd chill chased down his spine. He was being watched. He could feel it. With that awareness, he calmly pushed back his chair, lowered his hand to his holstered weapon, and casually glanced around. The place was swarming with people. It was next to impossible to tell who specifically was watching him, but someone was. That much, he was sure.

At last, his focus fell upon a man standing at the bar, and their sights locked. In the space of a heartbeat, Marc sized him up. Middle aged. Wealthy and dressed impeccably. No weapon to speak of. Not to say that he didn't have something hidden beneath his coat. All in all, the man didn't look to be a serious threat. In truth, he looked uncomfortable and completely out of place in a joint like the Starcruiser.

Suddenly, the man pushed away from the bar and began working his way through the crowded tables toward Marc.

"Banner? You in, or what?" Williams asked.

Returning his attention to the table and game at hand, Marc looked down at his cards and flipped ten credits into the pot. "I'm in."

"We were beginning to wonder," Williams added. "It's your turn."

"Excuse me." By now, the stranger was standing politely off to the side behind Marc. "I'm looking for Mister Marc Banner?"

Silence.

Again, Marc wondered what a man of obvious wealth and social standing was doing in a place like the Starcruiser—looking for him, nonetheless.

The man spoke again. "By chance, are you Mister Marc Banner?"

"Maybe," Marc responded without taking his eyes off his cards. "Who wants to know?"

"My name is Thomas Byers, and I would appreciate it very much if I could have a few minutes of your time."

"I'm busy right now."

Drawing another card from the deck, Marc carefully arranged it in his hand.

"Yes, I can see that," the man said respectfully.

He then reached into his pocket and withdrew seven gold coins and set them down one by one on the table before Marc. "Would this, by any chance, make it worth a small bit of your time?"

The table fell silent as Marc, without moving a muscle, lowered his gaze and calmly studied the coins. Together they amounted to well over a thousand credits.

Williams released a breathy whistle. "I'd be happy to give you a few minutes of my time, mister."

No one laughed.

At last, Marc laid his cards down on the table. "Deal me out." Scooping up his past winnings along with the seven gold coins, Marc rose from the table. "Okay, Byers, I'm listening."

"Thank you. If you would follow me, please."

Marc followed Byers out of the Starcruiser, down and across the street into Port Ireland's finest hotel.

"Please..." Byers said with a wave of his hand to indicate an ultra-modern settee located along the back wall of the lobby, "have a seat."

Marc sat down. It had been a while since he'd been in this hotel. His line of work didn't bring him through the front door of such extravagant places very often. Nevertheless, things hadn't changed much since the last time. Leaning back, he let his gaze wander. Just as he remembered, credits were not spared when it came to ambiance. The place glowed with crystal chem-lights, shiny chrome-like tables with iridescent tops, marble floors with lavish rugs, unusual potted plants, and soft blue chem-light chandeliers that cast the lobby in a mystical blue glow.

"So, what's this all about?" Marc asked, returning his attention to Byers.

"First of all," Byers began, "My wife will be here shortly. I'd like you to meet her."

"I see, and I ask again. What's this about?"

"Mister Banner, we've been told that you sometimes go to Aden for...uh, various reasons."

Marc lifted a brow. "Is that right?" Truth was, he did occasionally deliver large vessels of ice or salt to one or more of the major settlements on the desert planet. Often the delivery was used as a front when looking for someone or something believed to have been stolen by Adenian pirates. But, at the same time, other than delivering supplies, his trips to Aden for any other reason were not something he went around professing.

Byers continued. "We've also been told that you are very good at what you do. One of the best in fact."

Marc sat forward. "Look Byers, so far, you've used up about one and a half of those gold coins. Let's cut to the chase, shall we? Just what is it you want?"

"Okay," Digging into a coat pocket, Byers pulled out a folded printout of a notice. "This," he said, unfolding the printout and handing it to Marc. "*This* is what my wife and I want."

Marc quickly scanned the message.

Twenty-Thousand-Credit Reward

For the safe return of

Jenelle D'Anne Byers

Kidnapped by Adenian pirates eleven years ago.

Jenelle is now Twenty years old.

Last known to have honey blond hair and gray eyes.

Any information that leads to her recovery will earn the same reward.

Contact Thomas Byers c/o Interplanetary Law Enforcement

Marc silently studied the picture of the young girl posted above the notice. She was a pretty little thing with large gray eyes and a pink bow in her curly blond hair. The catch was, she was no longer the same little girl captured in this picture. Eleven years had passed. She would be a young woman by now. Nevertheless, it was the reward that held Marc's interest more than anything. A man could do a helluva lot with twenty-thousand credits.

Byers went on to explain, "Eleven years ago, my wife, daughter and I were returning to Earth when our commercial liner was attacked by Adenian pirates. They left my wife and me alive...but they took our daughter."

"How do you know it was Adenians?" Marc asked without lifting his sights from the printout.

"I personally saw the Adenian emblem on the side of their ship."

Marc nodded. "I see."

"I've heard they are brutal," Byers continued. "Why would they leave my wife and me alive and take our beautiful little girl?"

"My best guess is that most likely they were initially after something your ship was carrying in its hold, and while they were at it, they decided to take whatever else interested them." Marc glanced up from the printout. "I can guarantee, had the attack been in retaliation for something, you'd all be long dead."

"That doesn't answer why they would take our daughter."

Marc shrugged and glanced down at the printout again.

"Adenians have a weakness for kids. Not just their own, but all kids. Aden's a harsh planet, Byers, children don't always live long."

Byers groaned. "Dear God. Don't let my Karissa hear you say that. They took our only child, Mister Banner. We love her and want her returned. We've hired numerous men to find her, paid tens of thousands of credits over the years to no avail. You're our last hope. If she's alive we want her found and brought back. If she's dead..." he paused and swallowed hard. "If she's no longer alive...then—then, we need to know. For eleven long years there has been no closure."

Marc glanced back down at the printout. "Eleven years?"

"Yes."

"And she was nine at the time?"

"Yes sir."

Marc released a soft breathy whistle. "Eleven years, and no one's found her yet."

"No sir, but I don't think they tried very hard. I truly believe they took my initial deposit and ran with it."

Marc studied the notice again and slowly shook his head. "Eleven years..." At last, he looked up at Byers. "I don't know...that's a helluva long time."

"I'm well aware of that."

Marc rubbed the back of his neck, and continued. "You want my opinion?"

As though afraid to respond, Byers simply stared at him.

"You'd be wasting your credits. As well as my time."

"I'm asking for your help, Mister Banner. I'm willing to pay for it. Plain and simple."

"All I'm saying is, with the passage of all these years it's going to be damn hard to find a nine-year-old child who's now a young woman. If, by chance she *is* alive, I can assure you she's been absorbed by now."

"What do you mean, *absorbed*?"

"By now, she's one of them," Marc replied. "I'm telling you; chances are I'm not going to find her. Even if I do, it's possible she won't want to leave, might not even remember you."

"I'm sorry, but I can't believe that."

Marc shrugged. "Believe what you want. It's brain washing, mind control, hypnosis, whatever you want to call it. It doesn't matter what you choose to believe. It's the way it is, Byers, and it's strong."

"Look, Mister Banner. I'm good for the reward and to prove it, I'll pay you half of the bounty right now. I just need to know if you'll help us or not."

"I'm a freight pilot. Not a bounty hunter. Besides, how do you know I'm not going to run off with your deposit just like everyone else?"

"As I've said before, you're our last hope. We want our daughter back. If you're willing to take on this task—foolish or not, we'd have no choice but to trust you."

Marc glanced down at the printout again. "You don't know me, Byers," he said without looking up. "Why would you trust me?"

"You're right. I don't know you. I do know your reputation, and from what I hear, you're a damn good tracker. Whatever you choose to call yourself, we both know you're more than simply a freight pilot. Once again, I'm offering to pay in advance half of a sizeable bounty just for agreeing to help us. Plus, I'll add an additional thousand for expenses. That's eleven thousand upfront. One thousand for every year she's been gone. So, are you interested or not?"

"Since I'm not looking for a nine-year-old, this picture gives me nothing to go on other than her eyes and hair color. How am I supposed to know what she looks like today?"

When Marc glanced up from the printout, he found Byers looking away, his face softening as he rose to his feet.

He turned to see what had captured Byers' attention. A middle-aged woman dressed in soft blue leggings and matching tunic was making her way toward them. She had light blond hair and a slender figure. Marc watched as Byers stepped forward and enfolded the woman in his arms.

"Darling, I want you to meet Mister Marc Banner. He's the man I was telling you about."

Byers turned to Marc, "Mister Banner, this is my wife, Karissa

Byers."

Immediately Marc gained his feet to accept her extended hand. "Ma'am."

"I am very pleased to meet you, Mister Banner. My husband tells me that you might be able to find our daughter." Her voice was soft and husky as she spoke. Her green eyes were fringed with thick lashes. What caught his attention more than anything was the deep look of sadness in those eyes—an unconscious look that stirred a pain in his heart.

They all took a seat. Byers sat next to his wife and reached for her hand. "I was just telling Mister Banner how our precious Jenelle was taken from us."

Once again, Misses Byers turned luminous eyes on Marc. "Do—do you think you can help us?"

Unwilling to explain the slim chances of finding their daughter to Byers' wife, Marc asked, "Do you believe your daughter today might look like you?"

"It's possible. She favored me as a child. Of course, I can't say for sure what she might look like today—whether the resemblance is still there or not." Reaching up she unfastened a golden chain from around her neck that held a small heart-shaped hinged locket. "If this would help, it holds a picture of Jenelle and me," she said, handing it over to Marc. "The photo was taken not long before we—before she was stolen from us." With a deep breath, she folded her hands and placed them in her lap. "Please. You *will* help us, won't you, Mister Banner?"

Wordlessly, Marc accepted the locket and proceeded to study the picture encased inside. It seemed like an impossible quest—a waste of both his time and Byers' credits. However, if Jenelle were to look anything like her mother...could he be that lucky? What did he have to lose? If she does look like her mother, and if he were to find her and manage to bring her back, the balance of Beyer's hefty reward would be his.

Marc glanced up and studied Misses Byers for a long moment before responding. "I can't make any promises Misses Byers, but I'll make a run to Aden, scout out a few villages, and see what I can find out."

Tears filled her eyes. "Oh, thank you. Thank you, Mister Banner. My husband and I have great faith in you. I just know you will find our Jenelle."

Byers rose to his feet. "I'll draw out eleven thousand credits for you tomorrow. A thousand of it is for expenses. If you incur additional costs, let me know. Should you return with our daughter you will get the balance of the reward for a total of twenty thousand credits. One more thing...should you find her, would you give this to her."

He handed Marc an electronic tablet. It contains a message from her mother and me."

Marc accepted the tablet. "Yes, I'll see to it she gets this. I'll be leaving first thing in the morning." he said as he wrote something on the back of a business card. "Contact my brother at this number and he'll make sure the *advance* is deposited into my account."

Byers studied the name. "Clint Banner, Solarblaze Energy." He flipped the card over. "And this is the number I'm to reach him at?"

"Yes. I'll let him know to expect your contact." He held up the flyer. "Mind if I keep this?"

"No. By all means, take it."

Marc refolded the flyer. "So, how do I get in touch with you?"

"My personal contact information is at the bottom of the flyer. Day or night. No matter the time."

"As long as you don't expect to hear from me right away."

Byers nodded. "I understand."

Marc turned to Misses Byers. "Ma'am, do you mind if a get a copy of the photo in this locket?

"Anything. You can take the locket with you if it will help."

"I just need a copy of the photo." Marc started to turn away, then stopped. "On second thought. Do you think your daughter might recognize the locket combined with the picture?"

"I would hope so. It was a birthday gift from her and my husband. Please, if you think it will help, take it with you."

"I'll see that you get it back," Marc said as he placed Misses

Byers keepsake into his jacket pocket.

"Mister Banner," she added, "if I might ask...do you have any idea how long it might be before we know anything?"

The longing in her voice was impossible to miss. "To be truthful, I have no idea. It will take over eight weeks just to get to Aden from here. Could be six months or more before I know anything. It all depends on whether she's even on Aden, and if so, what settlement she's in."

He chose not to add that it also depended on whether her daughter was willing to leave. What if she's married and has a passel of kids? It could get complicated.

Thomas Byers released an exasperated sigh. "In other words, it's going to be like they used to say on Earth, *looking for a needle in a haystack*."

"Pretty much."

Marc turned his attention once again to Misses Byers. "I'll do my best to find your daughter, ma'am."

"Thank you," she said, tears welling in her eyes.

Thomas stepped forward. "Just one more thing before you leave," he said in a whispered voice. "Should you find her, I expect you to respect her. You *know* what I mean."

Marc frowned. "No, I'm afraid I don't," he replied in a conversational tone.

Byers' tone softened. "All I'm saying is that Karissa and I trust you to do the right thing by her."

Marc regarded the older man for a long moment. "Well, that's encouraging to know." With a shrug he added in a lowered, but serious tone, "Let me get this straight. First, *you* approached me. Not the other way around. If...*if* I should find your daughter, I have no intentions of violating her, if that's what you mean. However, knowing what I know of Adenian customs, by now she's already been violated." Marc gave the man a moment to mull that one over. "So, if you're having second thoughts," he continued as he offered the locket back in his open palm. "I'll just get on back to the Starcruiser."

"No, no. Please...Please forgive me. We desperately want you to find our daughter."

Their eyes held a moment longer, and then Marc turned to leave the hotel.

Karissa stared at the door, her eyes tearing again. *God be with you.*

~ * ~

Outside Marc stopped, shrugged the kinks out of his shoulders and patted his pocket for a cigarette. Finding one, he bent his head, lit up. Originally, he'd figured on heading back to the Starcruiser, but since his plans changed, he now had an early get-up in the morning. First thing, he'd need to head for Acacia to touch base with Nick and Zeke. Hopefully there'll be an upcoming ice run to Aden that he could make for them. As always it looked better if he had a viable freight delivery.

This was the fourth year in a row that Marc took on a variety of tracking jobs. Most were assignments to find stolen shipments off captured freighters. Occasionally, he'd been hired to search for men, women and even children who had been taken and sold at auctions. If found, he was often able to buy the captives from their owners. Occasionally, however, he had only sad news to bring back to families awaiting word.

He was dreading this assignment. First, there was a slim chance he'd even find the girl, and he hated the thought of having to eventually tell the Byers their daughter was a lost cause. He didn't know why he'd agreed to it. Why the devil did he do this to himself?

Because you're damn good at tracking, that's why. And because this job pays exceptionally well.

Yes, he had to admit that much. The credits were a nice incentive.

Before heading back to his ship, he withdrew the locket and once again studied the picture of Misses Byers and her daughter. Was she still blond like her mother, he wondered? He understood often light-colored hair was died black to blend in with the natives. If Lady Luck was still on his side, he'd find the young woman, bring her back to her parents, and end up with a tidy little sum of twenty thousand credits.

Stepping off the sidewalk, he crossed the street and headed for his bike. A few years ago, his older brother, Clint, transported the beautifully restored, shiny black 1994 Harley Sportster from Earth as a birthday gift. Marc cherished the bike and insisted on keeping it onboard his ship. Beside the sense of exhilaration and freedom when riding it, the bike was an easy and quick mode of transportation once he arrived at a port.

Now to get some sleep, and then head for Imperial to see if there's an ice or salt consignment he can deliver to Aden for Nick and Zeke.

CHAPTER TWO

Port Imperial – Acacia

"What do you mean Frank's coming with me?" Marc asked, staring at his older brother as if he'd lost his mind. "I'm pretty sure I can handle an ice drop without Frank."

"Not if you're taking the *Antara*. You're going to need Frank to get you through Aden's security."

"Since when?" Marc frowned. "Look Nick, this isn't my first delivery to Aden. They know me."

Nick huffed a soft laugh. "Of that, I have no doubt. Nevertheless, they've tightened their regulations since you last delivered a consignment for us. I guarantee without Frank to slide you in, the *Antara* will be denied access to the planet."

With a frown, Marc remained quiet for a long skeptical moment before responding. "I have no idea how long I'll be, Nick. For all I know, it could take months before I know anything. In the meantime, what the devil is Frank supposed to do while I'm off ship?"

"Nothing. Absolutely nothing," Zeke drawled as he entered the conversation with a mug of coffee in hand. "He can hold down the fort while you're gone. He likes doing that."

"And the best part is," Nick added, "we can spare Frank for as long as you need him."

Uneasiness hung in the air as the corner of Marc's mouth turned down in annoyance. "I don't *need* Frank."

"Nevertheless," Nick piped up, "we think you do. Therefore, Frank goes with the consignment."

Another long moment of silence passed as Marc mulled over their ridiculous mandate. "Fine," he said with quiet emphasis. "But you'd best make sure Frank understands I won't endure his insufferable lectures." Without waiting for a reply, Marc turned on his heel and stalked out of the office, their soft chuckles following him out the door.

~ * ~

Seven weeks later

It was early morning when Marc entered the helm. "Mornin' Frank. I'll take over now. Go get some sleep."

Although the *Antara* could have easily been programed to stay on course while they slept, Frank always insisted on taking the night shift.

"I don't know what the all-fire hurry is," Frank muttered as he rose from his seat, "but we'll be arrivin' in exactly twelve hours. In fact, thar she is right now." He jerked his chin to the vid screen above, where a sandy gray globe hung suspended against the star-studded blackness of space.

"The sooner the better." Marc murmured.

Frank Reno was an energetic man in his early sixties. He'd not only been a long-time friend of the Banner family, he'd worked closely with Nick's sidekick, Zeke Slater. No doubt about it, Frank was good at whatever task he was put to. Not only could he pilot almost anything, he'd also served as ship's cook, medic, captain's mentor and, last, but far from least, a trusted friend. However, despite his skills and rare likability, Frank had one downside, a tendency to be nosey, bossy and blatantly stubborn at times.

"Zeke said yer trackin' down somethun' important."

"He did, huh?" Marc ambled over to a back shelf where they kept the coffee and poured himself a mug.

"Thang I don't understand, is why y'—"

"Good night, Frank. I'll take it from here. Go get some sleep."

~ * ~

Six hours passed by the time Frank returned to the helm. Marc was at the controls, and they were close enough to Aden that it filled half of the vid-screen with its sandy-gray immensity. Scanning the readouts, Marc opened the COMLINK, tapped in a frequency, and spoke into the mic. "This is Captain Marc Banner of the *Antara,* Delta, Beta, Six, Niner Two, requesting a planetary approach vector." Marc turned to Frank, "Better grab a seat. Apparently, we're going to be needing you to confirm authorization to land or something?"

Frank stopped his mug of coffee halfway to his mouth. "We don't need no permission t' land."

No surprise there. Marc slowly shook his head and whispered a curse beneath his breath.

"What author-zation are y' talkin' 'bout?" Frank asked again.

"Nothing, Frank. I just thought it might be a precaution in case the *Antara* isn't recognized. It's been a while since I've been to Aden," he lied.

"Hell, long as y' got ice and salt tabs, they don't care whatcha' call yer ship, or where yer from."

"R i g h t..." Marc drawled. That was pretty much what he figured.

Frank took another sip of his coffee then ambled over to take a seat across the U-shaped cockpit from Marc "Who told y' that y'd need approval?"

"No one, Frank. Like I said, it's just that it's been a while since I've been to Aden, and the last time I was here, I didn't have the *Antara.*"

Frank could be an exasperating old coot, but no way was Marc going to tell the old man how Nick and Zeke insisted he go along. Marc could understand how the guys might need a break. Nevertheless, as insufferable as Frank could be, he didn't deserve the humiliation of being pawned off like this.

Leaning back Marc absently studied the controls while verbal communications continued between Frank and the spaceport. He had to admit, the old man knew exactly what he was doing when it came to manning the controls.

Gradually as time passed the swirly gray planet grew even larger until it completely engulfed the overhead screen. It was another two hours before a bark of static hailed a greeting. "Welcome to Port Jahara, *Antara*, please initiate your descent."

"Understood," Marc replied, continuing verbal contact while Frank began entering the designated coordinates. "Go ahead and take her on in, Frank."

"Yes sir, Boss."

Eventually, the inky blackness of space gave-way to Aden's luminous aura. As they commenced entering the planet's gravity and the various layers of Aden's upper atmosphere, the *Antara* began glowing like a fanned ember with flames licking off the bow and the leading edge of both wings. As usual, an eerie orange glow filled the cabin as the firestorm outside swept across the viewports. At regular intervals a soft chime broke the silence signaling designated drops in elevation.

"Y' got yerself a real nice transport here, son," Frank commented as they fought their way down through alternating layers of high winds and calm voids. "She's a well-oiled, smooth runnin' m'chine fer sure."

"Thank you, Frank. I make it a point to take good care of her."

Frank huffed a soft laugh. Reaching overhead, he made another adjustment to the controls, then relaxed for the moment. "Yep, it's the only way to treat a good woman." He took another tentative sip of coffee. "Which, by the way, has me wonderin' when y' gonna find yerself a good woman?"

Here it comes, Marc thought. Frank never failed to bring the subject up.

"What'er y' waitin' fer son?"

Marc released a heavy sigh. "I guess for a good woman to walk into my life," he replied, never taking his eyes off the controls. "In the meantime, I happen to enjoy bad women."

"Well, I guarantee, sure as 'ell, no good woman's gonna walk into yer life at the rate yer goin'."

"Well, that's good news," Marc replied. "Cuz right now, I happen to like my life just the way it is."

As they entered Aden's lower atmosphere, the firestorm outside the ship slowly began dissipating.

Another crack of static preceded... "*Antara,* you are cleared for Docking Bay Twenty."

"Understood."

A glance out the viewport, revealed vast dark regions staining the surface of the planet. However, the closer they got, the more those dark areas became the shaded sides of towering, sun-drenched dunes stretching out into the distance and disappearing beyond the curvature of the planet. Aden was a hot and harsh desert world with no mercy for the careless and unwary.

Soon the *Antara* was gently banking into a turn, her reversed thrusters inundating the cabin with shuddering vibrations and a low scream of protest as the ground seemed to rise to meet them. Geysers of sand and dust coiled about them as Marc guided the ship, inches above the surface, to its designated landing pad where he gently lowered it down onto its jacks.

"I understand we're lookin' fer someone's lost treasure?"

"That's right."

"So... Where do we start lookin' and what is it we're lookin' fer?"

"*We...*aren't looking for anything, Frank. I want you to remain onboard while I'm gone. You're holding the fort down. I can't say how long, but I'll keep in touch. However, if something comes up, I need you here to handle it."

With that, he grabbed his holstered weapon along with his taubear hide leather jacket. Taubear hide was one of few leathers that could hold

Aden's stifling heat at bay. It worked just as well on a glacial planet. However, now, Aden was anything but glacial.

"Think you can handle it?"

"Yes sir."

"Like I say, I have no idea how long I'll be. Contact me if there's trouble of any kind. Okay?"

"Got it."

Marc turned away and headed for the cargo hold where he kept his Harley. It was hard to miss the crestfallen look on Frank's face, not to mention the glum tone in his voice. It couldn't be helped. He'd be damned if he was hauling Frank from settlement to settlement on the back of his bike.

~ * ~

The settlement of Shapiro

Working on a new beaded ankle bracelet, Jaimin Ala Rashard sat in the shade of a desert palm tree outside her parent's home. The Annual Adenian Festival was less than a week away and she had been asked to be a junior celebration dancer, chosen to be one of the distinguished Veil Dancers for the opening ceremony. It was a high honor, and one Jaimin didn't take lightly.

Ahmed would be attending the festival. As far as she was concerned, it was he, she would be dancing for. Ahmed Farouk was a handsome young man, held in high esteem not only by the local heads, but also by every unmarried maiden in Shapiro as well as the nearby villages. Although over the years Jaimin had seen Ahmed countless times from afar, six months ago her parents and Ahmed's parents arranged for her to officially meet him. The mutual approval of both sets of parents meant that Ahmed could court her. She smiled, thinking that in just a few days she would dance for him as she had never danced before. He was so handsome, she thought, with his swarthy skin, black wavy hair, and his dark full beard.

Her face warmed at the mere thought of seeing Ahmed again, of wearing her beautiful ceremonial dress, and secretly dancing just for him. Who knows what the future would bring? But for now, she had to quit thinking about Ahmed. At this rate she would never get her lovely ankle bracelet finished in time.

Suddenly, in the distance, came a deep rumble of something slowly approaching. It was unlike anything Jaimin had ever heard. Glancing up she saw a stranger gradually advancing into the midst of the village on a loud, throaty-sounding, two-wheeled vehicle. A *motorbike*. She was sure of it. Although she had only seen a picture of one once.

The man sat with ease, his arms and hands outstretched upon extended handlebars, his legs spread upon raised foot pegs. He wore black pants, a dark gray shirt, and an open black leather jacket that exposed a holstered weapon worn low and tied down on his right thigh. Obviously, he was an outsider and Jaimin wondered how he had made it this far into the village without being challenged. Remaining in place, her heart beating wildly, she watched him slowly press forward. The closer he got, the more she could feel vibrations coming from his loud and rough-sounding motorbike.

Was the settlement in danger, she wondered? Should she warn someone. But then, he was riding in so blatantly, it was as if he was assured of a welcome. Surely someone must know him. Several men stopped what they were doing to watch him pass by. One raised his hand in greeting. A few young boys trotted alongside, waving, and laughing.

As he slowly progressed, Jaimin's gaze moved over him, more closely this time. His shoulders were broad. His hair was black, and although his dark glasses prevented her from seeing his eyes, what she could see of the rest of him, she suspected he was strikingly handsome.

As if aware of her perusal, he turned, offering her a cordial nod, and Jaimin knew, despite his dark glasses, their gazes had surely met, instantly setting off butterflies in the pit of her stomach. Dropping her unfinished ankle bracelet, she turned to quickly disappear inside her home.

~ * ~

Marc stared after the girl. Shapiro was the sixth settlement he'd visited so far, and unless he missed his guess, he'd just found his bounty—Byers' long-lost daughter. He didn't need to refer to the locket for verification. As luck would have it, the girl was an exact replica of her mother.

She had her mother's blond hair, although over the years, the sun had bleached it silver white. Her skin, which undoubtedly had once been fair, was nearly as dark as the natives—another gift from Aden's harsh sun. Unfortunately, he was too far away to catch the color of her eyes, but he'd be willing to bet they were gray.

He glanced about the village as he progressed toward the main pavilion. As usual, Aden's desert heat was intolerable. The air was heavy with a combination of incense, ripened fruit, and spices. Marc inhaled slowly, savoring the scent of local cooking. The compound had a communal atmosphere about it. Women throughout were preparing the afternoon meal, and the aroma was tempting.

Pulling up in front of the main headquarters, Marc cut the engine, jacked the kickstand in place, lifted his leg over the seat and dismounted. A young teenage boy came rushing up, offering to take the bike to a collective parking area.

"Leave it," Marc said in their native tongue. He tossed the kid a couple of Aden coins. "I won't be long."

With that, he quickly finger-combed his hair, turned and ducked under the flap into the large tent-like structure. The air was cool inside. Marc always thought it odd that most Adenians preferred to live in tents as their forefathers had on Earth. Yet, despite how religiously they adhere to numerous ancient customs, they didn't seem to have a problem letting other traditions go by the wayside.

Basically, these people had one foot in the past, and the other in the present. For example, air-conditioning wasn't the only contemporary convenience that replaced tradition. Another was their use of computers, and automobiles instead of camels. Although some still used camels, it seemed nearly every residential household had a shiny Land Craft parked in front.

Most middle-class families lived in tent-like structures located near the outskirts of the settlement, while the wealthier citizens lived in solid built homes closer to the settlement's center of operations. Byers' daughter had obviously been taken in by an affluent family. The home she ducked into was a large solid home that spoke of wealth.

CHAPTER THREE

Once inside the settlement's headquarters, Marc presented the necessary credentials to identify himself. While waiting for approval, he glanced about. It had been a while since he had visited Shapiro. Nevertheless, just as he remembered, a cheerful brightly colored carpet in a vibrant shade of green covered the interior floor. Assorted jewel-colored drapes sheathed the ceiling before cascading down the walls to the floor. Directly behind the counter hung a large portrait of the settlement's Shakari.

"I see that you unloaded a large consignment of ice and salt tabs in Port Jahara," the clerk commented as he studied the computer.

"That's correct," Marc said, returning his attention to the man behind the counter.

"From there you have visited Port Kahn, Medid, Port Zalain, Pirandaj, Port Faraqudah, and Barvisara. May I ask what brings you to Shapiro, Mister Banner?"

"I prefer to discuss that with your Shakari. Is he available?"

After a moment's hesitation... "I will ask. But first, you will need to disarm."

"I understand."

With that, Marc dutifully removed his holstered handgun, placed it on the counter, then removed a concealed knife called a *synthoblade* from its sheath, and placed it on the counter next to the handgun.

"Just these two?"

"That's it," Marc replied.

"I'll inform the Shakari of your wish to see him."

With a nod, the clerk turned and headed for the curtained doorway that sectioned off the Shakari's office from the rest of the structure.

Within moments, a burst of excitement drifted out into the main foyer. "Marc? Marc Banner." The Shakari practically knocked his clerk down, besting the man out of his office. "I thought I heard your voice. Where the devil have you been keeping yourself?" he demanded in English as he approached Marc with an outstretched hand and a warm grip.

The Shakari looked to be about Marc's age. In truth, he was young for such a prestigious position, but Shapiro was a small settlement, a perfect place for grooming a younger man for an impressive future within Aden's régime.

The two men embraced with an air-kiss on each cheek. Marc was the first to step back. "Saleem, I agree. It's been far too long. You're looking well. I heard from Nick about your promotion to Shakari. Congratulations."

"Thank you, my friend. Yes, many moons have passed since we were both young and played war games while our fathers talked business. What brings you to Shapiro? Are you taking on some of the deliveries now for Nick and Zeke?"

"No... Actually, I'm looking for a woman."

"...A woman?" A slow smile spread across Saleem's face. "Don't tell me you're finally looking to settle down?"

"Afraid not. This woman was kidnapped off a passenger liner by Adenian pirates eleven years ago. She was a nine-year-old child at the time."

Comprehension dawned in Saleem's eyes. "Come, let us sit down and talk," he said, turning toward a small conference area with a low table and large colorful pillows placed upon the floor for seating. "You speak of Jaimin Ala Rashard?"

"It's very possible if she's the one I caught a glimpse of on the way in. She seems the right age and fits the description I have of her." Marc removed the locket from his utility belt, opened it and handed it to Saleem. "This picture was taken not long before she was abducted. The woman is her biological mother."

Saleem nodded slowly. "Yes, the resemblance is strong. However, she no longer remembers her past life, or the parents she was taken from. Besides, I assure you, Zari and Hassan will not let her go. In fact, I suspect she will soon be promised to the son of an upstanding family. She's had a good life, Marc. She was adopted by affluent parents who at the time recently lost their own daughter of about the same age." Saleem studied the photo in the locket a moment longer. "It's a shame," he said, "but to be honest, Jaimin has fared much better than many others who have been stolen from their families."

"She has other parents, Saleem—biological parents who love and miss her very much. They've been looking for her for eleven years."

Saleem nodded. "Yes, but she is one of us now, Marc." His tone hardened as he handed the locket back. "You will not take Jaimin away without her absolute consent."

"I understand." Marc placed the locket back into his utility belt. He knew at the time he accepted the assignment it would not be easy. If he were to find her, he could not simply ride in, grab Jenelle, and make a run for it. Not if he wanted to be welcomed back on Aden again. Now that he found her under Saleem's reign, he would have to be even more careful to retain Saleem's respect and welcoming friendship.

Later that evening, Marc relaxed in the guest accommodations that Saleem provided. Nursing a mug of chilled Tenga tea, he mulled over his options. There had to be a way to convince Jenelle Byers to go with him. Bribe her somehow—even promise to bring her back if she didn't want to stay. Maybe cozy up to her, win her trust and entice her to go with him. Afterall, serious credits were at stake here.

He'd wondered if she was seeing anyone. According to Saleem, she was. That meant things could be a bit more difficult. Not that he couldn't do it. It wasn't competition that concerned him so much, it would just entail more time to get the task done—especially if things were serious between Jenelle and her boyfriend. He was just thankful she wasn't married yet.

Closing his eyes, her image flashed before him. He hadn't missed a thing—slender figure, white-blond hair, a pert little nose, lips that were... Suddenly. his gut tightened, and an intense lance of desire knifed through him. With a muttered oath, Marc shoved Jenelle's image aside. Pretty or homely, it made no difference. He had twenty thousand good reasons waiting for him to bring her back to the Byers. The sooner the better.

~ * ~

Jaimin rolled over onto her back and smiled into the darkness. In less than a week she would be dancing for Ahmed. She felt a giddy thrill of excitement and anticipation at the thought of Ahmed watching her dance. She understood it was because of the combined wealth of both sets of parents that he was permitted to court her. She overheard talk between her parents, Ahmed was their first choice for marriage. Yet Jaimin thought it strange she was finding the idea of courtship, and all that goes with it, more exciting than the idea of being married. Did all young women feel that way, or was it just her?

Without warning, her musings turned to the outsider she'd seen riding into the village that afternoon. With the memory, all thought of Ahmed was swept from her mind. She'd asked her father about him, and although he'd said he might have seen him before, it had been a long time ago. He had no idea who he was, much less why he was here.

Jaimin thought the outsider looked threatening, and yet in the brief moments she'd regarded him, there was something about him that seemed to call to her. She vividly remembered the loud, raucous noise of his motorbike and fancied, even now, that she could still feel the residual pulsations as he slowly passed by. And then, when he turned to look directly at her—dear Allah, this man addled her brain.

Now...now in the quiet of the night, Jaimin found herself assaulted by strange longings and unfamiliar desires unlike anything she had ever known. They were all centered around the outsider. Even Ahmed hadn't elicited such thoughts.

Rolling over, she closed her eyes and continued to wonder about the outsider. Just thinking of him filled her with an unsettling sensation.

He was unlike anyone she had ever seen before. Who was he? Why was he here? Where did he come from, and how long would he be staying?

He was still on her mind as she fell asleep.

~ * ~

When Jaimin awoke early the next morning, her first waking thought was of the outsider. Not exactly shocking since he was in her dreams all night long—outrageous and inappropriate dreams that had set her innocent heart to pounding. In this last dream, the one that awakened her, she had been riding behind him on his motorbike and they were heading into the dunes. Alone.

She vividly recalled having wrapped her arms about him and hanging on tight. *It was late afternoon and the trail they were on followed an endless expanse of rolling, sandy dunes with spots of coarse grass, dwarfed shrubs, and the flare of orange-flowered cacti.*

The next thing she knew, they stopped before a beautiful oasis surrounded by tall palms. Jaimin's breath caught as he set the bike on its stand, dismounted, and turned to lift her off. A blanket was already magically laid out in the shade beneath the towering trees.

Suddenly, he was carrying her in his arms as though she'd weighed no more than a feather. Ever so gently he laid her down on the blanket and followed her down. Jaimin felt her stomach clench as he leaned over her and tenderly kissed her.

Even now, her lips tingled with the outsider's phantom kiss. Dream or not, the kiss left her breathless. It seemed so real as she placed the tips of her fingers to her mouth, hoping to still the sensation.

Stunned by the sheer reality of the dream, Jaimin nearly forgot she promised the festival committee she would help gather wild Mercy fruit this morning so it could be made into the traditional cactus wine for the upcoming celebration. A quick glance at the clock sent her bolting from her bed. They would be here soon to pick her up.

She had no sooner dressed and was quickly fastening a ribbon in her hair when there was a soft knock on her door. "Honey, the group is here to pick you up."

"Thank you, mother. Would you tell them I'll be right out?"

Three hours later, while carefully collecting the prickly fruit of the Mercy cactus, Jaimin was knee deep in cacti when once again she heard an approaching rumble.

She turned, watching as the thunderous machine pulled to a stop across from her. Quickly glancing about, she looked to see where the others were. No one was nearby, let alone paying any attention to anything other than gathering fruit.

~ * ~

Having pulled onto the shoulder of the road, Marc shut down the engine, set the kickstand and dismounted. Hooking his thumbs in his belt loops, he hitched up his pants and entered the field of thorny cacti.

And all the while his target—this young woman-child—remained frozen in place, watching him with a strange, almost guarded fascination.

"Mornin'" he said in her native tongue. "You're Jaimin. Right?"

Silence.

Good lord, she looked as if she were ready to take flight. Did he look that bad this morning? Remembering he hadn't shaved in the last couple of days, he slowed to a stop a few yards from her. "Need any help?" he asked as he removed his dark glasses.

Still no reply. She quickly glanced about, as if suddenly aware of just how alone she was. The rest of the group were scattered a good hundred feet or more away.

"I'm Marc Banner," he went on amicably in her native tongue. "I'm a long-time friend of your Shakari."

That drew her attention back to him. Marc couldn't help himself, his gaze moved over her in a lingering perusal. She was gorgeous. Her likeness to Misses Byers was unmistakable. Unlike Misses Byers, however, long hours in Aden's harsh desert sun had darkened Jaimin's skin to a deep golden brown. It had also bleached her hair many shades lighter from what he suspected might have once been honey blond. Nevertheless, those gray eyes were her fathers. Oh yeah, there was little doubt but that she was the Byers' daughter alright.

"I dropped off a consignment of salt tabs in Port Jahara," he continued pleasantly. "It's been a while since I've seen my friend, and I decided to make the trip out for a visit."

His steadfast perusal persisted as he watched the color bloom in Jaimin's cheeks. He wondered if she felt it too...the lure that suddenly seemed to crackle like summer lightening between them? He couldn't help but ponder what she would do if he were to close the distance, but he remained anchored in place. Like a frightened *cawl,* poised to take flight, she stood there watching him with wide and uncertain, rainstorm eyes. He saw a pulse throb rapidly in her throat. It wasn't until his gaze moved to her mouth that she innocently moistened her lips with the tip of her tongue.

Almost as if sensing his thoughts, Jaimin took a step back.

Marc grinned and withdrew his keys from his pocket and put his dark glasses back on. "You're all alone out here f*atan*," he continued in her native tongue, using the Adenian word for beautiful. "Better hurry and catch up with the others."

~ * ~

Jaimin watched him turn and walk away. Dear Allah, he had a nice voice—deep and smooth. His eyes were blue, blue. He was tall and appeared powerfully built. She continued watching as he mounted and fired up his thunderous machine. She watched until his bike disappeared around a curve. It wasn't until the rumble had faded into the distance that her heart finally stopped its riotous pounding and her breathing returned to normal.

Oh yes, she vividly recalled him riding into the settlement yesterday, but it wasn't until now that she'd had a chance to really get a look at him. He'd taken her breath away—he was that handsome. His movements, as he set the kickstand, swung his leg over the seat and dismounted had been fluid and lithe, his muscles unmistakable beneath his white short sleeved T-shirt and dark jeans. Her friend, Aannisah, would have labeled him *hot*.

He was on her mind when Jaimin finally joined the others. Later that day, he was still on her mind while she finished working on her ankle bracelet. She thought about him mentioning he was friends with the Shakari, which led to wondering how often he visited. Had she, by chance, seen him before? No, she would remember that motorbike. Double *no*, she would remember *him*.

That night, as she crawled into bed, she found herself still wondering about him. Was he married? Did he have a wife and family waiting for him somewhere? Stars...she was spending far too much time thinking about a man she didn't even know. Yet she couldn't seem to stop herself.

Once again morning came early. A soft knock at her door brought her awake as her mother cracked the door open. "Hey sleepyhead, you'd better get up. Did you forget Ahmed was coming by at noon to take you for a drive and a picnic?"

"Oh. What time is it?"

"It's ten thirty, and you need to hurry. Do you know what you're wearing?"

"Yes, Mother."

CHAPTER FOUR

Jaimin toyed nervously with her hands in her lap while staring straight ahead as Ahmed followed a seldom-used backroad that wound through the dunes. This was the first time that she had been out with him alone.

Now they'd left Shapiro behind some thirty minutes ago. Other than commenting on the heat, or the upcoming festival, not much had been said between them. Jaimin dared a shy glance in his direction and caught him watching her.

"Have you ever been to Balar Falls," he asked?

"Only once. It's beautiful there."

Ahmed turned to her with a wide smile, "Yeah, but not nearly as beautiful as you."

Suddenly uncomfortable, and with a shy smile, Jaimin turned away to watch the desert scenery rush by.

"This looks like a nice place for our picnic, don't you think?" he asked as he guided the Land Craft off the road toward a tree-lined oasis. "The falls are not far from here. We can go see them after our picnic."

With that, Ahmed got out and walked around to open her door. Jaimin accepted his assistance when he extended his hand to help her out. But then, he didn't let go. Instead, he drew her close.

"Jaimin, my love," he murmured, "I never realized until now just how exquisite you are."

Drawing her closer still, he leaned forward, and Jaimin held her breath, wishing she could back away. Unfortunately, there was no escape. The open door of his Land Craft was directly behind her.

"Maybe we should get the picnic basket," she suggested nervously. "We could set up under those trees over there."

He smiled and pulled her even closer. "Later..." he whispered as his bearded face descended.

Jaimin braced her hands against his chest. "Ahmed, please...I don't think we should..."

His hold only tightened as he disregarded her rejection. "Sure, we should sweetheart. It's okay. You see, I planned to ask you to marry me today."

With that, he tightened his grip on her chin, forcing her to look straight up into his dark, lustful eyes. Grabbing her hair, he pulled back, holding her head firmly in place while bringing his mouth down upon hers in a brutal kiss.

The more she fought, the tighter he held-on, pressing her back against the open vehicle as he continued the assault. Jaimin struggled not only for breath, but for balance. Perhaps if she stopped fighting him, he'd loosen his tight hold on her.

"Don't fight me. Let me show you how good it can be."

With that, Ahmed forced his tongue into her mouth while at the same time groping the front of the beautiful outfit, she'd chosen to wear that day.

Jaimin's muffled cries died in her throat as he painfully squeezed her breast. A sharp portion of the vehicle was jabbing into her back as he leaned into her. There was no escape as he fumbled with the closures at the front of her ensemble. She heard ripping then his hands were fully on her.

At last, he broke the kiss long enough to run his mouth down her neck to the fullness of her exposed breast. "Ahmed, stop. Please."

"Quit fighting me and just enjoy it."

"You're hurting me," she pleaded, unable to keep the panic from rising.

"You know you want it as bad as I do. Stop fighting me, dammit."

"Please. Ahmed..."

Suddenly without warning, Ahmed released her, and was mysteriously ripped away, leaving Jaimin sinking to her knees. It wasn't until a loud whacking sound followed by a groan and a muffled thud brought her head up as she scrambled to her feet.

Ahmed was sprawled in the sand, and looming over him was a man dressed in black. The outsider. What was he doing here? Had he followed her and Ahmed?

Marc bent over Ahmed, grabbing him by his shirt. And with very little effort, he hauled the young man to his feet. A split second later, his fist slammed into Ahmed's face, launching him, once again, back to the ground. For a long moment Ahmed lay there, dazed and moaning as blood gushed from his nose and mouth.

"Stop it," she cried as Marc proceeded to advance on Ahmed.

With every intention of putting a stop to the brutal beating, Jaimin started forward. There was so much blood. If he didn't stop, he'd end up killing Ahmed. "Please. Stop."

Marc turned to look at her, dark spikes of hair hanging low over his brow. But it was his fierce, murderous expression as he took in her torn outfit that stopped Jaimin in her tracks and had her gripping her torn bodice.

After a drawn-out moment, Marc's attention returned to the stunned young man still sprawled on the ground. Once again, he hauled Ahmed back onto his feet as blood continued gushing from the kid's nose and mouth. Grabbing the front of Ahmed's shirt in his fists, Marc lifted him completely off the ground. "Didn't your daddy teach you how to treat a lady?" he snarled in perfect Adenian. At last Marc shoved him away, leaving the boy to stumble backward in an effort to keep his balance. "Friendly warning," Marc growled. "Stay away from Jaimin. If you *ever* lay a hand on her again, I'm coming for you."

Stunned, the kid remained where he was, glaring at Jaimin with one eye swollen closed. It wasn't until Marc began to advance on him again, that Ahmed bolted for his Land Craft and scrambled into the driver's seat.

"Ahmed. Wait." Jaimin called as the vehicle lurched forward.

But Ahmed wasn't waiting for anyone. He was fleeing for his life. And now, here she was, miles from her village, left all alone with the outsider. Her first thought was to run, but that would be crazy. Where would she go? Besides, she could never outrun him.

For a long moment Marc simply stayed there watching her. Suddenly, he turned and moved toward the lake where he crouched down at the shoreline and proceeded to wash Ahmed's blood from his hands.

Mouth trembling, Jaimin continued standing where she was, her shaking hands clasping her torn bodice. When he rose and turned toward her, her heart skipped a beat. Once again, the urge to run rushed through her. Instead, her feet remained rooted, unable to move.

"Are you okay?" he asked, stopping a respectful distance from her.

Jaimin stared up at him with wide eyes. Somehow, he didn't look as mean and violent as he had earlier. Instead, his features softened and, as his gaze rested on her face, a concerned expression replaced the furious glower she'd witnessed only moments before.

"Jaimin?" Taking a step forward, he reached out to her, his fingers barely grazing her arm. "You, okay?"

He'd hardly touched her, but the jolt that traveled up her arm was instant. Sucking in a shaky breath she stepped back. "Don't touch me." Stars, her arm was tingling.

"Are you hurt?" he asked softly.

Sudden anger swelled inside her and her head jerked up. "You were going to kill Ahmed, weren't you?"

Marc shook his head. "No, but I gave that son of a—I gave him exactly what he deserved."

"Well, he certainly didn't deserve the beating he received," Jaimin disputed.

"Didn't he?" He stepped closer. "I take that to mean one of two things," he said smoothly. "One: you had everything under control, which I doubt. Or two: you enjoy being manhandled. Some women do, you know."

"You're disgusting," she snapped. "We have been promised to each other and will soon be married. He would never—"

"Yes, he would." Marc cut her off. "You don't have any idea what your *prince* would have done. Do you?" He stepped closer. "Had I not come along when I did..."

Jaimin took an unsteady step backward, "He would not have hurt me."

"He already did," he said with a clipped nod to her torn dress.

She struggled for something to say. Yes, Ahmed overstepped his bounds. Yes, he had gotten carried away, but surely, he wouldn't have forced himself on her. He'd always been a gentleman. His advances today simply meant he loved her and was anxious to marry her.

Still, a nagging little feeling in the back of her mind troubled her more than anything. Why didn't she enjoy Ahmed's advances? Why wasn't she just as anxious for his kisses? Why didn't her body tingle as it had when this man, this outsider barely touched her?

"I can tell you one thing," Marc continued, "Where I come from, a man is brought up to treat a woman with respect. He doesn't do things or try to force himself upon her if she objects. And from what I saw, sweetheart, you were objecting."

"So... tell me, Mister Banner, how did you just so happen to be here in time for the rescue? Were you spying on us?"

"What? No, dammit, I was—"

"Enjoy the show?" she interrupted, cutting him off.

Refusing to qualify that with an answer, Marc turned and strode off toward the lake again. Jaimin watched as he followed the shoreline until he disappeared around a cluster of palm trees.

The next thing, she heard his motorbike start up, and within moments he was pulling up before her. "We need to talk."

Jaimin whirled about and struck out for the road. "I don't want to talk to you."

Refusing to let her walk away, he cut the engine, put the bike on its kickstand, dismounted and caught her by the arm. "At least let me explain something. Hear me out. Please."

"There's nothing to explain. Release my arm."

"First of all," he continued. I was here at the lake long before the two of you showed up. I wasn't spying on you, *Jenelle*."

Silence. Then... "What did you call me?"

"Jenelle?" he repeated. "Sound even a little bit familiar?"

"I don't know what you're talking about. My name's Jaimin."

Marc clenched his jaw. Maybe this was a mistake. Maybe he should have left the past in the past. Still, the Byers had a right to have their daughter back. "Jaimin, do you remember anything of your past? Anything at all?"

She frowned. "I don't know what you mean?"

"Jenelle's the name you were given by your birth parents, Thomas and Karissa Byers." Marc turned to stare out over the dunes, wishing he could protect her from the shock of learning the truth. "I'm saying that Hassan and Zari are your adoptive parents."

"That's not true."

Marc reached into his pocket and withdrew the locket that Misses Byers gave him. "Do you remember this, Jenelle?" he said, opening the locket to the photo and offering it to her. "That's a photo of you and your birth mother."

Jaimin cautiously accepted the locket. "I do not know this woman, and that is not me. Where did you get this?" she asked, turning to face him.

"Your mother loaned it to me, hoping you'd recognize it. Your real parents miss you very much, Jenelle."

"They sent you to bring me back?"

The panic in her eyes tore at his heart.

"Yes. Even if it's just for a visit. I'll bring you back here if that's what you want."

"I'm not leaving. This is my home. I am Jaimin Ala Rashard." She handed the locket back. "Even if what you say is true, I won't break the hearts of the two people who have raised and loved me."

"Are you sure? Aren't you the least bit curious about your real parents, Jenelle? Your real name is Jenelle D'Anne Byers. Wouldn't you at least like to meet them?"

"I don't want to talk about it. Besides, the Aden Festival is in two days, and I am expected to dance for the opening ceremonial dance."

"That won't be a problem. We can wait. Besides, I look forward to seeing you dance."

"I am promised to Ahmed," she continued. "We are expected to be married."

"Well, you think about it, Jenelle. It's not something you need to decide right now."

"Stop calling me Jenelle. My name is Jaimin Ala Rashard. Aden is my home, and I am not leaving."

"What do you say I give you a ride back to the village, since your *Prince* left you stranded. Maybe you should try doing something about your outfit first. It's torn. See if you can fix it enough to get you home." With a wink added, "You never know, someone could come along and get the wrong idea about us."

~ * ~

"Ohhh." With that she whirled about to fumble as best she could with her torn outfit. The nerve of him. Besides, it was his fault Ahmed raced off without her. He left her to get home any way she could.

"Now I'm going to have to apologize to Ahmed and his family," she mumbled more to herself before turning to stalk toward the road.

Marc gave her a sidelong glance of utter disbelief. "Excuse me?" Hurrying to catch up with her, he caught her arm, stopping her progress. "Apologize for what, may I ask?"

Jerking her arm from his grasp, Jaimin whirled about to face him. "For your outrageous treatment," she replied heatedly. "Poor Ahmed. Now I must salvage this mess you've made."

Leaving Marc standing there with his jaw dropped, Jaimin spun around. "Why are you so bent on ruining my life?" she snapped, as she started stalking away.

Two strides and he caught up with her again. "I'm not trying to ruin your life," he said softly. "Your father—your birth father, Thomas Byers, contacted me and explained how you were kidnapped eleven years ago. Your mother gave me the locket to bring with me in my search for you. You look a lot like your lovely mother. She's a beautiful lady and misses you very much."

"I'm sorry, but I have a mother and father who love me. My life is here. I'm to be married soon, and I will not allow you to expose this lie and endanger my future."

Marc stepped back, a muscle ticking in his jaw. "Well sunshine, if that's what's most important to you...then by all means, go back and grovel at their feet. Since both parents are behind it, I'm sure no harm has been done. I just hope it's worth the price you'll be paying."

With that, he turned and headed back to his bike.

"Good. Maybe now he'll leave me alone," she murmured as she began her trek down the sandy road back toward Shapiro. It would be a long walk, yes, but it would also give her time to decide how to handle things once she got there.

Moments later she heard that mechanical beast of his roaring back to life. The next instant, the brute materialized at her side. He kept it at a crawl to match her pace, his machine sounding as though rumbling the word, *potato, potato, potato.* "It's a long way back, *fatan*. Surely you don't intend to walk."

Ignoring him, Jaimin kept on walking.

"My offer still stands," he continued. "At this rate, it won't just be dark by the time you get there, it will be morning."

"I don't care."

Without another word he suddenly picked up speed, advanced ahead of her, and positioned the bike crosswise, in the middle of the road. Blocking her way, he sat there straddling his bike with both booted feet on the ground. "You're hardly dressed for a long walk in the hot desert sun. Let me give you a lift."

"Thank you, but no thanks. You've done quite enough as it is." Without looking at him, she began circumventing the bike. "Besides, I'm hardly dressed for riding on that—that awful contraption of yours."

In less than a heartbeat he'd cut the engine, set the kickstand, dismounted, and advanced on her. "You're not dressed for a long walk in the desert sun," he repeated.

She couldn't rally fast enough before he snatched her up, carried her to the bike and plopped her down on the back. Stunned speechless, Jaimin simply stared as he got on and brought the bike back to thundering life again. “There’s pegs to put your feet on,” he shouted over his shoulder. “Watch the exhaust pipes. They’re blazing hot, so keep your legs away from them. One more thing,” he added over the loping, roaring din of the bike, “make sure your dress is tucked beneath your legs, so it doesn’t get caught in the back wheel.”

“I am *not* doing this.”

“Yes, you are.” He revved the engine for emphasis. “You can thank me later.”

“Just what am I supposed to hang on to?” she snapped.

His eyes grew openly amused as he turned his head and slipped on his dark glasses. “Me.”

Jaimin swallowed hard.

CHAPTER FIVE

"All set?" he asked over his shoulder.

"No."

"Hold on to my waist."

She didn't want to touch him. Yet she had no choice, so sitting as far back from him as possible, she slid her arms about his waist, silently cursing this entire day.

Marc revved the throttle, swung out onto the main path, and began picking up speed.

He'd insisted she wear his leather jacket for protection from the sun and hot wind. Even though it was too big for her, it provided covering. But it also held his essence—an elusive trace of masculine cologne mingled with the heady scent of leather and tobacco smoke. To Jaimin, it was an unsettling combination that had her feeling as though she were wrapped in his arms.

It wasn't long before he geared down just enough to explain how to sway with the bike around curves. "Lean into it," he instructed. "Don't fight it, or you'll throw us off balance."

"I'll fall."

"No, you won't. I promise. Centrifugal force will keep you from falling."

Silence fell between them again, and as the miles flew by, she gazed out over the arid dunes that stretched away on both sides of the road. A hawk-like bird soared overhead, wings spread wide as it glided on the rising air currents. Suddenly, it changed direction, folded its wings, and dove down on some unsuspecting prey.

As time and the miles continued to pass, Jaimin found herself dealing with more of the same chaotic thoughts that she'd experienced the day before. This man was so different from any other man she'd ever known. Other than the dream she'd had the other night, these thoughts and desires were foreign. Ahmed had never stirred such feelings. Not once.

"Jaimin. Quit fidgeting. I'm tired of having to counterbalance every time you shift back there."

"Sorry."

After the dream she experienced the other night, she thought she knew it all, knew what to expect. Today she realized how wrong she was. There was a huge difference between a silly dream and the real thing. Reality was far beyond her small and untutored imagination. Reality was the steeled back her cheek was pressed against. The tempered, virile body her arms were wrapped about. The heady scent of his leather jacket—of *him*. It was the wind in her hair, the tang of fuel and oil. It was the deep growl and the pulsing heartbeat of the strong engine throbbing between her legs. It was no wonder she was squirming.

"You okay back there?"

"No." she shouted back. "I want off. Thank you."

He laughed. "If you'd prefer, I can let you off at the edge of the village. It would be a short walk home from there."

"Perfect."

Her reaction seemed to amuse him. With a slow grin, he briefly turned, and said over his shoulder, "That way, your reputation won't be ruined by being seen with the likes of me." Turning back around, he added dryly. "Your thoughts are as easy to read as print on a dispatch, sunshine."

Jaimin didn't respond. It was too noisy for conversation. So instead, she continued devising a plan for smoothing out the disaster this day had turned into. One thing for sure, he was right, she didn't need to have the village witnessing her arrival astride his motorbike—especially with her torn outfit bunched up to her thighs for all to see.

By the time another half hour passed, Marc began gearing down as they neared Shapiro. They made the trip in just under an hour. "Let me know where exactly you'd like to be dropped off," he called back.

~ * ~

He'd kept his word and let her off where she indicated.

"Thank you," she said softly, as he helped her off his bike.

"You, okay?" he asked and steadied her when she started to sway.

"I'm fine. I just need to get used to standing again."

Her legs were shaky, her body still feeling the lingering vibrations and hearing the constant thunder of his bike.

Marc studied her for a long moment. "Look, I know it's counterproductive, considering you don't want to be seen with me, but maybe I should take you home."

"No, I'm fine," she said, arching her back to relieve her aching muscles. "Besides, you're right, it would be counterproductive."

She started to turn away when he gently caught her arm.

"Jenelle? Do me a favor. Give some thought to what we talked about. Okay?"

"My name is *not* Jenelle. It's Jaimin, and I'm not leaving my home."

With that, she started off down the road. She suspected he was watching her because she didn't hear his bike start-up until she turned the corner and was out of sight. It was then she heard Marc Banner's departing bike fading into silence.

She hurried home where she slipped through the back door and into the kitchen unobserved. She could only imagine what her parents would think and say if they were to see her.

Rushing to her room, she quickly changed, then silently scurried back through the kitchen again and out the door before anyone saw her. It was a bit of a walk to the beautiful home that Ahmed's parents kept in Shapiro. Jaimin didn't mind as she hurried along, it gave her time to perfect what she was going to say and how to handle the situation.

Not for the first time did she wonder how Marc Banner just so happened to be at the same place Ahmed had chosen to stop. Was he there first as he'd said, or had he been following them? What difference did it make? Just look at the mess she was in now. She didn't blame Ahmed for leaving her. He was fleeing for his life.

When at last, she arrived at his residence, she stopped before approaching the home. Loud male voices could be heard coming from somewhere behind the home. Following the sounds, she discovered a small tent-like structure and stopped just before arriving at the closed entrance.

"How the hell would I know who he is?" came an angry, nasal voice drifting out from the shelter. "I swear, I've never seen him before. He looked rough, and definitely not Adenian."

"Okay. Okay. Keep that ice pack on your nose," came his father's deep voice. "You need to stop the bleeding. I'm sure your nose is broken, Ahmed."

Feeling guilty over Ahmed's injuries, not to mention the fact that she was standing outside eavesdropping, Jaimin started to enter the tent and make her presence known. The next words drifting out of the tent, however, stopped her dead in her tracks.

"I don't know why I ever agreed to go along with your scheme to marry her," Ahmed muttered through his plugged nose. "I don't love her, and I don't want to marry her. For all I care that sonofabitch can have her."

Jaimin's hand shot to her mouth, smothering her gasp.

"Let's get this straight," his father growled. "You're marrying her because of your obligation to this family. Why do I have to keep reminding you of this? As her husband, you'll be heir to the Ala Rashard wealth and power. Rashard, himself, is aware of the advantages and reasons for this match. It will combine the wealth of both of our families, and it makes no difference whether you love her or not."

"Jaimin is not one of us," Ahmed protested. "Just look at her. Her hair. Her eyes. Her coloring. She's not Adenian. Besides, I love Nijah. She's the one I want to marry. Not Jaimin."

Jaimin's knees weakened and she leaned against one of the exterior foundation poles of the shelter.

His father laughed. "Ahmed, Ahmed...you can still have Nijah.

I'm telling you; you can have Nijah too. Marry them both if you wish. Nothing is stopping you from having them both."

Jaimin had heard enough. On shaky legs and with tears falling, she turned and stumbled back toward the road that led home. In just one short day, her world—the world she thought she knew—had crumbled around her. Apparently, even her father was in on it—willing to go along with the match knowing, and not caring that love wasn't part of it. It would be a marriage for wealth and power.

Aren't you the least bit curious about your real parents, Jenelle? Banner's words stormed through her mind as she trudged back home.

Jaimin swiped at the tears. What if it's true? What if her life here on Aden was all a lie? What if she really had been kidnapped? Why didn't she remember any of it? She had to admit, she did sort of recognize the picture of the beautiful woman in the locket—her mother. If she had been nine years old at the time, wouldn't she also remember something so traumatic as being abducted? Even bits and pieces of it? Why didn't she remember anything?

Still, what if it *is* true? What if she wasn't meant to be here after all? Hadn't she always felt inferior to the others, like an outsider? Wasn't she always trying to prove that she was just as good as everyone else? So-what if her skin, hair and eyes were different.

Maybe it was time to step outside the comfortable, protective sphere of her parent's—*her adoptive parent's*—world and learn where she truly belonged.

Marc pushed his bike inside the guest accommodation that Saleem provided. From there, he dug through his travel pack until he found an old rag of a T-shirt. It made a good dust cloth as he lovingly dusted off and polished the bike's glossy black fenders and fuel tank. He then started in on the chrome.

The thing about diverting his attention to the bike, he'd managed to work through much of his anger and frustration over the thought of Jaimin apologizing to Ahmed. If that's what she wanted, there was little he could do about it.

Since he'd already accepted Saleem's invitation to stay for the

Adenian Festival, he felt obligated to stay. Unless Jaimin changed her mind—which didn't look promising—he'd be leaving Shapiro the following morning without her.

He'd simply gone out for a bike ride today to clear his mind. To think—hoping to figure out a way to convince Jaimin to at least meet her parents, if nothing else.

As he approached the lake, he chose a quiet spot in the shade of a few tall palms and pulled off the road, It wasn't until he'd heard loud voices arguing that he realized other people had arrived in the area. The sound of a woman's cry had him checking it out.

Marc flexed his fist. His knuckles still smarted. If he hadn't shown up when he did, Ahmed would have surely violated Jaimin. In truth, that asshole deserved more than a couple of missing teeth and a broken nose. The only thing that stopped him from doing even more damage was Jaimin's pleas for him to stop. How she could defend that dirtbag was beyond him.

Max Banner had always taught his boys that a woman was to be revered. Never hit or manhandled. Marc couldn't even remember a time when his father had even so much as raised his voice to his mother. Not that there hadn't been occasional differences of opinion between his parents. They share a deep love and respect for one another and have always worked their way through any problems.

Marc shook his head slowly. Taking on this rescue mission had been a big mistake. He didn't look forward to having to tell the Byers that he'd found their daughter alright, but she was unwilling to leave. Adenian brainwashing methods were strong. He pondered the idea of simply telling them that he couldn't find her, but then he wouldn't be able to let them know that she looked well. That she had been adopted by an affluent couple and raised with love as well as the best of everything.

And... soon to be married to a no good, sonofa—No. He couldn't tell them that.

Oh well, can't save them all. Might as well give Frank a call and see how things are going.

CHAPTER SIX

"Where the 'ell are y'?"

"I'm in Shapiro. They're having the annual Adenian Festival tomorrow. I'm going to stay for it, then I'll be heading back the next morning."

"Well, goodie fer you." Frank drawled cynically. "So, did y' find that lost treasure you was lookin' fer?"

"A wasted trip, I'm afraid. Anything new at your end?"

"Not a dang thang."

"Bored out of your mind, are you?"

"Whata' you think? There's no one here to talk to 'cept that noisy, foul-mouthed, red-feathered vulture y' insist on keepin' aboard. I locked him in yer cabin by the way."

Marc huffed a laugh. "I take it Ruckus is screaming his head off?"

"Surprised y' cain't hear 'im. 'Ee don't like bein' locked up, but that's the way it's goin' to be as long as I'm in charge."

"That's fine, Frank. Besides it's better he's locked up than flying loose when nobody's there."

"Whadaya mean by that?"

"If I arrange a ride for you, how would you like to join me tomorrow for the annual festival?"

"...Y' don't have t' ask twice."

"I'll make the arrangements to bring you out tomorrow morning."

"I'll be awaitin'."

~ * ~

The crowd was beginning to gather. Once seated, Marc scanned the elaborate banquet hall. Mingled with the essence of tobacco smoke, incense hung heavy in the air. An extravagant red and white marbled fountain stood in the center of the room; its bubbling geysers illuminated by subsurface lighting. Walls of stark white were off set by arched doorways decorated with what appeared to be gold carvings. Throughout the room were dozens of round tables, like the one he and Frank were at. They sat low to the ground and were surrounded by brightly colored pillows. His friend, Saleem, told him that only a privileged few were invited to join the opening ceremony inside the pavilion. Even at that, there must have been thirty or more candle-lit tables, each seating at least six. Thanks to Saleem, the table he and Frank were seated at had been reserved for them alone. It was situated near the front with a sweeping view of the raised dais where Shakari Saleem would be officially welcoming the guests and giving the opening speech.

Although Marc and Saleem had been friends for many years, Marc knew very little about Aden other than the fact it was an arid planet heavily steeped in legend and ancient customs. One rumor said that Adenians were descendants from the ancient Tuareg warriors on Earth who brought their culture and peculiar traditions with them to Aden. Another rumor said just the opposite, that the Tuaregs on Earth were originally descendants from Aden. No one ever bothered to question either theory.

It wasn't long before every table in the large hall was occupied, and soft native music was competing with the buzz of male voices. Marc glanced about, looking for Ahmed, but didn't see him. Without a doubt he'd be here, especially since Jaimin made it a point to apologize to him. Unquestionably the marriage would go through. With both of them coming from wealthy families, it didn't take a vivid imagination to see the advantages of combining their wealth. Jaimin had made her decision, and again, that left him with the task of telling the Byers that their daughter was getting married and choosing to remain on Aden, an undertaking he wasn't looking forward to.

"It's been many years since the last time I was at one of these shindigs," Frank said, glancing about the crowded hall. "If I remember correctly, they start out with something called the Veil Dance." After a moment of wistful silence, he added softly, "If I were only thirty years younger..."

Marc laughed. "I can imagine you were quite the operator back then."

"Y' better believe it."

A young serving girl, moving among the tables, approached to set down a beautifully enameled tray laden with a variety of desert-grown fruits. With an adoring smile, she topped off both of their chalices with more of the heady wine they had been drinking.

"If I remember correctly," Frank added, "this stuff is called Mercy wine." Lifting his goblet, he barked a hoarse laugh. "Friendly advice, son. Just in case y' didn't already know, it'll have y' beggin' for mercy 'fore y' realize it."

"Uh huh..." Marc replied loosely, his interest suddenly focused on something upon the raised platform.

"Yep," Frank went on, unaware of Marc's lack of interest, "I'll never fergit the time Nick, Zeke and I attended one of these ballyhoos in Jahara." He released another croaky laugh. "Y' shoulda' seen those two. They ended up so bombed, they spent most the night readin' the bottom of the table."

Marc wasn't listening. His gaze was caught and held by a pair of dark, luminous eyes. Who was she, he wondered? Wife? Daughter? Mistress? He hoped for the latter, although there was something about the veiled young woman that suggested she was anything but a mistress to the Aden ruler who was seated at her left.

"Hey. Y' wanna put yer eyes back where they belong 'fore someone decides to take yer head off?"

Marc was so mesmerized he took his sweet time acknowledging Frank's hissed warning. True to Banner form, Marc was accustomed to running his life by his own set of standards and code of ethics—a habit that usually had him crossing somebody's line of protocol now and then. Yet, there were some lines even he didn't cross. In short, wives were out of the question, and virginal daughters were more trouble than they were worth. A mistress...now *that* was generally fair game.

Ever so slowly he dragged his gaze away from the raven-haired beauty whose eyes kept straying back to his. He's known his fair share of beautiful women, bedding more of them than not, and yet never had he felt anything more than a passing attraction, usually satiated along with his body.

Damn, was it the wine playing tricks, or was this beauty really looking directly at him with those come-hither eyes? Like a moth to flame, he looked at this woman clothed in snowy layers of semi-transparent diaphanous fabric. He imagined the shape of her mouth as his appraisal slowly moved down the graceful drape of veil concealing the lower half of her face. She was a native. He was sure of it. Her olive coloring, dark almond shaped eyes and her raven hair left no doubt.

At last, his gaze moved to linger upon the delicate swell of her breasts.

It had the usual effect.

Suddenly an elbow slammed painfully into his ribs. "Dammit man, will y' quit gawkin' at her?" came Frank's low murmur. "Case y' ain't figured it out yet, y've been noticed. Hell, yer gonna get us both killed at this rate."

With great reluctance, Marc tore his gaze away and turned to Frank. "Who do you suppose she is?"

"Beats me, but I'd be willing to bet she belongs to someone important. Like maybe that Sultan-dude to her left."

Another young serving girl approached to refresh their chalices with more of the heady wine. Laying his palm over the bowl of his goblet, Marc declined the refill. Frank, on the other hand lifted his goblet for an easy top-off.

"Y' know..." Frank added. "She ain't the only one 'round 'ere. Why don't y' try checkin' out the rest of the dolls. Fer one; that little servin' gal ain't bad, and she was eyeing you, case y' didn't happen t' notice that either. Plus, if I remember correctly, you'll be offered one of the dancers for the night." Grinning, Frank reached for his wine. "Heck, if y' think yer man enough, y' can 'ave two." he added on a lewd chuckle.

Ignoring the challenge, Marc slowly digested Frank's comment. "Frank, I doubt very much that this is that kind of a dance." He doubted Jaimin would be involved if it were. "Besides," he added, "we're not spending the night. We've got an early get up, and I for sure don't need a roaring hang-over to deal with in the morning."

"Y' mean we're leavin' tomorrow?"

"That's exactly what I mean."

"Ain't y' afraid of offendin' yer Shakari friend if we don't stay?"

Marc refrained from rolling his eyes. Who was Frank kidding? Between the booze and the women, it didn't take a genius to know who would be upset. "I'm not worried. He'll understand, Frank."

"But..."

Suddenly the background music stopped, and the hall quieted as Saleem stepped up onto the stage to give the official welcoming address along with introducing Hassid Ala Shalem, ruler of the fourth sovereign of Aden. This was the man *Dark Eyes* was sitting next to, and as soon as Hassid was officially introduced, Marc's attention became divided as *Dark Eyes* quietly rose from her seat and made her way off the stage.

The instant the opening speech ended, suddenly a dozen or more veil dancers twirled their way out from behind the stage for the opening entertainment—the Veil Dance. Marc cast a quick scan of dancers. If it truly was as Frank had described, surely Jaimin wouldn't be involved. *Dark Eyes,* however...

~ * ~

Jaimin was grateful for the veil that concealed her look of relief. He was here. He had stayed for the festival after all. Last night she came to a decision, one that she thought she would never make. Now she depended on the outsider to help her carry out her resolution. After yesterday's fiasco, she didn't know if he was even still planning to stay for the festival. She hadn't seen him since he dropped her off at the edge of town.

He was here! Conflicting emotions surged through her—anticipation, fear, curiosity, and now a measure of hope.

Luckily, she'd had a chance to point the outsider out to Aannisah before the dance started. The plan was, when the dance ended, Aannisah would *choose* him, and with an adoring smile entice him to follow her.

Would he follow her? If he did, Aannisah would lead him backstage to where she will be waiting. Hopefully it wouldn't be too much of a problem since the outsider had been intently watching Aannisah ever since he noticed her on the stage.

~ * ~

Aannisah was in the middle of a synchronized pirouette when her arm was suddenly grabbed, and she was roughly hauled out of the lineup.

"That man will lose his eyes if he's not careful." came a whispered warning.

Her older brother's tone was as matter of fact as his statement.

"Let go of me, Jordain. He simply looks," she reasoned in low undertones. "After all, what is the harm?"

"Yeah, well there are looks, my sister, and then there are *looks.* That man is not just looking. He is devouring. Unless he stops, he will first lose his eyes, then his life."

"I say again. I see no harm." Aannisah threw a slanted glance her father's direction.

Had he, too, noticed the man's bold perusal? To her relief, her father was still on the stage talking to Saleem.

Once again Jordain was over-protective. Aannisah jerked her arm out of his grasp. "I've got to get back in line. Leave me alone."

"Fine. You just make sure you don't reward that man for his audacious behavior. You'll have only yourself to blame for his consequences."

With a sigh of frustration, Aannisah fell back in line.

~ * ~

Marc watched with avid interest as the dancers wove their way about the tables, their hips and limbs moving teasingly to the seductive beat of the music in the ancient art of unfolding an age-old story. It was stirring, a sensual feast, their bodies becoming one with the music as the exotic dance progressed and the story unfolded.

Each dancer wore a different color. Together, they became a vision of an undulating pastel rainbow. Once again Marc glanced about the hall. Was Ahmed here, he wondered? Had he accepted Jaimin's apology? If so, then the marriage was undoubtedly still on.

"Looks like that little doll's in the dance."

"And which one might that be, Frank?"

Frank huffed a laugh. "The one y've been tradin' heated stares with for the past half hour. As if y' didn't know."

"I don't know what the devil you're talking about."

Frank croaked another laugh. "Y' really need me to point 'er out fer y'?"

Ignoring Frank's taunt, Marc continued scanning the hall for Ahmed, failing to see him anywhere. Hopefully two black eyes, a broken nose and two missing front teeth had kept the sonofabitch home nursing his injuries.

Just then a second line of dancers entered the hall. Jaimin was in this second group—dressed in a delicate shade of aqua, her platinum hair arranged loosely about her shoulders. Marc noted that her dress was not quite as revealing as some of the others, and he watched her with avid interest as she joined the other girls, weaving their way about the tables.

Each dancer took her turn plucking filmy wisps of hip scarves from their costumes and tossing them into the air to float down among the honored guests.

~ * ~

"Let me guess," Jaimin whispered as she caught up with Aannisah, "Jordain is up to his usual big brother guard duties. Right?"

"Yes." Aannisah said through clenched teeth. "I get so tired of him."

"What's his problem this time?"

"The outsider," Aannisah grumbled while plucking a thin handkerchief of delicate fabric from the folds of her costume.

With a practiced smile and a flick of the wrist, she tossed it high in the air to drift downward among the guests.

"What did he do to earn Jordain's rath?" Jaimin whispered.

"I'll tell you later."

"Well, don't forget your promise. That's all I ask."

"I won't."

"Bring him back to me, Aannisah. It's important. I need to speak with him."

"I know, Jaimin. I *know*. Don't worry, I'll bring him, even if I must bind him up in a tangle of gossamer scarves."

~ * ~

A tissue-thin, diaphanous scrap of snowy white glissamer floated momentarily on a shelf of air before drifting downward directly in front of Marc. Neither willing nor capable of stopping himself, he reached out and lightly caught the scented wisp, inhaling its alluring fragrance.

Holding eye contact as she approached, Aannisah smiled as if discerning Marc's very thoughts. The seductive music pounded on, its beat primitive, hypnotic. Like a package being unwrapped, Aannisah plucked another swatch from her costume and released it to drift down upon Marc's lap. "I will come for you when the dance is over," she sighed in her most suggestive voice.

Having overheard, Frank let out a low breathy whistle. "Still wanna to go back to the ship, Sport?"

"Yes. Nothing's changed, Frank. We're not spending the night here."

"Whatever you say," Frank drawled with a sly grin that said he doubted Marc would be able to stick to his avowal.

Marc turned to glance at others seated nearby and would have laughed if he, too, wasn't beginning to feel the effects of the heady wine. Frank's eyes were glassy and half-lidded as he reached out to catch a peach-colored scarf drifting his way. What was that old Earth adage about a kid in the candy store?

"See one y' like?" Frank asked as he caught another thin veil of peach. "Or are y' gonna follow that little gal who's already chosen y'?"

Less wine, and a bit more restrained than Frank now, Marc simply grunted an answer as the rainbow of women wove their way about the tables. The floor was littered with a rainbow mix of delicate pastel scarves, but it was the snowy white wisp that Marc still held in his hand that had his attention. If she came for him, dare he go with her knowing, undoubtedly, that it would be an all-nighter, not to mention he'd feel like hell in the morning? Would it be worth it, he wondered?

With that thought, his gaze once again moved from the bevy of scantily clad women to the one dressed in purest white who had apparently made her choice. Him.

"She's a beauty fer sure," came Frank's murmured assessment as they both watched the dancers. "If she comes back fer y', y'd be a fool to turn her down, son."

Slowly Marc turned toward Frank, "I'm *not* staying. Soon as this dance is over, I'm outta here. I have things to do before we leave in the morning."

With a look of disappointment, Frank replied. "What if *I* stay?"

"You do what you want, Frank. We're leaving at O-Seven-Hundred. Make damn sure you're back by then."

"I'll be there. Not to worry."

With his shaggy iron-colored hair and full mustache, Frank, at nearly sixty-three, was still a stunningly handsome man. While each of the dancers divided their attention between the guests, this one dancer, dressed in peach, had eyes only for him. Marc couldn't help grinning as he watched Frank loop an arm around her waist and draw her down onto his lap. Between the potent wine and the beautiful woman in his arms, Frank was a goner.

Marc wasn't much better off with the angel in white hovering close by. In truth his attention was divided between her and wondering if Jenelle's apology had been accepted.

Jenelle...Damn. He needed to start thinking of her as Jaimin Ala Rashard, because that's who she was. She'd made it perfectly clear that she wanted nothing to do with her real parents, or the life she was born to. The life she would have lived if she had never been kidnapped.

Suddenly, the hypnotic beat began slowing as the dancers began twirling their way toward the exit. Without thought or even realizing it, Marc turned to search the crowd for the dark-eyed beauty dressed in white.

If she comes for you? a silent voice whispered. *You gonna go with her Pal? You might as well get something out of this trip besides a failed rescue.*

Just then, behind him a gentle hand rested upon his shoulder. "Please...follow me."

Mulling over her soft words, Marc slowly turned his head to look up at her. "Much as I'd love to, sweetheart, I can't."

Dark Eyes wasn't listening. Instead, she dropped to her knees beside him and placed her hand suggestively upon his thigh. In a beseeching voice she softly added, "There's something I want to show you. I'll make it worth your while."

Contemplating her promising words, Marc slowly dropped his gaze to study the beautifully manicured hand resting suggestively upon his upper thigh. The unspoken message was loud and clear.

Oh hell...Why not? It had been a while since he'd had a woman, and he doubted Frank would show up on time tomorrow anyway.

CHAPTER SEVEN

Marc followed *Dark Eyes* across the hall, stopping only when she paused at the closed entrance to a backroom behind the stage.

"Wait here."

Leaving him to wait, she disappeared behind a closed door.

Now what, he wondered? He could hear giggles intermingling with the prattle of feminine voices. Marc's head suddenly snapped up with a jolt of recognition. One of those voices sounded very familiar. Too familiar. Jaimin? What the devil was she doing back here? Easily understanding their native language, he focused on what was being said from behind the closed door.

"So, what do you want me to tell him?"

Marc frowned at hearing that he was the topic of discussion between *Dark Eyes* and Jaimin. If she had made her peace with Ahmed, he couldn't think of one good reason why she'd be looking for him.

"Bring him in, Aannisah. I need to speak with him."

"I sure hope you *know* what you're doing."

A moment of hesitation, then... "So do I, Aannisah. So do I."

Marc was about ready to open the door himself when the door swung open and *Dark Eyes* appeared. "You may come in now."

"Well, well, this is a pleasant surprise," he drawled as he strode casually inside the small chamber. He looked from one to the other. "So...do I get to choose? Or do I get you both?"

"Stop it!" Aannisah's tone was no longer soft and inviting as she turned to meet him toe to toe. "I can't begin to imagine why, but for some nonsensical reason my friend, Jaimin, feels a need to speak with you."

His eyebrows rose expectantly as he shifted his gaze to Jaimin. "Well then, I'm all ears."

All but wringing her hands, Jaimin stood by quietly, her eyes downcast. “I’d prefer to talk in private.”

The slight hitch in her voice didn’t go unnoticed. Whatever this was about, Marc’s curiosity was piqued.

Tight-lipped and scowling, Aannisah left the room, her snowy white costume swishing about her hips and legs.

“Could we maybe go for a walk?” Jaimin asked in the awkward silence.

“Sure.”

Clasping her hands in front of her, she ignored his offered arm and headed for the outside exit. Marc caught up with her in two strides and fell in step as they left the structure. Aden’s sun had set long ago, and the sky was a black inky canvas of glittering stars. Holding her chin high, Jaimin looked straight ahead as she walked.

“So... what’s on your mind?” he finally asked after they’d walked for a while in silence. “Let me guess. Prince Ravisher accepted your apology, and I get an invitation to the wedding.”

Jaimin stopped and turned to face him. “...Okay,” she said after a long moment of silence. “First, I need to apologize for being so ungrateful yesterday. I am truly sorry. You came to my aid, and I’m afraid I didn’t appreciate it, let alone thank you.”

Well, he sure hadn’t seen that one coming. An apology was the last thing he’d expected. There had to be an ulterior motive. “What happened, Jaimin? Didn’t Prince Debaucher forgive you after all?”

Jaimin’s gaze dropped to her clasped hands. “I didn’t apologize.”

The hurt in her whispered voice was unmistakable, but then she lifted her head and looked directly at him, grey eyes reaching out to him. “Tell me...” she asked. “Tell me about my parents. I mean, my real parents.”

Marc stared at her before answering. “I’ve only briefly met your parents.” He hesitated before asking, “Why?”

Unless he was mistaken, he strongly suspected she was hiding something.

“I’m just curious, that’s all.”

"I see."

She was picking her words carefully If only he could figure out what she *wasn't* saying. For now, however, he'd play along. "Well like I said, I met your parents only once. It was when your father approached me about finding you. They're good people, Jaimin. It's been eleven years and they've never given up looking for you. Eleven years and they still grieve your loss." Gauging her reaction, he paused, allowing his words to sink in. Tears shimmered in her eyes. Not the kind of tears a woman can turn on and off at will. These were real tears.

After a moment she sniffed, quickly swiped her cheeks, and lifted her chin. "If it still stands," she began, "I would like very much to take you up on your offer."

His brow lifted. "Let me get this straight. You want to come with me to meet your real parents after all?"

Her response was immediate. "Yes." Ignoring his look of astonishment, she went on, "but we need to leave tonight."

"Tonight? Why tonight?"

"Because I must leave tonight. That's why."

"I'm leaving first thing in the morning. Not tonight. Besides, I can't leave without Frank, and he won't be back until morning."

"Frank?"

"If you're leaving with me, you'll meet him soon enough."

"Well, tell him you need to leave tonight instead."

Marc laughed. "I don't think that'd be such a good idea."

"Why not? You're the captain, aren't you? Yesterday you were adamant that I go with you and meet my real parents. You said that's why you came here."

"Yes, and that's true, but I'm not leaving tonight. Besides, have you told your parents, Hassan and Zari, of your decision? I can't just grab you and run."

"Why not? Why do I have to tell anyone?"

"Your Shakari already knows why I'm here, Jaimin."

A gentle breeze tugged at the delicate aqua costume she was still wearing and sent her loose hair in tangles about her face. "So?" she asked, brushing the hair from her face.

"So...unless he's satisfied that you're leaving with me of your own free will, it would only stir up one hell of an inconvenience."

Jaimin turned away, her mind in a whirl. Overhead a raucous Aden nighthawk made its presence known with a screech that mimicked her own thoughts. "I don't understand, why would he care what I do?"

"Because it's his job to keep the peace, and I guarantee that if we're both missing, it will be assumed I abducted you. They'll come after us, Jaimin. Whether you say anything to Hassan and Zari is up to you, but if you're leaving with me in the morning, your Shakari needs to know, and it needs to come from you, not me."

~ * ~

A flutter of fear shot through her. She didn't dare tell her parents. They'd never let her go. Never. All along, her father had been in on this scheme with Ahmed's family. How could he betray her? *Her loving father.* He had to have known that Ahmed didn't love her, that she would not be happy. Was her mother in on it too?

At last, Jaimin asked "Can't I just leave a signed message or something? Must I talk to them?"

Marc stared at her for a long time. "A message to who?"

"Our Shakari and my parents. They won't like it, and I want to be gone before they find out. That's why I must leave tonight."

"Nobody's going to like it, Jaimin. As long as you make it known that you're leaving because *you* wish to, there's nothing anyone can do about it."

"But..."

"At any rate," he went on, "I'm leaving in the morning. So, if you're coming, make sure Saleem knows I'm not forcing you."

Clenching her hand to her mouth, Jaimin smothered a small sob. If only she could leave tonight. She would be long gone by morning, and Ahmed's father would not be able to stop her. "So where exactly do I meet you?"

"I'm staying in the third guest tent from the pavilion."

"Okay, I've seen your machine parked outside."

"Then be there no later than O-Seven-Hundred."

"I will..." she replied in a faint voice as she turned to leave.

Marc stepped forward and took her arm. "I'll walk you back."

"Thank you," she said, easing her arm from his grasp, "but I need time to think."

He dropped back. "As you wish."

It was a gamble to put her off when she was apparently ready to leave with him tonight. With Frank not due back until morning, he had no choice.

~ * ~

Jaimin arrived at the family home of her friend, Aannisah, a place of many sleepovers throughout the years.

"How do you know he isn't simply going to trade you off for a tidy sum on another planet somewhere?"

"Don't be silly, Aannisah."

"I'm dead serious. Hands on hips and a level stare, Aannisah faced Jaimin. "It isn't like it's never happened before you know."

Jaimin regarded her friend for a long moment of silence. "Well, I suppose those things do happen, but he would never do anything like that."

"Oh, I see. You know him that well, do you?"

Jaimin released a heavy sigh. "Of course not."

Aannisah frowned. "Look, I know he's *smokin' hot*, Jai. Even I must admit it, but—"

"What? ...That's not it, and you know it, Aannisah."

"No. I don't know it. The point is, I don't trust him. Anyway, what's the name of his ship?"

"How should I know? Why?"

"Well, I forget the name of this one pirate ship, although I'd recognize it if I were to hear it again. Anyway, not long ago a marauding ship attacked a commercial liner, along with two of our own merchant freighters—all in one day. And I heard that the captain killed the crews, stole all the cargo, and"—her voice lowered dramatically— "and ravished all the women."

Jaimin rolled her eyes and refrained from laughing. "Wow, how energetic of the captain." She turned to gather up a few of her personal belongings and stuffed them into a woven shoulder bag. Turning back to Aannisah, she held up a couple of outfits. "Do you mind if I take these two with me? I don't dare go back home. Besides, I already told my parents that I'd be spending the night here."

"I don't care. Take them." Aannisah released a frustrated sigh. "Jaimin, are you hearing anything I'm saying?"

A faint smile curved Jaimin's mouth. "Yes, I hear you."

"I don't like it, Jai. How do you know that this Captain Banner, isn't the same pirate who attacked those ships?"

"He isn't."

"But, what if—"

"Aannisah," Jaimin interrupted. "Whatever you're about to suggest, he isn't, and he won't. If he does, then you will have the satisfaction of saying I told you so. Do you mind if I borrow this tunic?" she asked, her attention returning to the task at hand.

"No. Take it." Aannisah watched helplessly-on as Jaimin continued packing. "You hardly know him, Jai. I don't like him. I don't trust him. He scares me."

"Oh honestly, everything scares you. If I were to believe all the tales I hear from you, I'd be afraid to go for a walk without a bodyguard. You always seem to ignore the facts surrounding these fanciful tales you stumble upon. One of these days your imagination will get you into trouble."

"You may be right," Aannisah replied tartly, "but not in as much trouble as your foolish determination will get you into. I just think you're rushing into something you're going to regret."

Jaimin shot her a resigned look. "Yes, I believe you've already said that, and as much as I love you, I'm not asking for your approval.

All I want, is for you to give my parents, and Shakari Saleem these notes that I've written."

Jaimin withdrew two handwritten notes from a pocket and handed them to Aannisah. "If anyone should question you about me, tell them the truth. That, against your compelling advice, I left of my own accord."

Aannisah accepted the notes. "Oh Jaimin, I..."

"Please, please don't say it. My mind is set."

"It's just—"

"You'll do this for me, won't you? Please? "

"Yes. You know I will."

"Thank you," Jaimin then withdrew a third note. "This one is for you. For your eyes only," she emphasized. "Hopefully it will help explain everything—why I'm leaving, and the truth about Ahmed."

Aannisah's head snapped up. "*Truth*? What truth?"

"No more questions. Read it after I'm gone. I promise all your questions will be answered, and you'll understand."

"Oh Jai...Will I ever see you again?" Aannisah cried, rushing over in tears to cling to her friend. "I'm going to miss you terribly."

"And I you. Although I don't know when, but once I get settled, I'll be in touch. I promise."

Dawn was barely breaking when Jaimin climbed out of bed. She'd been awake all night, her heart pounding like thunder. Unwilling to stay. Hating to leave. Terrified of the decision she'd made and praying that she knew what she was doing.

CHAPTER EIGHT

"What'er y' gonna do if she don't show?"

"She'll show."

"What if—"

"If she doesn't, then she doesn't."

Frank ambled over and sat down on the fender of the self-driving taxi that arrived earlier to take him and Jaimin back to Port Jahara's spaceport. "So, y' say y'll be about a day behind us?"

"Yes, about that. I have two stops to make for Nick that shouldn't take long." Marc was thankful Frank was with him after all. Without Frank, he'd have to haul Jaimin around with him on the bike. Either that or not run the errand at all. The thought of her riding on the back of his bike was bad enough, not to mention spending a night under the stars with her—which is what it would amount to considering the distance between stops.

"That'er comin' now?" Frank asked, his attention drawn to a young woman making her way toward them.

"Yeah. That's her."

"Looks like she must 'ave packed everything she owns in that case she's draggin' behind 'er."

Without comment, Marc hurried forward, meeting Jaimin before she joined them, Taking the travel case from her, he headed for the awaiting taxi.

"Frank, meet Jaimin Ala Rashard."

"'Ello darlin'" Frank said with a cordial nod as he took her offered hand.

"Jaimin, this is Frank Reno, my co-pilot," he said in her native tongue.

"Hello."

"Pleasure's all mine, honey."

Marc ignored the veiled looks of full-blown approval that Frank kept firing his way when Jaimin wasn't looking. You didn't have to be a mind reader to know Frank's thoughts. He was relentless when it came to matchmaking. Marc had watched Nick, Zeke, and Clint all go through it, and he remembered laughing at the time. Now he was the target, and it wasn't so funny anymore.

"Jaimin, I've got a couple of stops to make on the way back," Marc said as he hefted her travel case into the back of the small taxi. Frank will be taking you back to the ship."

"You won't be coming with us?"

"I'll join you and Frank at the ship sometime tomorrow afternoon."

"Oh."

"You'll be far more comfortable, and safer riding in that taxi than on the back of the bike. What's more, you'll arrive at the spaceport this afternoon."

"Plus, when we get there, darlin'," Frank interjected, "the ship will be airconditioned. You'll have a cabin of your own with your own lav, and a comfortable bed to sleep in tonight instead of the cold ground."

"Ground?" she asked softly.

"Yes, plus, I'm sure y'd have to share a blanket, since he probably only has one on the bike."

"Oh...I don't think that would work."

Marc grinned. "Frank's right. I don't think it would work either.

"Frank?" he said without breaking eye contact with Jaimin, "You and Jaimin go ahead and take off. I'll be right behind you until we get to the cut off."

"Yes sir, Boss. Here darlin'," Frank said rushing over to help Jaimin board the taxi. "Lemme help y'."

"Thank you."

"Don't y' mind the captain none." Frank whispered. "If he seems a bit surly this morning, I'll wager it's because he's hungover from last night." Frank grinned. "But I assure y' his bark is worse than his bite."

"He's not mad at me, is he?" she whispered back.

"Nah...it's just...well, he wants to make sure yer safe. That's all. We don't need no trouble."

"Is there going to be trouble?" she asked.

"Not if we can help it."

Jaimin stared off into the distance. The pre-dawn sky was still glittering with stars scattered across its deep blue pallet. It wouldn't be long before the flush of daylight would be silhouetting the distant dunes. "Is he really going to be sleeping on the ground? she asked.

"I would imagine. There ain't no inns near where 'ee's goin'."

"What about snakes?"

"You two about ready?"

Hands on the handle grips, Marc was straddling his bike. "I hate to interrupt, but we need to get moving." As if in throaty agreement, the bike's deep, loping idle expressed a mutual eagerness to hit the open road.

"We're all set, Captain." With that, Frank set the taxi into motion as Marc's loud and commanding motorcycle pulled in behind them.

~ * ~

Hands folded neatly in her lap, Jaimin turned her sights outward at the swiftly passing scenery, absently noting that the desert was in bloom. Cactus flowers made bold splashes of color against the dun-colored sand. Two days ago, she was happily preparing for the Aden festival, looking forward to dancing for Ahmed in the opening ceremony. Two days ago, she was anticipating marrying him. Now...her future was empty, and it scared her.

"I just hope you know what you're doing?" came the memory of Aannisah's troubled rebuke.

You and I both. In truth, she couldn't remember being as afraid as she was now. Although she must have been terrified if she truly had been kidnapped as Captain Banner said. She had no memory of that horrifying experience. Just the same, nothing in her recent life experience had prepared her for anything like this. She who had been cosseted and protected by loving parents. Even the parents she couldn't remember apparently loved her. At least that's what she had been told. Now here she was, racing away from the only home she could remember.

They had been on the road a couple of hours when Jaimin suddenly realized she no longer could hear that thundering beast trailing behind them. With the hot desert wind tugging at her loose hair, she turned about to see if he was still there.

He wasn't.

"'Ee turned off a while back, darlin'," Frank said. "Y'll see 'im tomorrow."

Face flaming, Jaimin swung back to face the front, mortified that Frank easily guessed her thoughts. "I was just curious since I didn't hear his machine behind us anymore."

"Uh huh."

The hot flush staining her cheeks shot from her eyebrows down to her toes. It was embarrassing—the press of laughter Frank was obviously restraining.

By mid-morning, the sun was already growing hot. Wishing the taxi had air conditioning, Jaimin removed a small length of cloth from a pocket and quickly mopped the back of her neck.

"Can I git y' somethun' cool t' drink? There's water on ice in the back as well as some sort of fruit drink, if y' prefer," he said as he brought the vehicle to a stop.

"Water would be wonderful. Thank you."

"The captain made sure y' had somethun cold to drink on the hot ride in," Frank went on, as he handed her an ice-cold thermos of water.

"I appreciate his thoughtfulness. Please, thank him for me."

Frank snorted a laugh. "Y'll see 'im tomorrow, darlin'. You can tell 'im yerself. I think 'ee'd appreciate it more hearin' it from you." He handed her a small tablet. "Captain said to give this to you too. "It's a tutor on learning to speak English all over again. It's only an introduction, but to start off with it will help you with basics and might help break the boredom of the trip into Jahara."

"Thank you."

The desert road dipped, dropped down into a deep gorge for a couple of miles, angled back up again, and now they were in a land of sandy gulches.

Three hours later, they were topping the last dune and Frank was pointing out the settlement of Jahara below. "Won't be long now honey. Soon y'll be relaxin' inside the air-conditioned *Antara and* sippin' on sumthun' refreshin'."

"That sounds wonderful."

Frank chuckled. "I thought y'd like it."

"Antara?" she asked.

"That's his ship. And way over there is the spaceport," he added, pointing at a vast levelled area shimmering in a watery mirage of late afternoon heat. As if to confirm Frank's announcement, a blast of thunder heralded the distant image of a large freighter as it rose skyward.

Within an hour they were entering the far end of Port Jahara's spaceport. By now, the sun was slowly slipping behind the distant dunes and the day had begun to melt into the amber-infused indigo of a hot desert evening.

The spaceport was far bigger than Jaimin ever imagined. Not only had she never been to Port Jahara, but she had also never been to a spaceport—leastwise, not that she remembered. Wide eyed with curiosity, she watched as the taxi cruised down an extensive corridor that was flanked on each side by rows of docking bays. Some of the bays were taken by smaller mail boats like the ones that she's seen occasionally at Shapiro's tiny spaceport. Most of the bays were occupied by nasty-looking long-haul freighters that looked ready for the scrap heap. As if they didn't look bad enough, Jaimin noticed they were perched upon massive, rusty-looking landing jacks that reminded her of ugly bird legs. Many of those ships appeared in need of serious repair, that's if those puddles of dripping lubricant were any indication.

"Where do all these ships come from, Frank?"

"Everywhere, darlin. Everywhere.'"

"Even Earth?"

"Yes. Even Earth."

Eventually the taxi came to a halt before a large black wall which soared more than a five hundred feet up the side of a dune that bordered the far-left side of the spaceport. "Well, darlin' this is where we get out. We're gonna walk it from here. There's an elevator in that wall straight ahead that will take us to the upper deck. From there it will be a short walk to the ship. Here," he added as he hurried around to help, "Let me help y' out, then I'll grab yer things."

"Thank you, Frank."

Even with the sun having dipped behind the dunes, waves of heat continued radiating off the scorched landing surface. Jaimin decided that between the combination of excessive heat, ugly freighters, and the stench of raw fuel, exhaust and ozone, the spaceport was a very unpleasant place.

"This way, darlin'." he said as he steered her into the elevator's marginally cooler interior. Within moments the doors reopened on the upper deck, and they were greeted with a renewed blast of residual heat. "We're almost there, honey. See that ship straight ahead? That's the *Antara*."

One thing she was relieved to note was that the *Antara* did not look anything like some of those dilapidated ships they had passed. No puddles of dripping lubricant. No rust or filth. It looked shiny and well-kept. "Well, at least we won't have to walk very far," she said.

Frank laughed and reached for his remote. "No, that's fer sure." With that he began punching in a code. "I promise, five minutes from now you'll be relaxin' in the coolness of that thar ship."

As they made their way toward the *Antara*, Jaimin watched in fascination as a boarding ramp slowly began descending from a dark and narrow rectangle below the main hatch.

"After you milady," Frank proclaimed with a theatrical bow and an elaborate sweep of his arm.

Jaimin covered her mouth to control her laughter. She loved Frank's gentle camaraderie and wit.

"Just go on up, honey. The hatch will slide open when you get to the landing. I'll be right behind you with yer things."

CHAPTER NINE

Overhead entry lights snapped to life the instant Jaimin stepped across the threshold. The first thing that hit her was a rush of cool air. Stepping deeper inside, she found that the ship was dark, except for the helm where the command console and overhead panels held a throng of pulsing tiny colored lights.

"Welcome to the *Antara* darlin'." With a wink and a grin, Frank added. "Lemme git some lights on and wake this baby up so y' can be properly introduced."

Frank set her case and bag down by the hatch and turned for the helm. The instant he sat down an electronic voice greeted him.

"Welcome back, Marc. While you've been gone, the outside temperature—"

With a flip of a switch, Frank cut off the computerized report. "Yeah, yeah...Y' don't 'ave t' tell me how hot it is out there. Right now, we got company, so how 'bout gettin' some lights on 'round here."

"Certainly. Do you want light in the helm only, or in the entire ship?" came the calm electronic response.

"The whole damn ship," Frank growled, "if it ain't too much trouble."

Jaimin started to laugh. Up until now both Marc and Frank had been communicating with her in Adenian. Thanks to the tutor, she had learned just enough English to sort of understand what Frank was growling at the computer about.

"Oh honey, I'm sorry. I gotta watch my language."

Amusement flickered in her eyes. "It's okay Frank," she said in her own tongue. "I hear it on occasion. Maybe not in the same language, but it means the same. "

"Now try sayin' that in English, darlin'". With a wink he added, "I don't understand Adenian that well."

It was a fib, and they both knew it. Frank and the captain both spoke flawless Adenian.

Between the tutor and Frank helping her on the trip-in, she found it easier to understand the words than to speak them. When she did try to say something in English, she found herself having to slowly pick and choose the right words, as well as how to pronounce them. The result, the words always came out sounding broken and awkward—even to her own ears.

"It's so frustrating. I'll never get it."

"Aww honey, sure y' will. Yer doin' better than I expected. Just one day and look at y'. Boss is going to be surprised when 'ee shows up tomorrow. I guarantee."

"You think so, Frank?"

"I *know* so. I want to work on something for you to say when 'ee gets here. Okay?"

She took a deep breath. "Okay."

"Now, how about a quick tour and show y' to yer cabin? With that Frank grabbed her travel case and shoulder bag. "This way, honey" he said as he led the way down the narrow corridor away from the helm. They approached three doors on the right that Frank explained were living quarters. "This first one," he said, "is the one y'll be stayin' in." With that he pressed the palm pad and opened the door to place her belongings in.

"Screech! Squawk!" A wild flurry of bright red plumage flew out of the open cabin door, shrieking a string of obscenities as it disappeared down the corridor.

~ * ~

Frank just hoped Jaimin couldn't grasp the meaning of such foul language. "Damn buzzard," he muttered. "I have half a notion to leave the Main Hatch wide open for 'im. Are y' alright, darlin'?" He turned to find Jaimin plastered against the bulkhead directly across from the open cabin. Both hands protectively thrown over her face. Frank quickly closed the distance between them. "You alright?"

No response.

"Jaimin?"

She cautiously opened one eye. "What...was...that?"

"That's the boss's foul-mouthed vulture. I was 'sppose to move him outta his quarters 'fore y' got here."

Jaimin jerked away from the bulkhead. "Are you saying that this cabin belongs to Captain Banner?"

"Yes ma'am'." It's the best one out of 'em all. Even has its own private lav. Boss wanted to make sure you get his cabin."

"Oh, he did, did he? Well, I don't think so." She rattled off in her native tongue.

Frank hesitated, clearly confused. "Y' don't think what?"

For several long moments, Jaimin simply stared at Frank in disbelief. Then... "If the two of you think I am going to share a cabin with him, you are both crazy. I'd rather sleep in the cargo hold."

"Share?" Frank frowned, looking even more confused than ever. "Darlin' he ain't stayin' in here with y'. 'Ee's movin' into one of the other cabins."

"That's why he left the bird here? Because he isn't planning on staying here?" For a moment Aannisah's wild tale of the pirate captain crossed Jaimin's mind. What was it she had said? That after all that looting and killing, he'd ravished all the women too? Men...were they all animals? She was beginning to think so after her encounter the other day with Ahmed, and now this.

With a compressed sigh, Frank tried to reason with her. "Darlin' I'm tellin' y' it's my fault. I was supposed to move Ruckus out of here. I promise you...the Boss ain't plannin' on staying in this cabin."

"Well, he'd better not."

"I'm sayin' he ain't."

"Alright. I believe you."

"Good. I've set yer things inside. Now you go take a nap, a

shower or whatever makes you happy while I make us somethun' to eat."

Before leaving, he quickly grabbed the bird's perch stand, seed, and water cups.

"Frank?"

"Yes?"

"I'm sorry." She managed a little shrug and glanced down at her clenched hands. "I think the heat, or something must have gotten to me. I apologize and want to thank you for all you have done for me today."

"Nah. Think nuthin' of it. A little gal like you, y've had a long, hard day with the heat and all. Get some rest now and I'll have sumthun' ready whenever y' feel like eating. By the way, just so you know, I cleaned the cabin from top t' bottom yesterday. Fresh towels and bedding. Even removed the captain's stuff from the lav. He grinned. "It's all yours."

"Thank you, Frank."

"It gave me something to do. I had well over a month of listening to that godawful buzzard of his, and nuthin' to do but wait."

"Well, thank you just the same."

Jaimin ended up taking Frank's advice. After a quick shower, she laid down for a nap with every intention of getting up to eat with him. As it turned out, her little nap lasted until morning of the next day.

It was the bird that woke her. He was squawking somewhere off in the distance. Next came the sound of a klaxon quickly disappearing down the length of the corridor, and Frank muttering, "Shut the 'ell up."

Jaimin had never heard a bird mimic anything before. It was so real sounding.

More screeching, then "Warning. Warning. Brace for collision. Shriek." the sound getting louder as the bird was obviously flying back up the corridor.

Unable to control her laughter, she knew for positive why the noisy bird had been confined to a cabin while his owner was away.

Frank was a vision of pure frustration by the time Jaimin made her way into the galley. Quickly putting on a cheerful smile she entered with, "Something sure smells good, Frank. What are you fixing?"

"Roasted Ruckus," he growled as he poured himself a mug of coffee and turned to face her. "That damn—uh, darned bird. He woke you up, didn't he?"

Jaimin laughed. "No, I was half awake anyway. Ruckus? That's his name?"

"Yes, but I could come up with a few names of my own that better suit 'im."

Jaimin was still laughing when Frank turned to flip something he'd been tending on the cooktop. "You hungry, darlin'? Grab a plate over there. I made some temberberry muffins. There's eggs and fried taters on the cooktop and whatever you like to drink—coffee, tea, juice, they're on the counter behind me."

"Maybe just a muffin and some tea."

"Whatever sounds good to y'. Y' just help yerself, honey. I made plenty so when captain gets back, there's enough for him too."

Jaimin sat across from Frank, breaking her muffin in half, she took a tentative bite while waiting for her tea to steep. "This is wonderful," she said lifting the muffin for emphasis. "I've never heard of temberberries." "They're a local berry on Terra Four." Frank said as he filled his own plate and came to sit across from her.

"So do you have any idea when Captain Banner might return?" Jaimin asked.

Frank leaned back with his mug of coffee. "Well, if everythang goes accordin' to plan, I figure he should be pullin' in sometime mid-afternoon at the very latest."

Jaimin set her tea down. "Seriously, he should have his cabin back."

Frank shrugged dismissively. "It's a done deal, honey. Besides, 'ee's the one who ordered the switch." With a wink he added, "I just follow orders."

"But—"

"Think about it," he said gently. "Do y' really want to give up that private lav? Yer very own shower? Once we get on our way, yer lookin' at about two months of sharin' tight quarters with the likes of us.

There will be times when it ain't gonna be pleasant. Y' sure y' want to give up that spacious cabin? It'll be yer escape..." he chuckled, "from the two of us."

She released a heavy sigh. "It's just that I don't feel I should be kicking him out of his private quarters."

He slowly nodded. "For our needs, Capt. and I have plenty of room in the smaller cabins. We have the entire ship to get away from each other when needed. Plus, we'll be constantly tradin' shifts at the helm. Where you, on the other hand, could spend as much time as y' want sleepin' and relaxin' in that roomy cabin and not be bothered by us."

Jaimin burst into laughter. "What you *really* mean, Frank, is that you two wouldn't be *bothered* with me being underfoot. Right?"

Frank smiled. "Wrong. Jaimin. A pretty thang like you could never be a bother. I guarantee underfoo*t* has nuthin' t' do with it. I'm not namin' names or anythang, but darlin' just *knowin'* yer onboard is gonna *bother* one of us in particular." A look of mischief came into his eyes and with a grin he added, "but I suspect in a good way."

"Screech! Two minutes to impact. Squawk!" Without warning, a flash of bright red suddenly soared into the galley. "Squawk! Phasers on stun." Dipping above their heads, the beautiful bird gracefully circled the area twice before settling with a flap of its wings onto Frank's shoulder. "Stand down and prepare to be boarded. Squawk!"

No longer afraid of him, Jaimin laughed. Although unable to fully understand the language, she thought it funny simply to hear a bird speak.

"Damn buzzard. Scuse' my language."

With a wave of his hand, Frank shooed the bird off his shoulder. It took to air once again, exiting the galley to soar down the corridor in a screeching frenzy.

"Where does he learn those things?"

"Some of it he hears from the computer."

Just then the bird returned, and with a graceful swoop, it landed on a nearby shelf and began softly muttering. From the scowl on Frank's face, Jaimin surmised they weren't good words.

Confirmation came when he glanced over at her, his expression grim. "Darlin' I hope you didn't understand what he just said."

"Honestly, I heard him speak, but I couldn't tell you what he said," she assured him as she reached for the other half of her muffin. "Certainly, he doesn't learn vile things from the computer. Does he?"

Frank shook his head. "No, ma'am. He does not. 'Ee's been deliberately taught. It's not that I have tender ears. 'Hell, on occasion, I'm guilty of usin' a few of those words m'self, but that damn bird needs to be caged or locked in a cabin when there's a lady present."

"So, how old is Ruckus?" Jaimin asked.

"Don't rightly know for sure." Dragging a hand through his shaggy hair, Frank stared at nothing in particular, yet seeing the years of time slide away. "'Ees not real young. That much I *do* know. Marc got him as a fledgling, maybe thirteen or fourteen years ago..."

He paused, momentarily reliving the memory. Frank's countenance suddenly hardened along with his tone as he continued. "'Ee, uh...brought the bird back from Earth. Without so much as a word to anyone, Marc and a few of his so-called *buddies* just took off one day. They apparently hitched a ride on an Earth-bound freighter. Gone for nearly a year by the time he showed back up. Never contacted his folks even once during that time."

"How awful" she said, halting her mug of tea halfway to her mouth. "I imagine everyone was worried."

"Yeah...His dear mother was near sick with worry. His father..." Frank paused for a deep breath that he released in a heavy sigh. "His father was angry more than anything."

"Well, surely Marc wouldn't have taught his beautiful bird to say vile things."

Frank huffed a laugh and drawled, "Oh yes he would 'ave. In fact, he took perverse pleasure in seeing the shock and disapproval on the faces of those within hearing range." Frank's curt nod avowed his statement. "Marc was in his mid-teens at the time, and he had an oversized chip on his shoulder for some reason. He was a handful back then—rebellious, cocky, and belligerent as all 'ell."

With another heavy sigh, he reached for his mug of coffee. "Y' wouldn't 'ave known him darlin'. Back then, his hair was so long it spilt over his shoulders. ...Surly, know-it-all kid," he added beneath his breath. "He was runnin' wild with a rough bunch who were up to no good one hundred percent of the time. You'd never guess he was the son of a prominent and successful businessman,"

"Oh my... So, tell me—"

Lifting splayed hands in surrender, Frank cut her off mid-sentence. "Darlin', I've said way too much already."

"I understand." She rose from the table and began gathering up their plates. "You've known his family a long time, haven't you?"

"Years...years."

She took a deep breath and let it out in a sigh. "Well, anyway I don't care what he teaches his bird to say if I can't understand it. By the way, where should I put these?" she asked, indicating the plates in her hands.

"Just leave 'em. I'll get 'em. Besides," he added with a lopsided grin, "we got t' work on yer language, darlin'. Y' need to be able to communicate. Plus...the boss'll be here sometime this afternoon and you were going to work on sayin' thank y'—in English, 'member? For that icy cold water, he made sure you had fer the trip out?"

Awkwardly, Jaimin glanced up at him. "Frank, can't I just thank him in my own language for now?"

"Sure, if that's what you want to do."

With a deep breath she continued, "I mean, Marc speaks flawless Adenian as it is. Plus, I'll have plenty of time in the weeks ahead to learn your language."

"It's yer language too, honey. Y' just don't 'member it."

"I know, but for now I want to thank him in Adenian. I don't want to be stumbling over words that I find hard to pronounce. I can learn English later, when I can take my time."

"Well then, sounds like a plan to me," he said, rising from the table. He glanced down at his watch. "Right now, I'd say we got about four hours t' kill 'fore the boss will be pullin' in. What do you say we use a few minutes of those hours and complete the tour that *buzzard* interrupted yesterday?"

"Oh, I'd love that."

The morning passed quickly. After the tour, Jaimin helped Frank clean up the breakfast mess. Later, to pass the time, he taught her how to play Bounty, patiently explaining which cards were more important than others, and what exactly she needed to be holding in her hand to win. She surprised him by being a quick study—even beat him twice.

Still sitting at the table, she was in the middle of memorizing the values of the different planetary designs on the cards when an abrupt and unfounded sense of panic seized her. Suddenly, it was hard to think, yet her mind raced with horrible worst-case scenarios. One after another, each one bringing her back to one name. Marc.

Rising to her feet, she made her way down the corridor "Frank?" she called, assuming a calm voice.

"In here, honey." He poked his head out of his open cabin door. "What can I do fer y'?"

"I was just wondering if you have heard anything from Marc."

"No. I wasn't expectin' to. Why?"

"Nothing. Just wondering. You said you think he'll be returning sometime this afternoon?"

Frank glanced at his watch, "Yep, I look for 'im to be pullin-up within the hour."

Jaimin nodded. "Thanks." And with a sigh she turned and headed back toward the bow of the ship.

The fear and sense of panic wasn't going away. Like a living thing, it was creeping down her spine and settling low in her stomach. Why did she have this jumpy feeling—the kind of feeling she might have if she were falling off a cliff? Whatever the reason, Jaimin felt sure it had to do with Marc. Maybe he was having trouble with his bike. That wouldn't explain why her heart was pounding so hard. People have trouble all the time, things that even cause them to run late. Yet, what she was feeling had nothing to do with running late. She was sure of it. Every nerve in her body was on edge.

Either something was happening now, or it was about to happen, and it scared her.

CHAPTER TEN

Marc just left the settlement of Dubhan, having delivered the last package for Nick. Now to get back on the road and head for Port Jahara.

He'd refueled in Dubhan and was about a half hour down the road when he glanced once again in his mirror. Was he being followed? He'd been keeping his eye on a white ground runner maintaining pace with him about a half mile back.

There was only one way to find out. Up ahead there was a break in the brush and cacti growing along the roadside. It would be better to pull off the road now and meet whoever face to face. With that, he began gearing down. Guiding the bike off the road, he killed the motor, engaged the kickstand, and dismounted. At this point he had two choices—either act as though he had motor trouble, or head for the bushes to pretend he was relieving himself. The bushes, he decided, were his best bet. Maybe he was overreacting. Maybe they'd simply drive on by. If not, he stood a better chance meeting them on his feet instead of crouched down, pretending bike trouble.

He'd no sooner assumed the position at the bushes when he heard the approaching vehicle slowing down. Sand and gravel crunched beneath the tires as it was brought to a halt on the shoulder of the road. Pretending to rebutton his fly, Marc turned around, taking his sweet time to acknowledge the intruders.

"Well, well...look who's here," came a stuffy, lispy-sounding voice.

Marc glanced up to see three young men headed his direction. There was no mistaking the one with the nose bandage and two black eyes. Ahmed Farouk. What was he doing here? Last he knew Ahmed was nursing injuries.

"You're looking good, Farouk," Marc drawled as he slid his shades back in place and continued making his way toward his bike. "Although you sound a little funny. Must be hard trying to talk through a broken nose and two missing front teeth."

Ahmed's expression hardened. "We have a score to settle."

"We do?" Marc frowned. "Here I thought we'd settled that the other day." Behind Ahmed stood two rough-looking young men, their drawn-weapons trained on Marc. "I see you brought some buddies with you."

"I did."

One of the men came forward, and with a leer, withdrew Marc's gun from its holster. "You're going to wish you'd never messed with Ahmed," he hissed.

Well, so much for defending himself. "Let me guess, Farouk, they're going to help you settle the score."

Ignoring Marc's sarcasm, Ahmed responded. "Wrong. They're here for the entertainment. You see, I have a special plan for you. You're going to love it."

"Oh yeah? I can hardly wait."

"Well, wait no longer." Looking smug, Ahmed reached into his pocket and withdrew a small slender weapon. "Ever seen one of these little babies?"

Oh shit! Marc's arrogant smile vanished. Adrenaline rushed through his veins with lightning speed, racing across every interconnection, alerting every nerve in his body. A lifetime of memories, thoughts and information rushed through his brain all at the same time, all categorized and recorded within a nanosecond.

"Yesss...I can tell by the look on your face, you know exactly what this is." Ahmed laughed with glee. "And just in case you're wondering, this is the latest and most advanced model of the *Ripper*. Nothing but the best for you."

Silence. Marc was fresh out of cocky comebacks.

~ * ~

It wasn't that Jaimin was feeling better. She wasn't. If anything, the butterflies of panic in her stomach were getting worse. Nothing like this had ever happened before. With Frank not worried about anything, he would think she was crazy—that she had lost her mind. So, she put on a happy face and tried pushing the butterflies aside.

"Darlin', you sure y've never played Bounty before?" he asked as he came forward to join her once again in the galley.

Jaimin feigned a laugh. "Never."

Frank nodded. "A greenhorn, huh? He headed for the coffee. With a slow shake of his head, he added. "Shoulda' known better. Greenhorns always win. Did y' know that?"

Jaimin faked another laugh. "Oh, you're just trying to make yourself feel better."

"Darn tootin' I am." Coffee in hand, Frank turned to face her with a mock frown. "It's embarsin' gettin' beat by an itty-bitty girl."

"Aww, poor guy. Come on back, and let's play another round? Surely, you'll win this next time."

"I dunno, you're awfully good for a beginner," Frank said as he returned to the table with his coffee and a container of homemade biscuits. "Can I git y' something to drink, darlin? Here, have a biscuit."

"I'm fine. Sit down, Frank. We've got a game to play."

With that, she began shuffling the cards.

~ * ~

"Oh, this is going to be even better than I'd planned," Ahmed chattered on. "I've got you scared, don't I? As you should be. Let's see...I wonder what happens if I press this button?" With that, he thumbed one of the pressure pads and was delighted when the weapon started humming. "They say these little toys won't leave a mark on you, but at half blast you'll be paralyzed with pain."

Shit. Heart pounding, it took a minute for the adrenaline to level out. Marc tried to steady his breathing, then waited for his thoughts to catch up. He was well aware of the pain and dangers of a *Ripper.*

"Now, I wonder," Ahmed continued with his animated, nasally, lisping voice, "what happens when this little light goes from red to green? Let's find out, shall we?"

With his friends cheering him on, Ahmed fumbled a little longer with several pressure pads, watching as they, too, lit up in response. "I'm going to set this baby on the lowest setting for now. That way you and I can have fun while I play with it."

His focus never straying from the weapon in Ahmed's hand, Marc forced himself to remain in a relaxed, casual stance while continuing to look death head-on.

"Hmm...I wonder what happens now? This is the lowest setting." Ahmed grinned. "Let me know if you feel it. Okay?"

Continuing to watch Ahmed's movements with distinct awareness, Marc dropped, rolling to the side the very instant Ahmed engaged the pressure pad. Despite his attempt to avoid the *Ripper's* deadly current, nevertheless Marc's body jolted with the impact. Hell, if this was the lowest setting, he didn't want to know what the highest setting was like. Yet he had a sinking feeling, he was going to find out.

So...is this how you're going to check-out, huh pal? No weapon? Unable to even defend yourself? No one will ever know what happened to you. The greegs will find your body and there'll be nothing left but picked bones. Looters will haul your bike off.

Ahmed all but giggled like a girl over the effects of his new toy. "That wasn't too bad now, was it? Let's see what this next setting does."

Marc braced himself as Ahmed engaged another button.

This time, the invisible current surged through him with the force of a runaway freight sled. His body spasmed with the shock, muscles contracting as pain knifed up his torso. It was like being trapped in a vice while every part of his body was seized in the grip of unbearable pain. His legs buckled and he went down.

He had no idea of the passage of time. Even after the shockwaves stopped, the pain seemed to intensify. Dear God, he didn't know if he could take much more. As it was, he was on the edge. These little tests were tearing him apart. If Ahmed doesn't stop playing around and get on with it, the next little test will have him crying like a baby. As it stands, the way he sees it, he has two choices. One: try to hold up as best he can, and hope Ahmed will grow weary of the game. Two: say something insulting and foolhardy and get it over with fast.

And right now, choice Number Two was looking better by the moment. With that, he managed to stagger to his feet. He'd be damned if he was going to lie there and take it. If he was going to die, he'd die on his feet. Better yet, if he could just get something started with one of Ahmed's buddies, he could easily take-on either one of those two clowns—both if he had to—and get his gun back. At the moment, one of them was lighting up a cigarette while waiting for Ahmed's next plan of attack. Marc studied him. The kid was too sure of himself, waving his gun around while talking to his friend. That's the one he'd provoke. His sloppiness would be his own downfall.

Now to wait for the chance to get something started.

~ * ~

"So," Jaimin began, "how did you happen to meet the Banners? You said you've known them for years."

"Marc was just a toddler when I first came to work for his father."

"Is Marc an only child?"

Frank exhaled a croaky laugh. "At the time there was a total of three young mischievous boys all under seven. Marc being the youngest."

"He's got brothers?"

"Yes. Ma'am, Clint, and Nick."

"I can't imagine having three busy boys underfoot at the same—"

With a sharp intake of breath, Jaimin—mid-sentence—sprang from her chair and began pacing.

"What's goin' on with y' girl?" Frank asked. "Yer as jumpy as a *neural firefly*."

Jaimin stopped her pacing to turn to him. “Something terrible is happening.”

Her words hung between them in the silence. The only sound was the constant hiss of the ship’s ventilation. She couldn’t even explain it to herself, much less to someone else.

Without dropping eye contact, Frank cleared his throat, “Jaimin...y’ wanna give me a bit more detail on what exactly yer talkin’ about?”

“That’s just it. I have no idea what I’m talking about. I just know that over the last half hour I’ve felt nothing but pure panic for no reason, a feeling of impending danger.”

“Impending danger? For who?”

She shrugged as a resigned sigh escaped. The whole situation was either a bad joke or a bad dream. “I don’t know, Frank. Call me crazy, but I can’t help but feel that maybe Marc’s the one in danger somehow.”

“Marc? Hmmm, I tried messaging him about twenty minutes ago. No response.”

~ * ~

Marc shifted positions, figuring he’d start with, “Hey, can a guy at least get a last smoke?”

“You get nothing but a slow trip to hell.” Having said that, Ahmed leveled the weapon on Marc’s chest. “Ready or not,” he recited in a nasally, sing song voice, “here it comes.”

There was no time to provoke anyone into a fight. He was just thinking he could sure use a cigarette about now when everything suddenly exploded. Without so much as the flash of a laser beam, or the force of a heavy slug slamming into him, Marc’s body buckled with the invisible impact of the *Ripper.* In a world of intense agony, he felt himself sag to his knees. At first the descent seemed in slow motion, then, suddenly like a two-by-four, he smashed face-down onto the ground.

Nothing could have ever prepared him for the pain. Dear God, it was as though he was being eaten alive. He could feel invisible teeth tearing and ripping away at his flesh. If he were a screamer, now would be a great time for screaming.

For several stunned moments he laid there, trying to gather his thoughts—a task that was impossible, given the fact that his brain was now completely disengaged—off flying around somewhere trying to escape the pain.

A heavy boot slammed into his ribs forcing the air from his lungs. In a far distant corner of his mind, he could hear Ahmed laughing as he and his friends walked away. Next came the sound of a vehicle pulling away. He tried getting up but discovered one small problem. He couldn't move so much as his little finger, let alone get up. Ahmed was right when he said he'd be paralyzed. He couldn't even blink the sand from his damn eyes.

Crap. Was he dead and this was hell? Sure, felt like it. Not that he didn't deserve hell, he just always thought he'd have plenty of time to make up for all the depravity over the years. Thirty-one years. He was too damn young to die.

~ * ~

"If we find he's unable to ride his bike back," Frank was saying. "He'll need to ride with you."

"I just hope we find him, Frank."

"Me too, darlin' Me too. I'm hopin' we'll pass 'im on the road comin' in. He'll think we're nuts worryin' about 'im."

They'd been on the road about two hours, desperately scanning both sides while there was still light. By now the sun had dipped behind the distant dunes and the desert sky was growing dark. Frank brought a bright search light with him and was casting a brilliant beam on both sides of the road as they progressed.

"Not much farther 'til we get to Dubhan." he said, running his hand through his steely gray hair. It dropped right back over his brow. "I checked the ship's records before we left. He'd refueled in Dubhan about three hours ago. So, we can assume he was alright at that time."

"So," Jaimin began, "if we don't find him before Dubhan, we'll still look beyond, won't we? Just in case he's been abducted or something and they've doubled back where they came from?"

"I'm not giving up. We're gonna find him...alive."

"Good," she replied, thinking Frank had somehow aged in just the last couple of hours.

"Wait." she shouted as she pointed to the left side of the road. "Over there. What's that? Quick, shine the light over there—to the right of that brush."

Before Frank could bring the taxi to a halt, Jaimin was out and dashing across the road. "It's his motorbike," she called out as Frank cut the engine and joined her at a run.

"That's his bike alright. Do y'see Marc anywhere?" he asked swinging the spotlight wildly about the area.

"What's that over there?" Jaimin asked as she took off again with Frank close behind. "He's over here!" she cried, dropping to her knees beside Marc's unresponsive body. "Oh Frank...I don't know if he's unconscious or..."

"Here, let me roll 'im over—get 'im off his stomach." Once he had Marc on his back, Frank quickly checked for a pulse, finding it wildly racing. "'Ee's alive thank God, but we gotta git him to a hospital. I don't know what's wrong, but somethun' ain't right."

"What about Dubhan, Is it big enough to have a hospital?" she asked.

"That's where we're goin'," Frank said. "I've been there and know exactly where it's at. Stay here with 'im while I bring the taxi around."

Within moments Frank had the vehicle positioned as close to Marc as possible.

"What can I do to help?" she asked as he hopped out of the vehicle and approached Marc.

"Nuthin' right now, honey."

Frank seemed to know just what to do. Jaimin watched as he began pulling Marc into a sitting position so that his back was resting against Frank's legs. From there Frank reached around, giving Marc a bear hug. It was a maneuver that allowed him to heft Marc into a standing position. After that, a series of quick and precise moves had Marc's inert body slung—chest down—across Frank's back. With Marc's arms draped over his shoulders, Frank grabbed hold of each wrist, stabilizing his load, then with a groan of supreme effort he straightened to a full height.

"Frank, do you need help?"

"Noo," he rasped. "I got 'im." Exhaling sharply, Frank turned for the taxi with his unconscious cargo. "You go ahead and get in. 'Ee's completely unresponsive and I'm going to have to brace him against y'."

With a final groan of exertion, Frank all but dumped Marc onto the seat next to Jaimin. It took another few minutes of precious time for both Frank and Jaimin to maneuver Marc so that he was leaning against her, his head resting upon her shoulder.

"Okay," he said, winded. "I've already programmed the cab for the trip to the hospital. You don't have to do anything except stabilize Marc. Y' ready?"

"Yes."

"Let's get the hell out of here. I'll be right behind y'."

He thanked God that Marc's bike was still there, and still on its kickstand. Had it been tipped over, no way would he have been able to right it. It would take two men to get the job done. Frank mounted the bike and pulled in behind the taxi. It was so strange, he thought, not one moan or sound from Marc when he was being moved. If he has internal injuries, it would be painful. Yet not a sound. Even unconscious, people sometimes moan in pain. And then there was his racing heart. Hell, it's a wonder it hadn't exploded by now.

After being on the road a good half hour, the lights of Dubhan came into view. Frank had already notified Emergency that they were coming in and to be ready.

As they entered the settlement Frank goosed the bike, pulling ahead of Jaimin and leading the way to the hospital. It was a small hospital. The parking lot was practically empty when they arrived. Not surprising considering the time of night, and it being a small settlement. Pulling beneath the portico, he stopped the bike and quickly jogged back to see how Jaimin was doing.

“You okay back here,” he asked, never taking his eyes off Marc who by now had slid down on the seat, his head resting in Jaimin’s lap.

“I think so.”

Her arm was looped about his torso, keeping him anchored.

“Hang tight. I’m going to let ‘em know we’re here.”

“Please hurry Frank, His heart rate is scaring me, I can feel it pounding against my arm.”

“I know, honey...I know. Just stay put. I’ll be right back, and we’ll get that boy off y’.”

“Just hurry,” she whispered as he raced toward the emergency entrance.

CHAPTER ELEVEN

Frank and Jaimin hung back as they wheeled the gurney into an examining station.

One hour later one of the doctors came out asking if anyone knew what exactly happened. Frank told them what little he knew, which was basically nothing.

Nodding slowly, the doctor went on to explain they were able to get Marc's heart rate leveled out, but he suspected once the meds wore off it would rise again. As for him being comatose, they had no answers. A dark bruise across a couple of cracked ribs suggested foul play. However, there was no head trauma or anything that might give clue as to why he was unconscious.

"Mister Banner is about as stable as we can make him for now. My advice is to get him into Jahara as soon as possible. They have a bigger and more sophisticated hospital and will be able to help him better than we can."

On the way back to Jahara, over the constant drone of the bike, Frank spent the time mulling over scenarios that could possibly explain Marc's condition. What the hell happened? It didn't make sense. Obviously, it wasn't a robbery. His bike would have been gone.

They were forty-five minutes out of Jahara when a thought crossed Frank's mind. What if someone had used a *Ripper* on Marc? Several years ago, Marc's brother, Nick, had a *Ripper* installed in his ship. Now, as Frank thought back, he recalled Tressa accidentally triggered the damn thing and suffered the consequences.

Suddenly a cold knot formed in his stomach. What if...What if all this time Marc is suffering from the effects of a *Ripper*? Hospitals would have no clue how to help him. Oh, they might temporarily get his heart rate down, but they wouldn't know how to save Marc's life—if it's even possible.

Frank didn't know much about the *Ripper*, although he'd heard that the newer models were more than just a deterrent to burglary, the newer models were an inhumane death sentence.

It made sense the more he thought about it. Since he had no knowledge himself of what could or couldn't be done, there was only one person he could call. Doron, a local licensed naturopath, who was often referred to as a Medicine Man.

By the time they arrived back at the spaceport, Doron was waiting for them. "Good thing I was in the area when you messaged me."

"I agree. Thank you for comin'."

"No problem. So, you think someone used a *Ripper* on him?"

"I have no idea. It's just a thought," Frank paused, once again running a hand through his hair. "Alls' I know is that the hospital had no idea what was wrong with 'im, let alone what to do about it."

"I see. Is that him in the cab?"

"Yes."

"Let's get him inside so I can see what's going on."

Immediately, Frank withdrew the remote and lowered *Antara's* boarding ramp. They had Marc out of the vehicle and up into the ship in a matter of minutes.

"Where are his quarters," Doron asked as they started down the corridor

"Second cabin."

Jaimin raced forward to open the door and flip on the overhead lights in the darkened cabin. She'd no sooner done so when... "Awwk! Warning. Thirty seconds to impact. Screech!" A startled flurry of vivid red flew out to disappear down the corridor in a shrieking turmoil. "Dammit. This ship's in trouble. Squawk."

"What the hell was that?" Doron muttered.

"That was our resident devil," came Frank's grumbled response as they entered the quarters and positioned Marc on the bunk.

"Is there anything I can do to help?" Jaimin asked from the open doorway.

"Yes. Would you run out to my vehicle and get my medical case out of the back while Frank and I get him settled?"

By the time Jaimin returned, they had removed Marc's boots and stripped off his shirt. Frank was standing at the foot of the bunk, his face long as he watched his friend examine Marc.

At last, Doron straightened and released a deep, compressed breath.

"Well? Whata y' think?"

"Well, he's got two fractured ribs. That much I know. He's in bad shape, Frank."

"So, do y' think it was a *Ripper*? Will he be, okay?"

"Yes. And... I don't know yet. Plus, I suspect whoever did this had it set on the highest setting." Doron paused a moment. "Do you have any idea when this might have happened?"

"I dunno, but ship's records show he was in Dubhan, refueling at about two o'clock this afternoon, so it would 'ave been after that."

Doron nodded. "It's eleven thirty now. Okay. Well, his heart rate has risen again, so tonight I've given him an injection to bring it back down." Doron looked pointedly at Frank. "I won't sugarcoat this, Frank. Your boy's got a long road ahead of him. He's going to need both you and the girl to help him through this."

"Yer saying he'll live. Right?"

"I'm not making promises. Had we gotten to him sooner..." With a shake of his head and a heavy sigh, Doron glanced away. "Look, I might be branded a *medicine man* because I work with crazy stuff like snake and spider venom, but I am not a miracle worker by any means."

"Sometimes for one reason or another," Doron continued, "those potions work, and sometimes they don't. It also depends on how strong the patient is—whether he has what it takes to crawl up out of that dark hell hole he's in. To be honest, Frank, I suspect his attacker intended to kill him. Why he's still alive I don't know—especially after all the hours that have passed since the incident occurred."

"We wasted a bunch of time at that hospital for nuthin'."

"I wouldn't say for nothing, Frank. They got his heart rate down—long enough for you to get him back here. Anyway, I'm leaving some vials of serum that he might need before this is over. They need to be kept refrigerated. Would you set them aside for me."

"Sure."

With that, Doron transferred three vials of serum into Frank's open palm. "It's strong stuff," he added, "and has some interesting side effects. I hesitate to use this unless nothing else works."

"What do y' mean interestin' side effects?" Frank asked as he gazed down at the four ampoules of iridescent liquid in his hand.

"If we must use it, I'll explain then. Now this one..." Doron held up yet another syringe. "It needs to be given to him four hours from now. The syringe is already loaded and ready to go."

Frank nodded. "Okay. What's that for?"

"Several things," Doron replied. "It's a tough combination that should help lessen his pain, help with his heart rate and blood pressure, and hopefully start to ease the paralysis."

Stepping just inside the threshold, Jaimin asked, "If he's really paralyzed, is he still feeling pain? I mean, how can he feel it and be paralyzed at the same time?"

Doron turned to her. "Oh yes, he's still feeling pain. Very much so in fact. He may be unresponsive, but I assure you his mind is wide awake and in a world of agony right now. I'm hoping the injection I just gave him will at least start to relieve the intensity. See to it one of you gives him the second injection in four hours. I'll stop by first thing in the morning to see how he's doing."

Frank followed him to the main hatch. "Again, I can't thank y' enough for takin' the time to come out at this hour."

"Well, don't thank me just yet. Besides, I don't get many *Ripper* cases, I'm as anxious as you are for him to recover, and to see how well these mixtures work on a *Ripper* victim. See you in the morning, Frank."

Other than the constant hiss of the ship's ventilation, or an occasional ping from the command console, the *Antara* was deathly quiet. Frank, in a world of worry, retreated to Marc's quarters and was sitting in a bedside chair. He'd tried convincing Jaimin he could handle things, and for her to go get some sleep while she could. Instead, she remained where she was. Worried. Dr. Doron said Marc was in bad shape. He'd confirmed Frank's suspicion that he'd been hit with something called a *Ripper,* and that most people die from the *Ripper.*

"Frank?"

He was leaning over, studying his hands that were clasped between his spread knees. "Yes, darlin'," he responded, raising gloomy eyes to meet hers.

"I've heard both you and Doron speak of something called a *Ripper.* What exactly is a *Ripper*?"

Frank leaned back in the chair and fell silent for a moment. Inhaling deeply, he began... "A few years back a *Ripper* was no more than an extra powerful stunner. Mainly used as intruder and theft protection onboard merchant ships. An electronic guard dog so to speak. Since then, there's been a number of so-called *improvements* in the models they make now. Basically, today they're an illegal killing instrument."

Jaimin listened while Frank went on to explain.

"It's called a *Ripper*, but in truth it's an acronym for Radial Impulse Primary Protector Relay. R-I-P-P-R."

"But...he'll be okay, won't he? I mean, Doron said—"

"Darlin, believe me we're doin' everythang possible."

Jaimin nodded and silently remained in the doorway for a while before finally turning away. With four hours of worry on her hands she headed for the galley, to make a mug of hot tea, take a seat at the table and began nursing her worries.

The space was obviously designed for efficiency and functionality. Just as detailed as the rest of the ship, she imagined. The walls and ceiling were made of a sleek, metallic-like material. The lighting was subdued, casting a warm soothing glow over the room.

To the right was a storage system along with what looked like some sort of automated food dispenser, both unlike anything Jaimin had ever seen. On the left was a cooking station, no doubt also controlled by the main computer system.

Glancing about, she saw a small shelf with what looked to be a Memory Gem sitting on it. Aannisah had a Memory Gem, and Jaimin knew exactly what the sphere-shaped object was and how to work it.

The base had been leveled so that it could rest on a shelf or desk. By itself, the Memory Gem looked like a globe of liquid crystal, but Jaimin knew that upon holding it, body heat became the catalyst in bringing both still photos as well as videos to life. Intrigued, she picked up the object and very carefully clasped it in both hands. Holding her breath in anticipation, she waited as the picture gradually materialized within its transparent depths. The first picture was of Marc as a young boy, maybe ten or eleven. There was no mistaking his smile, even at that young age. He was standing with a friend about the same age. Smiles on both of their faces, arms draped over one another's shoulders. They looked happy. One had dark hair, the other had sandy-colored hair. Marc not only was the taller of the two, he had a rascal look about him. His hair was slightly wavy and hanging over his brow. His shirt was hanging out. There was a small rip in the knee of his pants. The other boy was much more put together. Not only was his shirt tucked in, his hair was in order, and there were no rips in his pants. Obviously, despite their differences, it was apparent their friendship was strong.

The next was a silent video of a teenage Marc. He was shirtless with his dark hair hanging long and shaggy upon his tanned shoulders.

A black motorcycle stood on its kickstand in the background. It looked different from the bike he had now, not as big, or heavy. A racing bike perhaps, especially since Marc was holding up a very tall and shiny trophy for the picture. He looked proud and was grinning as he said something to the person doing the videoing. Jaimin continued watching as a soft breeze tossed several spikes of hair down across his forehead. He was exactly as Frank had described him, right down to the bright crimson Ruckus perched upon his bare shoulder. So, she thought, if he has Ruckus, this must have been taken after he'd come back from his year-long trip to Earth.

In fascination, she saw sunlight glint off the dark teak of tanned skin and youthful muscle. So detailed were the images, she could even glimpse a fine sheen of perspiration dappling his shoulders and face. It was his face that commanded most of her attention. Even at his young age—despite that cocky, self-assured grin—Marc Banner's rugged good looks held heartbreaking promise.

A small girl entered the scene and Jaimin watched with interest as Marc drew his arm about her and said something that made her laugh. A younger sister, perhaps? Jaimin was pondering that question when the scene changed again. This time he was sitting astride a shiny red motorcycle. Muscular arms stretched out to grasp tall widespread handlebars. Marc's hair remained unfashionably long although a bit shorter in this video, and with a toss of his head he flipped an errant lock away from his face. He remained youthfully rangy, nevertheless the black short-sleeved T-shirt he wore clung flawlessly to muscular biceps that belied his youth.

Most of the photos and videos that followed were of Marc with various motorcycles. In several shots he was posing astride a shiny black bike that she thought looked a lot like the one he has now. She'd be willing to bet, too, that the bike was idling at the time the photo was taken. She could almost hear the deep, loping rumble of the strong engine begging to hit the open road. And the more Jaimin remembered her own experience on Marc's bike, the more she could all but feel the engine's throaty heartbeat vibrating through the photo. Her gaze shifted back to Marc in the video, and if she didn't know better, it was as if he could not only see her, but knew her thoughts. His brow lifted and his mouth curved into a wolf's smile so devastating that her heart skipped. She could almost hear him ask, *Wanna go for a ride?*

Slowly advancing through the selection of photos and videos trapped within the crystal sphere, she noticed that there were several photos where three other young men were posing with Marc. All four of them were on their motorcycles. Two of them looked enough like Marc to be brothers. The third was equally handsome with tawny collar-length hair. Together, the four of them made a heart-stopping impact.

The final two photos were of Marc standing at the helm of what looked to be the *Antara.* The other photo showed him standing with his foot braced possessively on the base of a massive landing jack. No doubt the *Antara* again. In both pictures Marc's hair was in a crew cut.

Finally, with a sigh, Jaimin placed the globe back on the shelf. Marc was not only older now, but according to Frank, he was very different from the arrogant young man shown in those earlier pictures. The passage of time could bring about many reasons for shaping one's decisions in life. After all, in less than a week hadn't her own life been turned completely upside down?

Next to the memory gem, there was a small stack of reading material which she discovered was nothing more than a collection of motorcycle books featuring a motorcycle that looked very much like Marc's. Jaimin might not be able to read the words, H A R L EY D A V I D S O N boldly printed across the covers, but she did recognize the letters along with the trademark emblem. They were the same as what she'd seen on his motorcycle.

Replacing the books on the shelf next to the Memory Gem, Jaimin wandered out of the galley and into the corridor. If she turned left, she would end up in the helm. Turning right would take her down by the cabins and even further into the cargo bay.

Deciding the helm would be much more interesting, Jaimin made her way forward until she came to a sunken helm. Choosing not to trespass on what she suspected was sacred territory, she remained on the landing above. Three small steps led down into the heart of the helm, but she could see just fine from her perch above.

The helm was a complex, high-tech system which she assumed was designed to manage the entire ship. The command console was glittering with tens of tiny blinking lights along with numerous toggle switches and keys. Overhead was a darkened viewscreen along with more busy little lights stretching across the alcove. Every now and then a soft ping would calmly announce the completion of some mysterious task. It was mind boggling, and Jaimin wondered how anyone could remember what to do with all those controls.

Finally with an exhausted sigh she returned to the galley where she took a seat once again to wait out the remaining time before Marc's next injection. Closing her eyes, she laid her head down on the table—forehead on her folded arms.

Two and a half hours later she was awakened by a muffled ringing coming from the direction of the cabins. Suddenly, it stopped. Frank must have set an alarm. She glanced at the time on the wall. It was time for the next injection. With that, she rose and turned for the corridor.

Tap, tap. "Frank?"

"Yeah?"

"Are you awake?"

"Yes ma'am," came his gravelly response. "Come on in, honey."

Jaimin pressed the wall-mounted entry pad and entered when the door opened. "How is he?" she whispered.

Frank slowly shook his head. "'Bout the same I'm 'fraid. 'Least 'ee's still breathin'."

"Well, it's time for his next injection." Jaimin said as she stepped further into the dimly lit cabin. 'I wonder what time Doron will come by?"

"I dunno, but, far as I'm concerned, his strange, naturopathic methods are far above traditional medicine. If we had left Marc at a hospital, we'd 'ave lost 'im fer sure by now."

"Thank Allah that you thought to call Doron." She handed him the syringe that Doron left. "I know absolutely nothing about giving injections, Frank. I hope you do."

"Yes ma'am. I surely do."

She started to turn for the door, then stopped. "Can I bring you anything? Something to drink maybe?"

Frank grinned. "Yeah, a stiff shot of whiskey." At her hesitation he wheezed a graveled, laugh. "But I'll settle for coffee."

Five more hours passed before Doron arrived. "Any changes?" he asked as he entered the ship.

"Not that I can tell," Frank replied as he led the way down to Marc's cabin. "'Bout the same, if y' ask me."

"You gave him the final injection?"

"Right on time."

Doron nodded. "Okay," he said softly, lost in thought as he continued to study Marc's lifeless form. "We need to wake him up. The longer he remains unconscious the less his chances are of recovery."

Jaimin remained at the door, listening to the conversation between the two men.

"So, what are y' thinkin'?" Frank asked.

With a compressed sigh, Doron turned to Frank. "I was looking for a little more improvement by this morning. I'm thinking that we're going to have to go with those vials after all."

Frank turned to Jaimin. "Honey, could you bring them here for us? They're in the refrigerator."

"I need only one." Doron then turned to Frank. "It's strong stuff and I was hoping we wouldn't have to use it at all."

Doron turned away to rifle through his medical supplies. Finding what he was looking for, he proceeded to take Marc's blood pressure and temperature readings.

Jaimin returned with one of the ampules of serum.

"Thank you, darlin'."

Frank turned to Doron. "What's in this stuff anyway? Snake venom?"

Doron smiled. "That, among other things."

"So, is this the stuff y' said had interestin' side effects?" Frank asked.

"Yes. I'm going to brief you both on it shortly."

With that, he took the ampule and proceeded to load it into a syringe.

Having injected it into the muscle of Marc's upper right arm, he then remained by Marc's side for a while, watching for any sign of immediate rejection or any adverse reaction. When there was none, Doron finally turned to Frank and Jaimin. "Okay. Now to let you both know what to expect."

CHAPTER TWELVE

"First of all, I want to say, again, that using this is a last resort. I'd hoped that we might have seen even a small improvement by this morning, but his heart rate is right back up, his blood pressure's over the top, he's still comatose and I strongly suspect he's remains in a world of pain. This serum should give him a fighting chance. As I was saying, it also comes with side effects."

"Like what?" Frank asked cautiously.

Doron cleared this throat and began speaking in Adenian so that Jaimin could also understand. "The one thing that will be the most noticeable is that Marc is going to act and feel as though he's just fine. Unfortunately, he won't be fine. He'll be like he's had too much to drink. It won't happen right away. Usually not until the third injection is in his veins."

"That ought to be fun," Frank muttered.

"Not knowing Marc," Doron added, "I can't tell you how he will be affected—whether he will be belligerent, gutter drunk, funny or an amorous drunk. If you're lucky he'll be quiet and brooding."

"I see. So how long is this supposed to last, this *bender* 'ee's gonna to be on?"

Doron inhaled deeply, letting it out in a compressed sigh. "Could be a week or two. Maybe longer. It just depends."

"So, are we gonna have t' wait here in port durin' this time?"

"At least three more days. Maybe four," Doron replied.

Frank pulled Doron aside and spoke in a lowered tone. "Reason I ask is, we was originally plannin' on bein' gone by now." He cocked his head toward Jaimin and continued. "Y' see, the girl was abducted as a child. Her folks have hired trackers over the years to find her. All of them, dead ended until Marc was hired. Thang is, we need to be gone 'fore the cavalry shows up to snatch 'er back."

Doron nodded. "I don't know what to say, but I seriously don't recommend pulling him out of my care too early."

"That brings up another question," Frank piped up. "Is he gonna be sittin' 'round drinkin' up our stash of scotch?"

At that Doron laughed. "No. Not with that brew cruisin' through his veins. Your scotch is safe. However," he added as an afterthought, "it wouldn't hurt to put it out of sight." He lowered his voice. "Look Frank, with the young lady on board and all, I don't like the idea any more than you do, but I'm fresh outta ideas, and time is critical right now."

"I understand," Frank replied with a heavy sigh.

He did understand. If Ahmed starts snooping around, they can't be sitting here waiting for him. Then, there was the little matter of what the devil he's supposed to do to protect Jaimin from Marc for a week or two? If it was just him and Marc, no problem. He could handle Marc just fine. Now with her on board, he'll be constantly having to run interference. And what if Marc decides to pursue a bit of entertainment? There was a very real possibility that drunk, Marc could end up wanting Jaimin and it could get complicated quick.

Frank understood technically he was just a ride-along. Nick and Zeke weren't fooling him with that phony excuse. Until now, it was no problem. It could end up being a problem—a big problem if he were to give Marc too much trouble. He had no command over anyone—leastwise the captain. Marc was the one in charge, and under the influence or not, Marc could rid himself of trouble by setting *trouble* off-ship here in Aden, if not the nearest port.

Would he do it? Probably not. Could he do it? Hell yes.

Oh, he'd find his own way home alright. That wouldn't be the issue. The real issue would be that Jaimin would then be left all alone at Marc's intoxicated mercy. Would he even have mercy? Doron couldn't predict how the potion cruising through Marc's veins would affect him. Everyone reacts differently.

But the real kicker was, that little gal was anything but a

spaceport doxy. He didn't have Jaimin pegged as the type to enjoy a little *strip in the ship*, without suffering a thousand regrets afterward. In truth, he had a pretty good idea she's been sheltered and protected from some of Aden's more carnal customs and traditions. Now was not the time to introduce her. Hell, she'd be traumatized.

He may just have to lock her in her cabin the whole time. That would do it. She'd be madder than an angry *neurowasp*, but she could thank him later.

Frank and Jaimin followed Doron down the corridor toward the exit. "So, when does this stuff y' gave 'im supposed to kick in?"

Doron shrugged. "I believe it already has. Just in the short time since the injection, his blood pressure has already begun dropping. The next thing will be his mind will begin to wake up. Hopefully he'll feel less pain at the same time."

"Good, that's good. Maybe y' won't have t' give 'im more than just the one injection then?"

"We'll see. At any rate, I'll be back this evening. If things change, or you need to get ahold of me, don't hesitate."

Frank and Jaimin walked Doron to the main hatch. It was still early morning, the beginning of a new day. They remained at the open lock long after Doron left. The morning sky cast a warm orange glow upon the stark surroundings of the busy spaceport. Eventually, the moment was spoiled when a cool breeze, laden with the stench of exhaust, hot metal and ozone drifted in through the open hatch.

"Darlin'," Frank began as he closed the hatch behind them, "y' might as well try t' get some sleep. Y've been up all night. Me, I'm used to long nights, and besides I was able to grab a few winks. I'm going to stay up and keep an eye on 'im."

"Thank you, Frank. If he should wake, would you let me know?"

"Yes, darlin. You know I will."

~ * ~

Panic. He was trapped inside of himself. Just like a *chromafly* ensnared in a spider's web, he was imprisoned inside his own body. He couldn't think straight. He couldn't speak. Could barely hear. Couldn't move. Regrettably, he could feel. Oh yes, he could feel—pain, unending, excruciating pain. It was wearing him down. If he could, he'd be curled up in the fetal position about now, bawling like a baby. The truth was, he couldn't even cry. All he could do, was silently endure.

Time had no meaning. It could have been an hour or a day. As though in a far-off fog, he suddenly thought he could hear...snoring—Frank. At least he wasn't alone. He couldn't bare being alone. Frank. Thank God Frank hadn't left him.

~ * ~

It had been two hours since Doron left.

"Tap, tap...It's me."

"Come on in, darlin'."

Jaimin stepped inside. Soft lighting along the ceiling cast muted light within the darkened cabin. "How is he?" she whispered; her gaze riveted on Marc's still form.

Frank nodded. "I don't know. I thought I heard him moan a bit ago."

"Frank, let me take over the watch, and you go get some sleep."

"Nah, I'm fine. I've been catching a few Zs now and then."

"No. You need to lay down and get some real sleep. I promise to wake you if there are any changes. Okay?"

With a heavy sigh he decided she was right. Besides, it would do no good if he ended up caving-in from lack of sleep. "Alright, but. I want yer promise to wake me if there are any changes. Good or bad."

"I promise."

"I mean it, Jaimin. Any changes at all. This stuff Doron's got 'im on, is nuthin' to fool around with. If 'ee should wake up, y' wouldn't know what to do with 'im honey."

"I know. I promise to wake you."

Frank held her gaze for a drawn-out moment. "I don't like it," he muttered softly as he turned for the door.

~ * ~

"I'll be fine, Frank," she said, crossing the small cabin to stand at the foot of the bed. Frank had left the door open. Light from the corridor cast a rectangle of brightness upon the floor. Muted lighting along the ceiling created soft shadows throughout. Jaimin glanced about noting that unlike the captain's comfortable quarters that she'd been given, this cabin was not only small, it was sparse—only the bare necessities.

So, she wondered, did he really give up his cabin? Was that something Frank had taken upon himself? Oh well, she didn't want to think about it now. If it was Frank's idea, then she'd gladly trade cabins and give Marc his quarters back. In truth Marc was in no shape to complain about anything.

She turned her gaze upon Marc and moved closer to the bed, losing herself in a silent perusal that began with a strange tattoo on one gleaming bicep. Upon a closer look she wondered at the writing and made a mental note to ask Frank.

The skin surrounding his eyes appeared bruised, and she suspected that if he were awake, he'd be weak. Suddenly. A shudder coursed through him, and if she didn't know better, Jaimin would have said she felt pain course through her body at the same time he did.

Marc was lying on his back. The bedding having been folded down to the foot of the bed. They'd removed his boots and T-shirt. A startling white *medi-patch* had been placed over his fractured ribs. Doron had also attached a small square-shaped heart monitor on his chest. A tiny red light in the center of it was blinking with the cadence of a pulse.

Marc's black hair was damp, and several errant strands lay across his brow. Her gaze drifted south visiting a hard, flat-planed stomach, noting how his low-riding, faded black jeans were stretched across lean hips. She tried shifting her eyes away from his naked chest but lost the battle to curiosity. His chest was lightly dusted with soft black hair. It tapered to a fine silky line that arrowed down his stomach. Without realizing where her eyes were taking her, she dared to follow the dark *arrow* until it disappeared below his low-riding jeans.

She might not know everything that went on between a man and a woman. She knew enough from whispered hearsays and shared fantasies with other girls to know that this man was exactly the sort they would have whispered, giggled, and sighed about.

Again, he shuddered as a lance of pain coursed through him. Once again, Jaimin felt it. Even unconscious, he radiated a sense of strength that had once been. Her gaze settled on a hard-muscled thigh, and a jolt settled low in her belly. What would it be like, she wondered, if that tempered, virile body were...

"One more thing," Frank said, popping back inside the cabin. "if 'ee tries getting out of bed, don't try to stop him. Y' come and get me. Pronto. Okay? 'Ee's not to get up. "

"Alright."

Frank startled her, catching her swooning over his boss of all things. Frank wasn't dumb, and she could just imagine her scorching cheeks were a dead giveaway. He probably grinned all the way back to his cabin.

She was mortified at the direction her thoughts had taken. Marc was fighting for his life, and what had she been doing? Conjuring up visions of what it might be like to have him make love to her. With a weary sigh, she padded over to the chair Frank had vacated, and sat down.

CHAPTER THIRTEEN

Jaimin had fallen asleep in the chair when a low groan awakened her. Three hours had passed since she'd taken over the watch. She paused as a strange sensation swept through her. An image rose in her mind, struggling through layers of white pain and enshrouding blackness. It surfaced briefly then dissipated.

Marc awoke to blackness, pain and an intense thirst brought on by the fever raging through him. He stirred restlessly on the soft bunk. Suddenly, a shadowy figure materialized. A soft hand rested gently on his brow for a brief moment then a cool cloth tenderly sponged the heat from his face and neck. He heard her voice, and recognized the blurred outline of the angel who was constantly there to cool him down and encourage him.

"Marc..." she whispered, as another low moan broke the silence.

Panic curled within her just watching his chest heave with a broken gasp. His fists clenched and unclenched as they twisted into the bedding. "Marc," she whispered again, studying him closely. "Can you hear me?" She pressed her palm to his bristly, unshaven cheek. "You're safe."

"Don't...leave me." he gasped brokenly, his dry throat working between words.

Marc's breathing became ragged. To offer comfort, Jaimin reached for his hand, only to have that very hand snake-out to capture her wrist in a vice-like grip that all but cut off her circulation. His palm was callused, his fingers long and strong. The contact sizzled through her like a bolt of hot lightning. "Stop!" she cried, working to pry his fingers loose. "Marc. Let go."

His chest rose and fell as he desperately clung to her. Jaimin cried out as an unexplainable fiery current once again passed between them.

"Don't...leave," his voice deep and raspy.

Forgetting her arm and the pain he was causing, Jaimin inhaled sharply as yet another intense current passed between them—a strange link bringing with it frightening, and fearful visions and feelings that...weren't hers.

"F r a n k!" she called out. "F R A N K!"

Ruckus who had been asleep on his perch near the bed, took to the air in a flash of scarlet. "Screech!"

~ * ~

Frank came running just in time to see the bird circle the bed twice before settling upon Marc's chest with a flap of his wings. With an ear-piercing shriek Ruckus muttered something Jaimin suspected was outrageously obscene, then fell into silence as if sensing approaching doom. The instant Frank burst into the cabin, Ruckus took to the air in a screeching flurry, this time soaring out and on down the corridor.

"That's right. You get outta here. I heard what y' said, you foul-mouthed vulture." Frank was glad Jaimin had no idea of the filth that bird had just spewed. But then again, upon a closer look, he could see she wasn't aware of anything but the death grip Marc had on her wrist.

"Please," she whimpered. "Do something."

Frank raced forward. Grabbing Marc's hand, he loosened his grasp. "Honey, pull yer hand free."

Wrenching her hand from his hold, Jaimin stumbled backward.

"Are y' alright, darlin'?"

With her heart pounding, she stared down at Marc while rubbing the fresh bruises on her wrist.

"Jaimin? Are y' okay, honey?" he asked again, this time with a fatherly touch to her shoulder.

As though in a trance, Jaimin looked from Marc to Frank. "I—I saw a glimpse of his world," she whispered. "How could that happen?"

"Y' what?"

~ * ~

"I saw and felt what he is feeling, Frank."

Still shaken, Jaimin took a deep breath and sat down. For an instant she *knew* his world as if she were right there with him. For a moment she felt the excruciating pain he was enduring, the agony and panic of being imprisoned in darkness. Of being all alone.

She experienced his fear, as if it were her own.

"Darlin', yer tired. I think you should get some ice on yer wrist, then maybe some rest. I got in a couple hours, I'm good as new."

"I'm fine, Frank."

"It's mid-afternoon. Go get some sleep. Besides, it won't be long before Doron will be back. Anyways, I'm thinkin' it best if I take over from here."

"I want to stay, Frank. Maybe somehow, I can help him through this."

"Honey, I guarantee 'ee's gonna be more than y' can handle."

"Yes, I know, Frank. That's why I'm hoping you will stay here with me." Instinctively Jaimin knew Marc would not be able to hold on without her there.

"Y' *know* I'll stay with y'."

Marc emitted a low, husky groan and Jaimin's eyes were drawn back to him as his body jerked hard against unseen bonds—shackled in hell by elusive tormentors.

Catching her lower lip between her teeth, Jaimin once again came to stand at his side, her heart pounding.

~ * ~

"I want that bike of his," Ahmed growled through his missing teeth and bandaged nose. It was the morning of the next day. He turned to Jabbar, his friend and coconspirator. "We need to get it before thieves find it."

Jabbar rose from his chair and pulled his keys from a pocket. "I say, let's go now while it's still early."

It was a two-hour drive to where they left Marc's body and his bike. Ahmed laughed, "I was so happy to see that *neuro-heretic* go down, I completely forgot about the bike."

"We'll you can get it now. God willing," Jabbar assured him. "I doubt anyone would have found it yet."

"Did anyone ever find out the name of his ship?" Ahmed asked.

"Yes. It's called the *Antara*."

"Good. It shouldn't be hard to find if it's still sitting in port."

"So, are you still going to marry her?"

"Marry who?" Ahmed asked.

"Jaimin."

"I have no choice. Both my parents and hers are complaining about this mess. I've got to find her, Jabbar."

"What about Nijah?"

Ahmed grinned. "I'll marry her too."

Jabbar laughed. "Two women to keep happy. You will be one busy man."

Despite his facial injuries, Ahmed joined him in laughter.

By now, they were well over the two-hour drive back to recover the bike when Jabbar turned to Ahmed, "We should have come upon the bike by now, don't you think?"

"I don't know, do you think we passed it? I honestly don't remember where we stopped."

"It wasn't this far," Jabbar said. "I think we should turn around and backtrack."

"I agree."

They soon learned that backtracking wasn't the answer. Nor did it provide any clues as to what happened to the bike or to Banner's body. Both were nowhere to be found. And Ahmed was furious. "I can understand the bike being taken, but why is his damned body not here?"

"Maybe animals drug it off," Jabbar offered. "That's always a possibility,"

They'd pulled onto the shoulder of the road in an area that looked very much like the place they'd found Banner and were wandering around looking for signs of what might have happened—animal prints, anything. There was nothing to be seen. Sand didn't hold impressions well.

Ahmed released a compressed breath. "Someone found that bike," he snarled. "We need to keep our eyes open for it. It's bound to show up somewhere eventually."

~ * ~

In the meantime, Frank decided to go ahead and engage a couple of *Antara's* stealthy illusions. With a simple flip of a switch, the first thing he did was change the name of the ship on the outside of the hull to read in a foreign language, "*STAR BANDIT*." Under that new name, he then requested a change to a different landing pad on the opposite side of the spaceport. With another flip of a switch, he engaged a messy lubricant leak and added the illusion of rust and darkened burned areas here and there on the otherwise pristine hull of the ship. There were several other clandestine changes he could make if he had to, but hopefully nothing more would be necessary. With any luck, it would be enough to throw off anyone looking for the *Antara* and Jaimin.

~ * ~

Frightful images rose out of the darkness to torment him. Marc was entrapped in a deep void of darkness, restrained by unseen bonds, poised on the edge of reality while fiendish demons with glowing yellow eyes bared their teeth and tore at his flesh.

It was all he could do to hold back a silent cry of agony as another intense thrust of pain shot through him. His thoughts blurred and he felt himself drifting, deeper and deeper into a beckoning black hell. Dear God, death would be a mercy.

Suddenly, she was at his side again—his angel. He felt a cool caress on his face, heard her soft angel voice as she smoothed a lank of hair off his sweaty brow.

Although temporarily repelled by this angel of mercy, the demons weren't about to give him up without a struggle, their eyes glittered in the distance.

Marc strained, fixing his attention as best he could on the gentle voice offering strength and encouragement. Feeling her cool touch on his face and body, he gasped in relief and hung on, silently begging his angel to stay with him.

"Marc, can you hear me? I'm right here."

Sensing his response to her nearness, she hesitantly reached for his hand and continued talking.

Ever so slowly he succumbed to Jaimin's presence. Although he remained unconscious, his struggles seemed to ease, his moans and ragged breathing decreased. There was no doubt that her presence was having an effect on him. He knew she was there.

~ * ~

Still holding his hand, Jaimin remained at his side, struggling to make sense of it all. It was as if some sort of channel had opened between them, and she'd had a first-hand glimpse of hell. His hell.

She stayed at his side long after his breathing returned to normal, and his fingers had gone lax in her hand. Frank brought in a second chair for himself and was snoring. Sleeping in a chair might be okay for him, but she needed a real bed. She just hoped Marc would be able to sleep peacefully now. Stifling a yawn, she gently released Marc's hand and rose from her chair to silently make her way into the corridor and down to her cabin. A hot shower and sleep were calling.

Two hours later, a continuous drone of male voices filtered into the sleep-filled corners of Jaimin's mind. Eyes closed she groaned and rolled onto her back, the sheet tangling with her feet and bare legs. From somewhere off in the distance came the sound of high-pitched screeching and squawking.

Ruckus.

Marc.

Her eyes flying open, Jaimin found herself staring directly up at a poster affixed to the ceiling above the bunk. The subject was an exquisite, half-nude blonde with perky breasts, sitting shamelessly upon a jet-black motorcycle. The poster was faded and appeared vintage—like, a long time ago vintage.

Jaimin was still contemplating the poster as she jumped out of bed. Opening her travel pac, she dug out a pair of jeans and a soft yellow T-shirt. Thank goodness Aannisah had clothes to give to her. Quickly dressing, she brushed her teeth and ran a comb through her hair. At last, she turned for the door and hurried up the corridor to Marc's cabin.

"Jaimin, honey, come on in. Did y' get enough rest?"

"Yes, thank you."

Her gaze fell upon Marc. "So, how is he?"

"Doron says 'ee's not out of the woods yet, but 'ee's better."

Frank turned to Doron. "So Whadaya' think the next step is?"

"I'm giving him the next injection. We'll see how it goes from there."

"Y' really think 'ee needs more of that snake poison?"

"I do. The potion's working, Frank. Not only is his blood pressure and heart rate down, but he's also showing signs of beginning to wake up."

"Yeah, he sure as hell is ..." Frank complained as he pointed to Jaimin's wrist. "This little gal, here, has a bruise to prove it."

Doron looked genuinely sorry as he took a closer look at the dark bruise on Jaimin's wrist. "Get some ice on that."

Frank snorted. "Yep, woulda' done that when it happened, but Marc was goin' through *hallucination hell* at the time, and no way was she gonna' take the time to let me take care of 'er wrist."

"Well, do it now," Doron said. "It won't help the bruising, but it will help the swelling."

"Alright." Jaimin turned for the galley to get an ice pac.

~ * ~

When she was gone, Frank turned back to Doron. "Speakin' of hallucinations, have you ever heard of—man, I know this sounds crazy—but has anyone ever said that they've experienced a hallucination right along with the person having it?"

Doron's expression stilled. "Yes. Why?"

"Cuz that little gal's havin' them right along with Marc."

"Interesting," Doron pondered. "From what I understand, it could be a couple of things that can cause that. One of them could be a genetic thing. I don't know much about it, but I will say one thing, it could complicate things for you."

Frank groaned. "Yeah, tell me about it."

Before leaving, Doron gave Marc the second injection with strict orders to keep a close eye on him. "Frank, I'm going to stop back in six hours. If things should change for the worse, you let me know immediately. My *Messenger* is always on."

Four hours later, Marc awoke slowly in a cold sweat, reality seeping back by small increments. Where was he, and why the devil did his entire body feel as if he'd been on the losing end of a barroom brawl. Swallowing hard, he lay still for a long moment, feeling as weak as a newborn baby. What the hell had happened? Reality was a fog. He vaguely recalled bits and pieces of a confrontation of some kind. The details were a dark void as he struggled to remember.

Just then, the name, Jaimin, surfaced.

That opened his eyes, and with it came a wave of agony and his sight blurred. Suppressing a groan, Marc squeezed them shut again as blackness threatened to pull him back under. Swearing silently, he fought against the pain and lightheadedness. It was all he could do to hang on as flashes of memory continued to surface, only to disappear. He vaguely remembered the *Ripper,* but not who fired it. What about Jaimin? Where was she? Was she safe?

For that matter, where the hell was, he? Marc ordered himself to open his eyes again and uttered a silent oath when his body wouldn't cooperate with his brain. He wanted to call out her name, but even that effort was beyond him.

There was no mistaking the problem. He understood all too well why his body was failing to respond to commands. The problem was a little matter of dispersion. Somehow his mind was in pieces, scattered about in every direction. To accomplish anything, even the smallest, he needed to concentrate on gathering himself back together. Only then could he focus his energies on doing one little thing at a time.

Setting his mind to the task at hand, he began, bit by bit, arranging the pieces of what little memory he had into some semblance of order. Focusing on his senses first, he became increasingly aware of his surroundings. Gingerly peering through slitted eyes, he discovered that he was in a dimly-lit room.

Hearing came next as he centered his attention on the constant hissing of life support. Okay. He recognized that sound. He was on-board a ship.

"Darlin' y' hungry? Can I get y' anythang?"

Frank. Even at a whisper, Marc easily recognized Frank's lazy drawl. Who was he talking to?

"No thanks, Frank. I'm good," came a whispered response.

Angel. The one who had been there for him when the pain was at its worst. The one who had wiped his brow and body with coolness when he was burning up, and who had whispered words of reassurance and encouragement when he didn't think he could take much more.

"Well, y' just holler if y' change yer mind, honey."

"I will. Thank you, Frank."

Marc felt a gentle hand briefly press to his brow. With a sigh he relaxed under her touch. She was still with him, his *angel.* Nothing like having an angel to get you through the worst of it. If he didn't feel so lousy, he would have been content for hours of simply lying there while she hovered over him. Feeling as though he needed to get up. He moaned as another lance of pain shot through him.

"You're awake."

Weak and unstable, he managed with herculean effort to lever himself into a sitting position. So, Jaimin was the angel who'd been at his side when he needed her most.

"What are you doing?" she asked when he began swinging his legs over the edge of the bunk.

Silence.

"Marc, you're not supposed to get up. Frank said that you—"

"I don't care what Frank said," he hissed through gritted teeth. Completely exhausted, he was sitting on the edge of the bunk. Shoulders hunched, he blinked lethargically and continued staring at the floor between his feet.

Jaimin frowned. "Tell me what you need. I'll get it for you."

He ignored her. With a heavy sigh he said, "I don't know if I'll be able to stand on my own." There was another pause and then, "I may need your help."

"You shouldn't be doing this. Let me get—"

"Don't worry about it, I'll manage by myself." He pulled in a breath, and with what appeared as another monumental effort, stood up, swaying.

Jaimin rushed to his side to help stabilize him as he started toward the cabin door. "Marc Banner, you are absolutely the most stubborn man I have ever met," she said. "Where are you going?"

"Do you know—where Ruckus is?" he asked between labored breaths.

"Ruckus?"

"Has anybody fed him?"

"You need to worry about yourself. Not Ruckus."

They were part way up the corridor when he shrugged out of her support and staggered across the corridor to the communal lav on the other side. Once there, he pulled in a labored breath and leaned a shoulder against the open doorframe.

"This is crazy," she muttered. "Do you want me to get Frank?"

"I don't need Frank. I need you to go find Ruckus and make sure he's got seed and fresh water."

"Don't worry about Ruckus. Frank's been taking good care—"

"Still, I want you to check on him for me. Will you go do that?"

"Yes. Of course, I'll check on him for you."

"Good. Now get going."

"What?"

She stood there, hands on her hips staring at him.

"I gotta take a leak. Now, you can either stand there and watch if you want, or you can go check on Ruckus like I've asked. He straightened away from the doorframe and began undoing his belt, his hands all but trembling with fatigue. "I can't close the privacy panel, Jaimin. It's busted." Despite how awful he felt, he managed to grin his wolf grin. "So, if you're gonna watch, you should have a pretty good view."

Jaimin's jaw dropped.

"When you come back, I need you to—"

"Well just maybe I won't be back. You seem to be getting along just fine by yourself, and just maybe I've got other things to do that are more important."

"Oh yeah?" he said with a half grin. "Like what?"

"Like...Like—doing my nails."

Belt dangling from the loops, he reached for the top stud of his jeans, "You'll be back."

"And just what makes you so sure?"

Top stud undone; he went for his fly. "I just know."

"You're awful." Her face hot, Jaimin turned and fled down the corridor. "You can get your own self back to your cabin," she called over her shoulder. "I'll be busy doing my nails."

He laughed, entered the lav, and with a single yank, jerked open the remaining row of studs.

She had half a notion to leave him to his own methods of getting back to his cabin. If she were here, Aannisah certainly wouldn't be helping him. However, Jaimin knew she couldn't leave him stranded like that. Marc looked ready to pass out by the time she'd turned to leave. He would need help getting back.

You're too soft hearted. That's always been your problem.

CHAPTER FOURTEEN

Now to find Ruckus. The first place she looked was the cabin Marc took over. The perch that Ruckus roosted on was empty. She then checked the captain's quarters.

No Ruckus. Although, she hadn't expected him to be there since she always kept the panel closed for that very reason.

Remembering that the bird always disappeared down the corridor toward the cargo hold, she decided to check out the last spot she could think of to look for him.

"There you are you crimson devil. Ruckus lifted his head from beneath his wing to look at her as she came forward. He'd been sleeping upon another one of those standing perches. This one was positioned to the right of the hatch into the hold. "You spoiled little imp; your owner thinks you've suffered while he's been gone. But you've been well cared for, haven't you?"

As if he understood, Ruckus replied with a sleepy squeak.

"I'm going to refresh your seed and water," Jaimin explained, "and if you'll stay right where you are, everything will be fine."

With that she turned back toward the cabins to freshen his seed and water. And Ruckus, being the good little birdie that he is, tucked his head back under his wing.

~ * ~

One step at a time. Marc knew from personal experience that one step at a time was the best way to get from point A to point B. When you have roughly a hundred and eighty pounds of body weight attached to your legs, and when those legs aren't receiving your brain's message to move, it's pure hell. Plus, one minute he was on fire, and the next he was freezing cold. He clenched his teeth against another spasm shooting through him. And who the devil was beating on a drum somewhere nearby?

He thought he had a jacket at one time, but somebody must have taken it. That, and his gun. Where the hell was his bike? Had somebody taken that too? A guy just couldn't win.

Nanoflies were buzzing in his head. He liked *nanoflies*. They were cool. Anything that could fly with the speed of a *nanofly* was A-okay far as he was concerned. He liked watching them. Those little buggers can hover, bank, and pull a vertical drop better than most pilots he knew.

Suddenly his legs buckled, and he slid to his knees. As though in slow motion, his body followed the pull of gravity until he was face down in the sand. Nothing like a good ol' crash and burn when your legs are on strike. Nothing quite like just sprawling out and calling it a day. The sand felt warm, and for the moment he welcomed the heat.

~ * ~

Having refilled the seed and changed the water, Jaimin quickly exited Marc's cabin and turned for the lav.

"Marc!" she rushed to his side. He'd obviously attempted to make it back by himself. Instead, he ended up lying flat on his stomach in the middle of the corridor.

His angel. What was she doing here? He groaned as his body endured another shock of pain.

Jaimin inhaled sharply as she, too, felt the jolt hurl through her body. "You need to get up, Marc. You can't just lay here like this."

Lay like what? What was she talking about? The sand was warm, the tremors would stop soon—and he was comfortable. Why the hell couldn't he lay here like this? How else was he supposed lay? *Lay*...yeah, he liked that word. It was a good word. It reminded him of *Laid,* which reminded him of—

"You either get up now, or I'm going to get Frank."

He opened one eye to stare at a pair of stocking feet standing before him. They were attached to legs that were attached to Jaimin. "Nice footgear, Jai," he mumbled. "But you should put on some shoes. Sand gets hot. Even the *hyperscorpians* hide during the day. Good thing too. Ever been stung by a *hyperscorpian*? Mean little suckers..."

He was barely aware of his own voice babbling on about nonsense. He struggled to focus, then deciding it was too much work, he gave up.

"Marc, are you listening to me? You must get up."

He managed to roll onto his back and open both eyes. A dark gray metallic ceiling greeted him within his field of vision. Next came his angel with her platinum hair and unusual storm-gray eyes. She looked worried.

"Marc. If you don't get up, I'm going after Frank."

His poor little angel. Couldn't blame her for being worried. Even on a good day he didn't exactly instill trust. Here he was lying on his back, half crazy, going on about hot sand and hyperscorpians, He felt like he was jazzed-up on some sort of serum and couldn't make himself shut up. It was as if his voice was going on and on with nobody in charge—nobody home.

He couldn't help laughing at the whole situation, but it was a laugh that sounded strange even to his own ears. Another body-racking tremor convulsed through him. He ignored it as best he could and waited for it to pass.

Jaimin felt it too, but she was sure it wasn't quite as intense as what Marc felt. "Marc, please. Get up."

There she goes again. Nagging him to get up.

"Captain Banner," she said in her best loud and commanding voice. "Did you hear what I said?"

Yak, yak, yak...His brain struggled to focus on one thing at a time. It seemed everything was a confused blur. He was so damned tired. His head ached. His body ached. And he was hot and cold at the same time. Was that even possible, he wondered?

~ * ~

Suddenly, he sat upright and stared down the corridor. Jaimin saw him jerk as another lance of pain shot through him. As crazy as it was, once again she felt it at the same time he did.

Out of the blue, he started talking again. "The day Mitch died..." he began, "we were swimming in the reservoir east of town."

Who was Mitch, she wondered.

"We knew we weren't supposed to be swimming there." He frowned and paused for a labored breath. "Too dangerous. Signs posted everywhere. We'd always gotten away with it in the past. There was never a set time for opening the water gates, and it was always a challenge to go swimming and be out of there before the gates opened. But that day..." He inhaled an agonized breath and paused for a long, drawn-out moment. "The hell of it was, Mitch didn't want to go swimming that day...I talked him into it anyway."

Jaimin listened. Whether it was the *Ripper*, the snake venom, or the fever raging through him, she sensed that Marc, without even realizing it, was baring his soul about the loss of a friend.

"I didn't want to go to the funeral," he went on. "It was like..." He lapsed into another moment of silence as his mind traveled back in time to that day. "Dad insisted. So, we went as a family. It was just as awful, just as terrible as I knew it would be."

Another agonized breath preceded another moment of deathly silence. He was looking as if he were seeing a moment in time that only he could visualize. "I can still see his mother's face," he murmured despondently. "I *knew* what she was thinking. I *knew* they didn't want him running around with me. Mitch...he was a good kid. He was the Zen to my chaos. I was the wild one, always testing and breaking the rules, always daring Mitch to try something new and forbidden." Once again Marc fell silent for a long moment.

"...He was my best friend, and I killed him," he said in a hoarse whisper.

He turned to look at her, his pain-filled deep blue eyes suddenly lucid. "I should have been the one who died that day. Not Mitch."

Jaimin felt helpless. What could she say as he poured out his heart, his grief? Here she was sitting on the deck in the middle of his ship's corridor, while he exposed his soul. It was so private. So personal and had been buried for so long. Did he even realize what he'd just shared? Did he even know he was crying? That she was crying with him?

She hardly knew Marc. Other than that unnerving motorcycle ride back into town, there had only been one other occasion when she had even talked to him. They were strangers. Nevertheless, as broken as he was, how could she not be there for him? She eased closer and pulled him to her. Grief-stricken, Marc buried his face against her neck. It wasn't sexual. Hot with fever, his bristled cheek rough against her neck, he clung to her like a grieving child.

Ever so gently Jaimin brushed a damp lock off his hot forehead and made a mental note to ask Doron about the fever. She suspected the *Ripper* was responsible for the residual physical pain, and maybe even the hallucinations. What was causing the fever? Why did it come and go? He could be burning up one minute and normal the next. Wasn't there something they should be doing for it?

She sighed softly and thought about his grief and guilt over Mitch. About how he confessed that he should have been the one to die that day. They were just kids being kids, and yet he'd carried the guilt all these years, buried so deep that no one would ever see it.

Those years of rebellion that Frank spoke of earlier—could it be that it was Marc's way of punishing himself over Mitch's death? Even Frank had no viable reason for Marc running with the wrong crowd like he did. The things he involved himself in were undoubtedly both dangerous and illegal. He was the son of a successful businessman. The world would have been his to do and be anything he wanted.

"Did you know that a *psykobee* is both male and female?" he muttered against the side of her neck, his voice deep and raspy.

Her neck burned from the chafe of his unshaven cheek.

As if someone had flipped a toggle, Marc's mind had switched gears from his grief over Mitch to *psykobees*. "It's true," he went on. "They can have babies without sex. Now ain't that just warped? Can't imagine life without sex, can you?" He snorted. "What the hell do they do for fun?" His laugh was rough.

Suddenly, topics changed again. This time small nonsensical matters took priority as he rambled on and on about mundane things, placing their level of importance right up there with galactic security and the on-going slave trade along the rim worlds.

"Marc, you cannot stay here like this. You didn't do yourself any favors by insisting on getting out of bed. You don't look so good."

He released a labored breath. "I don't feel so good either. What's this damned blinking light on my chest?"

"It's a heart monitor. Leave it alone. She helped him get to his feet. "Here, lean on me. We'll get you back to your cabin."

"You should call Frank to do this."

"He's sleeping." With that she slung his arm across her shoulders and grasped him about the waist. "It isn't that far. We can do this."

Despite Marc's weakened condition, not to mention the pain from his fractured ribs, Jaimin was acutely aware of the hard-muscled body hugging her from hip to shoulder as they made their way back to the cabin.

He'd insisted on sitting for a while on the edge of the bunk. He looked none too steady, but his mind had seemed to have returned, at least for now. He blinked lethargically and looked up at her. "So, how—how long have I been here?"

"You've been on board the ship going on two days."

"I see. So, where did you find me?"

"About a half hour this side of Dubhan."

He nodded. "What about my bike?"

"Your bike's safe. Thank goodness it wasn't touched. Frank rode it back, and it's safe in the hold."

"Frank?" He pondered that bit of news for a moment. "Didn't know Frank could ride."

"Frank knew exactly what he was doing."

"No kidding."

He took a deep breath. Big mistake. He winced and drew his arm protectively against his ribcage.

"Doron said you have a couple of fractured ribs. That's why the protective medi-patch. Do you remember what happened?"

"No."

"Well, you probably should lay back down."

"Who's Doron?" he asked as she helped ease him back down onto the bunk.

"He's a doctor friend of Franks. You'll meet him when he comes by in a couple of hours, In the meantime, try to get some sleep. Okay?"

Marc let his head ease back onto the cool pillow, released an exhausted sigh, and closed his eyes. Nothing like having an angel fussing over you. Makes the going easier. He wanted to tell her so, but the words just wouldn't form. His brain was confused and scattering all over the place again. All he wanted to do was check-out.

"Whadaya' mean 'ee was layin' on the deck?"

"He needed to use the lav, and I helped him get there. He sent me to check on Ruckus, and by the time I got back, I found him collapsed in the middle of the corridor."

"Ruckus? 'Ee sent you to check on Ruckus? What fer?"

"I was going to wait for him in the corridor, and he said the door to the lav was broken."

"Oh yeah...I'll fix that door today. In the meantime, no more supporting him when 'ee can hardly walk. 'Ees too much fer y'"

"Okay."

"Good. Now, Doron should be 'ere before long. I'm gonna go wake Marc, and git 'im ready.

CHAPTER FIFTEEN

Jaimin remained in the ship's galley while Frank and Doron were with Marc. She listened to the murmur of male voices drifting in from Marc's cabin. From what she could gather, Doron seemed satisfied with Marc's progress.

She'd had a chance to voice her concern over the alternating fever episodes Marc suffered. Doron explained that the injections were the cause. If steps are taken to keep the fever under control, there's nothing to worry about. The *Ripper*, however, is responsible for both the physical and mental pain. He went on to explain the injections are also causing temporary changes in his mental state. This last injection, especially, will be rough.

"Why is it necessary to give him the injections when they are only complicating his condition?" she asked.

"They're not complicating his condition, Jaimin. The injections are interfering with the residual effects of the *Ripper*. I suspect that whoever did this to him, intended to kill him. Why he wasn't already gone by the time you and Frank found him, I don't know.

"It's a three-step process," he went on to explain. "Each injection's a bit stronger than the one before it. Had we not started him in on them, he would have died by now. I feel sure of it."

Jaimin listened as Doron explained the procedure in easy-to-understand terms.

"These injections are made of snake venom?" she asked.

He smiled. "In part, yes." He gave her a moment to mull things over. "Like I said, it's necessary to complete all three injections, Jaimin. I am, however, suggesting that Frank take over Marc's care for the next few weeks."

"Okay."

He took a moment to study her reaction to being pulled off duty.

He hadn't forgotten Frank's concern over the telepathic connection between Jaimin and Marc—how she told Frank that she physically felt Marc's pain and emotions at the same time he did.

After Doron left, Frank returned to Marc's cabin and Jaimin headed for the galley to make herself a mug of hot tea. She wondered why she would no longer be helping Frank care for Marc. It wasn't like she didn't know what to do. She knew the routine. Frank took care of Marc's personal needs, and she handled most everything else. it was because she hadn't been there to help Marc back from the lav, and now they thought she was unreliable. Could that have been the reason?

She had no sooner decided to ask Frank about it, when he entered the galley to get coffee. When he turned to leave she stopped him. "Frank, I need to know. Was it because I didn't make it back in time to help Marc to his cabin?"

He turned to face her. "What?"

"Is that why I'm no longer allowed to help care for Marc?"

His expression turned tender. "Oh, no darlin'. It has nuthin' to do with that. Absolutely nuthin," he repeated.

"Then what?"

"I'll explain it to y' later. I promise." He inhaled deeply, "In the meantime I suppose this is as good a time as any to give this to y'. I'll be right back." He left the galley long enough to retrieve a small package. Inside was a hi-tech message tablet which he handed to her.

"It's from yer folks. Captain was going to give this to y' once we put into space, but with all that's happened..." Frank shrugged. "Anyway, I think now's a good time as any to see this message. It's fer yer eyes only, darlin. Will y' take a moment to listen to it?"

"Yes," she said, and glanced down at the tablet in her hands.

"These folks are yer real parents," he said as he turned for the exit. "Oh, by the way, I switched to Adenian language so you can easily listen without trying to make sense of new words."

"Thank you, Frank."

With a heavy sigh, Jaimin opened the tablet. First thing to greet her was a video of a handsome gentleman and a beautiful woman standing side by side.

Hello Jenelle, my darling. Your father and I can only assume that if you are seeing this, then Mister Banner has indeed found you. We cannot begin to describe the joy and excitement we feel knowing that you have been found and are on your way back to us. It has been eleven long years since we last held you in our arms.

Next, her father began speaking. *We have missed you every single day and are overjoyed at the thought of finally being reunited with you. We want to remind you of who we are, Thomas and Karissa Byers, your birth parents who have been searching for you tirelessly since the day you were taken from us. We don't know if you have a different name now, but you were born Jenelle D'Anne Byers. We remember the day you were born like it was yesterday, and how you filled our lives with so much joy, love, and laughter. We would spend hours playing with you, reading to you, and watching you grow and discover the world around you.*

Again, her mother. *We hope you might remember some of the happy memories we've shared together. More than that, we want you to know that no matter how much time has passed, our love for you has never wavered. We have never stopped hoping and praying that one day you would be found and we would be reunited.*

As you make your way back to us, please know that we are waiting with open arms, ready to embrace you and make up for lost time. We cannot wait to meet the young lady you have become.

With all our love, Momma and Poppa

Jaimin remained motionless for a long time, simply staring at the two faces frozen on the screen. Faces she barely recognized. She listened once again to their message.

She just hoped she knew what she was doing, because right now she didn't think she could live with people she didn't know. Their cheery smiles and happy chattering only said more than she wanted to hear.

Jaimin knew she should recognize them and be just as excited to be reunited. In truth they were strangers, and their overexcitement frightened her.

Whether he knew it or not, Frank was her anchor. For now, she didn't need or want anyone else.

An hour had passed by the time Frank came back into the galley. "Are y' gittin' hungry?" He flashed her a grin. "I lived on those damn—er, excuse me—darn automated meals the entire time the boss was off galivanting around looking fer you. Tonight, I thought I'd fix somethun different. A favorite from Earth."

"Well, I'm starved."

Frank laughed. "That's good."

"Y' remember ever having a hamburger, honey?"

"A what?"

"A hamburger. It's sorta like a sandwich, but..." At her blank look, he stopped. "Y' don't know what a sandwich is." It was a statement, not a question.

Jaimin shrugged. "I'm afraid I don't."

"No... I suppose y' don't. Okay," he said, "this is it in a nutshell. So, instead of lamb, goat or camel meat, a hamburger is made with good ol'—hard to get nowadays—beef. And instead of flatbread, it's put on a split bun and just a'drippin' with all sorts of good stuff."

Jaimin laughed at his enthusiasm. "Sounds good, Frank."

"Yes, indeed. The best part is that it's quick and easy to fix."

Elbows on the table and her chin resting in the palms of her hands, Jaimin watched through peaceful eyes as he washed his hands and began gathering supplies and ingredients for his mystery recipe. She loved the camaraderie she had with Frank. He was a mixture of opposites. He was rough around the edges and take-charge strong, and yet at other times, he was an ol' softy. To prove it, she'd seen him age ten years or more the instant they learned of Marc missing. It was during those times there was no hint of weakness, no backing down from his purpose when it came to finding Marc and coming up with a plan to save his life. Frank was a gentle warrior, so different from the men in the world she'd grown up knowing.

Men held a superior status in Aden's society. Women, not so much. She never realized it as a child. Recently she had to face a harsh reality that her worth to the Ala Rashard family was no more than a pawn to combine the wealth of two prosperous families. A merger that neither she nor Ahmed wanted.

"So, y' think y'd like to try somethun new, huh?" he said as he added a few spices to the meat mixture he was working with.

She laughed. "Yes. I'm looking forward to it."

They made small talk while she watched Frank put together hamburgers and some sort of fried sticks that he called French fries.

"Here y' go darlin'. Yer very first burger and fries. Give it a try and see what y' think," he said as he took a seat across from her with his own burger and fries.

Reaching for a fry first, Jaimin took a tentative bite, then quickly reached for another. "These are good."

"Yep, and they're the real thing too. Made with real potatoes instead of parsos."

Parsos were a white root vegetable that tasted like a potato and commonly used in place of potatoes.

"Potatoes? I know what parsos are, but I've never heard of potatoes."

"That's because the only place y' can get 'em is on Earth," he said as he stuffed two fries in his mouth at once. "Captain made a trip to Earth a few months back," Frank went on, still chewing as he reached for his mug of coffee, "and he brought back a supply for everyone."

He'd cut her burger in half, and by the time she finished the first half, she was quickly reaching for the second. "Frank you're a wonderful cook. I love this meal."

"Nah... just a simple little meal."

"Well, nevertheless, Marc is lucky to have you onboard."

Frank laughed. "That's what I keep telling him."

Suddenly, Jaimin gasped as a lance of pain shot through her. "Frank. We need to check on Marc." Launching herself to her feet she turned for the corridor.

~ * ~

Marc stirred as once again fearsome images rose to torment him. Entrapped in a deep void of darkness, restrained by unseen bonds while fiendish monsters refused to give him up. The pain...it was all he could do to hold back a cry of agony as another intense thrust of it shot through him. "Jai-min..." he moaned brokenly.

With Frank on her heels, she rushed to Marc's side, feeling the jolt of pain that he was feeling. "Marc, I'm here," she whispered. "I'm right here."

He felt the coolness of her hand upon his brow. Then she took his hand again. "I'm here, Marc."

She glanced up at Frank and whispered, "Should you call Doron, and let him know what's going on?"

Frank shook his head. "No. He said that this final injection could bring about some repeat symptoms as his body adjusts this final dose."

"He was so much better. Now, it's like he's regressed."

"I know, honey. Doron said it will pass. So, let's do what we can to make him as comfortable as possible. If he doesn't get better, then we'll let Doron know. That sound, okay?"

She nodded reluctantly. "I don't care what you or Doron say, you're not sending me away. I am staying right here with him, Frank."

With a heavy sigh, Frank conceded. As much as he fretted over the bond that had begun to form between Marc and Jaimin, he couldn't deny the fact that on some level Marc needed Jaimin here with him. Ever so slowly he seemed to yield to Jaimin's touch, her soft voice, and meaningless words. Though he remained unconscious, his struggles seemed to ease, his moans and ragged breathing calmed once she took his hand. There was no doubt but that he knew she was there.

Jaimin continued murmuring soft words to him, and slowly Marc's fingers clamped about her hand, but this time not unbearably tight. She watched as he relaxed—seemingly pacified as he drifted into a quiet sleep. Jaimin remained at his side long after his breathing returned to normal, and his fingers went lax in her hand. Even then, she continued to stay.

~ * ~

Two hours later Marc awoke, reality seeping back by degrees. The cabin was dimly lit making it easy on his eyes as he glanced about. To his right, Frank was asleep in a nearby chair, snoring. To his left, Jaimin had fallen asleep in the chair next to his bunk, her hand lax, but still clinging to his. He felt the tension drain from his body as he quietly studied her with soft eyes. Jaimin. his angel. The one who was always quietly sitting by his side, soothing his fevered brow, offering words of comfort, bringing him meals, and insisting he eat and drink more water, demanding he stay in bed, or to wait for Frank.

Whether lucid or delirious with a raging fever, he was constantly aware of her quiet presence. Through blurry vision he continued appraising her. She wasn't what he'd call glamorous. She was just...just really pretty, her rainstorm eyes always sympathetic whether she was sponging him with a cool cloth or alleviating his thirst with numerous cups of water. Always, she was there when he needed her—her voice soft and low. Even when he was wandering down the dark corridors of hell, he was somehow always aware of her presence lingering nearby.

What did he ever do to earn the constant care and concern of this beautiful angel. He thought of the times when the pain was at its worst and he didn't know if he could hold on much longer. It was then he'd hear her soft voice comforting him, telling him to hang on. When he was burning up with a raging fever, it was then he felt a gentle hand on his brow, felt a sense of stillness as she sponged his fevered body. There were times when he vaguely recalled rambling on and on in confused delirium.

Marc witnessed, more than once, how people often react with a raging fever. God only knows what incoherent and pointless chatter he'd raged on and on about, not to mention the rough language he'd probably used as well. Yet, she remained steadfast by his side through it all.

Jaimin, his angel. He didn't deserve her faithfulness. Yet here she was. he couldn't name even one woman he knew who would have been there for him, let alone remain by his side at a time when he was not pleasant to be around.

With a gentle squeeze he enfolded her delicate hand in his and felt her fingers flex in response, watched her rainstorm eyes open, and saw the very instant recognition set in.

"Marc." she breathed. "You're awake." Sitting forward, she whispered. "How are you feeling? Are you hungry? Can I get you anything?"

The deep concern in her beautiful eyes warmed his heart.

"I'm feeling much better. Thank you. No, I don't need anything."

CHAPTER SIXTEEN

Suddenly, Ruckus blew in with a shrill screech to land on his perch near Frank. "Squawk! Flaming supernovas. Screech!"

Frank awoke with a start.

"Marc's awake, Frank."

"'Ee is?" Frank rolled out of the chair and came around to the foot of the bed. "How y' feelin', son?"

"I'm feelin' good, Frank. Damn good."

Jaimin rose from the chair. "Well, I'm going to get some coffee started."

"No more pain? Fever?"

"No. Like I say, I feel great."

"Maybe a bit too great?" Frank asked, suspicious.

"Yeah... You might say that." Marc sat up and swung his legs over the edge of the bunk. "Which one of you laced the coffee? I feel...like..."

Frank wheezed a laugh. "Like yer plastered?"

"Yeah, sorta."

"Doron will be coming by in 'bout an hour. He'll give y' a rundown on what's going on, and what to expect."

"Doron?" he asked, breaking a long moment of silence. "Do I know him?"

"Y' should. He's been tending to you for the past three days. I suspect y've been in another world, and don't remember now."

Marc gained his feet. "Right now, all I want is a shower."

"I moved some of yer clean things over from your quarters to the drawers and closet here."

Marc nodded, and cautiously turned for the closet and storage area along the aft wall of the cabin. "I take it you got her all set-up in the larger cabin?" he asked as he began selecting clean things to take with him to the lav.

"Yep. Plus, I moved all yer personal items over to the corridor lav. And," Frank added. "I fixed the privacy panel. With the little gal onboard, we need to be able to shut it."

"Thanks."

"Y' look a little unsteady there, son. Sure, you don't want some help?"

"I got it, Frank."

"Okay, but holler if y' change yer mind."

"Yeah..."

Meanwhile, Jaimin hung out in the galley, obsessed with cleaning, putting things away, wiping the table and counters down. Not that they were dirty, but it gave her something to do after she'd made the coffee. It wasn't so much what Marc did or said even. It was...vibes. She sensed his interest in her suddenly.

Doron arrived on time, and presently was in conference with Marc and Frank. Every now and then she would hear a burst of male laughter over something one of them said. Overall, it seemed that Doron was satisfied with Marc's progress.

An hour later she wandered up front, finding Marc in the helm, leaning against the back of the captain's seat, quietly scanning the controls.

"Frank said you're doing much better."

Marc turned to look up at her.

"Doron thinks you're over the worst of it. That's wonderful, Marc."

"You think so?" He turned away from the command console and came up the steps to the landing.

"Yes, don't you?"

He measured her for one hot moment, then slowly his heavy-lidded gaze slid over her. It wasn't hard to read his mind. "I don't know," he said, "I'm still a little unsteady." He flashed her a wolf's grin. "I may need your help getting back to my cabin."

Jaimin wasn't sure about this change in him. Worse, she wasn't sure about the change in herself. As much as she didn't want to be, she was drawn to him regardless, almost as if someone else was in charge of her thoughts. The direction they were going both scared and thrilled her at the same time. She blushed under his candid gaze, wondering if he could read the indelicate thoughts tumbling through her mind right now. He appealed to something raw and earthy deep within her. She backed up a couple steps only to find herself against the bulkhead.

He matched her pace.

"You're drunk, Marc."

With a deft movement he placed his hands against the bulkhead on both sides of her face. "Haven't had one drop, sunshine. Not one drop." He frowned as if trying to remember... "You didn't by chance slip something special in my—"

"No, I certainly didn't, and I don't think you should be doing whatever it is you're doing."

He leaned suggestively into her, "Just one kiss. That's all I ask. One little kiss."

"Marc..." she whispered. "Please don't."

Yet she made no move to avoid the hand that reached out to stroke the curve of her cheek. Nor did she turn away when he bent to kiss her.

Her heart jolted when she felt his mouth graze her cheek, then work its way down to the sensitive skin of her throat. He returned to her mouth and ever so gently wet her lips with his tongue. "I want you, Jaimin," he whispered leaning into her, pressing her against the bulkhead as he spoke.

He took her mouth again. This time in a kiss that was both tender and brutal at the same time. And she allowed it.

Hating herself, Jaimin allowed Marc to lead her down the corridor from the helm to the cabin and bed she'd been using—*his* cabin, *his* bed. Willingly, she sank down on the mattress as he turned to secure the lock on the panel. Later, she would be ashamed of the brazen way she responded to his touch, would be embarrassed to recall the love words she whispered in his ear. Only not now.

With provocative deliberation, Marc began slowly undressing her, caressing her T-shirt up over her head, then her lacy bra, kissing each inch of exposed flesh. He then ever so slowly began removing her jeans, and for a moment, his fingers stroked her naked belly and thighs. Jaimin stared up at him, her entire body quivering and on fire under his burning gaze.

Never taking his eyes from her, he stood up and began pulling his shirt from his pants. Within moments, he was standing before her in simply his jeans and bare feet. She marveled at the span of his shoulders. Although he no longer wore the heart monitor, she took in the stark white medi-patch over his ribs, the length of his legs, the strength in his arms. With a little cry, she reached for him, pulling him down beside her on the bed, loving the touch of his skin against hers as she explored his bruised torso with shameless abandon.

Despite his scars and recent bruises, she thought his body was beautiful to behold. Lying beside Marc, feeling his hand caress her flesh, tasting his kisses, she felt loved and protected. And for the very first time, she felt terribly female. He was so completely masculine, so virile it made her more than ever glad to be a woman. It was breathtaking to know that he found her desirable. She gloried in the easy strength of his arms as he enfolded her, brushing his lips against her neck. She reveled in his gentle attention. It seemed her entire life had been spent trying to prove that she was as good, and desirable as any of the other girls. Then to overhear Ahmed say that he never loved her...

Tap, tap. “Jaimin?”

Shaking his head, Marc grinned. “Frank...” he whispered.

“Yes?” she called out.

“Honey...have you seen Marc?”

It was all Jaimin could do to control her laughter. “Uh...No. Maybe he’s in the cargo hold. I think he was wanting to check on the temperature issues back there.” She clapped a hand over her mouth to hold her laughter at bay.

“I’ll go look.”

~ * ~

As soon as they heard Frank's footfalls heading down the corridor, Marc grabbed his shirt, picked up his boots, and with a heated parting kiss, turned and tiptoed out of Jaimin's cabin to disappear into his own.

It was absolutely infuriating to think that his life had been reduced to slinking around like this. In his own damn ship. If it had been anyone else other than Jaimin, Frank could take a flying leap. The hell of it was, it wasn't someone else. It was innocent Jaimin. As much as he hated admitting it, it was a good thing Frank interrupted them after all.

The next morning, Jaimin was sitting at the table staring into a cup of cold coffee remembering Marc's kisses and caresses. Wondering what exactly happened. The feelings of desire that had swept through her the night before were shocking. They were so unlike her. Never had she felt such a desire, such a desire for something she knew so little about. It was more than disturbing—it was humiliating. It defied common sense. She should not have allowed him to lead her down the corridor to his cabin, nor allowed him to undress her. It was as if she had been under some sort of mind control. What would have happened if Frank hadn't interrupted them?

She wondered, too, about her future and what it held. She didn't want to live with people she didn't know. Just watching the video made her feel smothered. What choice did she have? She couldn't stay here on Aden. Plus, Frank told her Marc would notify her parents before long, and the trip to Earth would take about eight weeks.

"Darlin'?" Her thoughts were interrupted when Frank entered the galley. "You okay How y' doin' t'day?"

"I'm good, Frank."

Frank studied her for a long moment. "Honey, he's just not himself right now. It's those damn injections."

"Yes," she said quietly. "I know."

Oh, did she know. She also suspected that Frank knew more than he was letting on. He hadn't been fooled for one minute when he tapped on her panel and asked if she knew where Marc was. He knew. He knew exactly where Marc was.

"Unless I'm present, I think it best if y' stay clear of him for a while. I know it won't be easy, given the ship's cramped quarters and all."

"I understand."

"The next stage he'll be goin' through will most likely be low energy and feeling drained. 'Ee's gonna need rest, but I guarantee 'ee won't wanna' take it. Doron wants to make one more trip tomorrow to check on him, then if all goes well, we'll put into space the next day. Bet yer getting' excited to meet your real folks, huh?"

Jaimin nodded. "Yes. Frank, by the way do you know how long this change in him will last? I mean..."

"I know what you mean. According to Doron, there's no way to predict how long a side effect will last. Everyone is different. It could last a couple of days or a couple of weeks 'fore he's back to hiself." Frank offered her a sympathetic grin... "We'll just have to put up with him I guess until it wears off. "

"At least you don't have him looking at you though half-lidded eyes like he wants to eat you up."

"No... Thank God." Frank threw back his head and let go a hoarse laugh. "I'd be runnin' if he did."

Jaimin joined him in laughter. "You mean you'd leave me all alone at his mercy?" It wasn't just the way Marc looked at her, it was the vibes that she was beginning to realize she was privy to.

"Mercy?" Frank repeated and shook his head slowly. "In his condition? There'd be no mercy? I'd take y' with me."

"Well, I would hope so."

With a grin, Frank turned for the corridor. "I'm gonna see if that boy's hungry."

"He's hardly a boy, Frank," Jaimin whispered softly as she got up from the table.

It was obvious that he thought of Marc almost as a son.

Jaimin headed for the cooking station and began putting

something together. For the past four days that he'd had been onboard, Marc had only been given broth. Even so, he would only accept a small portion of what was brought to him. Time to get Frank's *growing boy* back on solids again. Since she knew nothing beyond what she had grown up with, Jaimin searched the cupboards for something that would suffice as solid food, yet easy on the stomach. That's when she came across something that looked like it would make a bowl of hot cereal. Perfect. She'd look for cinnamon to sprinkle on the top, making it more like an Adenian dish.

She'd just finished setting the place for Marc at the table. when Frank and Marc entered the galley. Either Frank or Doron must have had another little talk with him, as Marc hardly looked at her when they came into the galley.

"Oatmeal?" Frank said on bark of laughter. "Good choice?"

Jaimin shot Marc a quick glance as he silently eyed the bowl of mush and a plate of toast sitting on the table. Finally, he turned to Frank, "Is this yours?"

"Nope. I believe it's yers."

Silence.

Jaimin turned and busied herself at the sink, and decided to let Frank handle this one.

"I thought you said solid food." Marc grumbled, eyeing the mush with obvious distaste.

"That-thar *is* solid food. Whad' you have in mind, steak and eggs? This is about as solid as yer gettin'. You haven't had anythang in yer stomach but broth for goin' on five days. Take it or leave it. "

Frowning, Marc sat down at the table, and after a long-drawn-out moment, spooned up a bite of oatmeal, grimacing as he swallowed it.

Frank sat down across from him while Jaimin left the galley for her quarters. She fought back a smile as she headed down the corridor. Of all things...Frank telling his captain to either eat the mush or go without? As a result, reluctantly the captain started eating? As her friend Aannisah would say, *Hell must have frozen over.*

Aannisah...would she ever see her friend again?

She wondered if she would ever see anything familiar again. No longer would she see the home she grew up in, her cozy warm bed, the beauty of a desert at sunrise, and the happiness she thought she knew...Hassan and Zari, the only parents she knew. To think that Hassan, and probably Zari too, were in on the marriage arrangement, knowing there was no love involved. So, in the long run, she guessed there was no big loss for her there.

Six days ago, it was the only life she knew. It was a happy life. The happiness ended when Marc Banner showed up. No, her happiness ended when she'd overheard Ahmed and his father discussing the real reason, he was to marry her.

Maybe it was just as well that Marc happened to be there that day. Maybe it was a blessing in disguise. She couldn't imagine now going through with the marriage. Especially after overhearing Ahmed explain that he didn't love her, that he loved someone else.

So now what did the future hold for her? Her mind was a crazy mix of hope and fear. She didn't want to go live with people she no longer remembered. Yet, what choice did she have? Where would she go?

Frank...She'd talk to Frank about it. That's what she'd do.

CHAPTER SEVENTEEN

Jaimin remained in her cabin, determined to stay out of everyone's way. Doron had been there most of the morning and was just leaving. She could overhear Frank and Marc walking him to the main lock, their voices drifting in through her closed panel.

"Hot dog! Finally." Frank's voice held a rasp of pure excitement. "I'm sick and tard of sittin' here in this damn spaceport. It'll be good to be on our way. Y' want me to take 'er out?"

"I got it, Frank." Jaimin easily recognized Marc's low-pitched voice. "We'll be leaving within the hour. Better let Jaimin know to secure anything loose and come up front to strap-in when finished."

Both he and Frank knew, as always, it would be a rough lift given the waves of scorching heat rising off the planet.

"I'll let 'er know, boss." Frank replied as he busied himself in the galley, securing anything loose.

It wasn't long before Frank tapped at her door. "Honey, it's me."

"What did Doron say?" she asked as she opened the door.

"He gave us his okay to leave."

"So... Marc is better now?"

"Most of the side effects are over, but they won't be completely gone for maybe a week or so. Regardless, I'll be keepin' a watch on him, darlin'."

"Thank you."

An hour later Jaimin stood in the corridor just outside of her cabin, her eyes on Marc. He and Frank were engaged in a conversation—just far enough away that it was impossible to overhear the exchange.

Arms folded, Marc had a shoulder braced against the bulkhead and was responding in lowered tones. Occasionally, he would nod at something Frank said.

Unable to resist, she drank in the sight of him. As always, he was wearing his standard *uniform,* black jeans, and another white short sleeved T-shirt with rolled sleeves that stretched across his biceps. In comparison, Jaimin thought Ahmed Farouk looked like a five-foot-eight, one-hundred-and-fifty-pound weakling with his head wrapped in a turban and his face hidden behind an ugly full black beard. How she ever could have thought him good-looking was beyond understanding.

Without realizing it, she took her perusal of Marc even further. Starting from his booted feet she slowly worked her way up long, muscular legs, past broad shoulders and finally coming to rest upon Marc's ruggedly handsome face with its five-day shadow. His dark hair was still damp from his shower, lying untrimmed and shaggy against his tanned neck. In truth, Marc Banner simmered with a sensuality that Jaimin barely understood. He was, without a doubt, the most blatantly handsome man she'd ever seen. Unable to keep her eyes from him, her heart caught each time he glanced in her direction.

Whether he'd been under the influence of the drugs or not, she was haunted by the memory of Marc's open-mouth kisses, the weight of his swarthy body pressing her against the bulkhead, his sapphire eyes alight with desire, his hands gliding over her flesh, arousing her while at the same time sending a flutter of fear through her.

He probably has a girl in every port just waiting for his beck and call, a silent voice reminded her.

Not that she was interested in being one of them, but curiosity had her wondering just what he considered appealing in a woman.

"Y' can come on forward, darlin'. It's okay. No need to hang back there. Y' need to take a seat and get strapped in." He grinned. "We'll be liftin' off this god forsaken hellhole shortly."

Frank took his place in the helm to the right of Marc. Jaimin descended the short flight of steps into the sunken helm and was seated on the port side behind Marc. Her heart was pounding as a mixture of emotions raced through her mind. She was scared to remain on Aden. Afraid to leave and had no idea what the future held for her once she got to wherever they were taking her.

Marc's very presence continued to be both disturbing and exciting as she watched him go through the process of sealing the ship. Determined not to go dropping at his feet in worship, she had no sooner formed her plan of immunity when Marc swung about to face her, the smoky timbre of his voice calmly breaking the silence. "It's going to be a rough lift," he said as he reached over, pulled her safety harness across her lap, and fastened it in place. "You ever been off-planet before, Jaimin?"

"No. At least I don't remember it."

"Well, then this will be a new experience for you. First, like I said, it's going to be rough to start off with. Nothing for you to worry about. It's all normal. Okay?"

Jaimin nodded. "Okay."

She shot a glance over at Frank, and noted that he was talking to the controller, and busily entering info into the ship's NAVCOMP.

"Any questions before we leave?" Marc asked.

Jaimin shook her head. "No."

"Okay then. In the meantime," he added with a smile, "Try to relax."

She nodded. "I'll try."

With that, Marc swung back around and returned his attention to pre-lift procedures.

Turning to glance out the viewport. Jaimin watched a tiny pulsing strobe light snap to life, marking the tip of the swept-back port wing. Four high-intensity landing beams came alive to instantly bathe the landing zone in bright light.

By now the day had worn away to evening. Dusk was casting the surrounding spaceport in a muted blend of soft oranges that faded into the deep blues of a hot impending night. Jaimin pressed closer to the window as she surveyed the surrounding spaceport for the last time. Nearby docking bays were occupied with everything from large freighters to small mail boats, to private yachts. Several docks were a bustle of activity. As she continued watching, a large freighter lifted, its loud roar barely heard inside the *Antara* as they awaited their turn to lift.

Frank was still talking to the spaceport as a subtle vibration became the low rumble of ignition. She turned to watch Marc flip an overhead switch. In response, a bank of tiny green lights came alive on the console. When he tapped a final key, the low rumble of ignition slowly began building into a muffled high-pitched whine.

Marc opened the com-link. "This is Linc McKenna of the *Star Bandit, Delta Beta, Eight-Niner-Four,* requesting clearance to lift," he said, using his newly registered name and ship I.D. that Frank recently relocated the *Antara* under.

"That's an affirmative, *Star Bandit,"* came a masculine voice. "You are cleared for vertical lift to thirty-thousand feet. After that you're on your own. See you on your return trip, Banner."

The controller had no sooner given clearance than the sound of the ship's powerful thrusters began escalating. Although the rumble was muffled inside the cabin, Jaimin suspected from the vibrations alone, the noise level on the outside was rising to a deafening roar as the *Antara* lifted skyward, escaping the confines of being planet bound.

Pinned to her seat, Jaimin watched in fascination as the lights of Port Jahara became smaller and smaller, gradually disappearing into the distance as Frank set the course for the trip ahead. Within mere minutes they had risen above Aden's horizon, and bright, direct sunlight now flooded the inside of the ship through the starboard viewports.

Suddenly the ship shuddered violently. White-knuckled, Jaimin grabbed hold of the edges of her seat. She had no sooner recovered from that, than another violent jolt traveled through the ship. "Is it always this bumpy?" she asked nervously.

"It's the heat rising off the desert." Marc said without taking his eyes of the controls. "Not to worry. It will get better as soon as we get above it."

For the moment she lost herself as once again her eyes wandered over him, from the defiant tattoo on one gleaming bicep, to the clean but worn white T-shirt.

"Relax darlin'. We've got a long way yet to go. This is only the very beginning." Frank explained. "You'll be an old pro by the time we get to our destination."

"How long of a trip is it?" she asked.

"Depends on where the rendezvous is." Marc replied. "Frank...I'm going to need you to take over."

"Not feelin' well?"

"I just need to lay down for a bit."

With that Marc rose from the captain's chair, made his way out of the sunken helm and headed for the corridor. "Wake me if anything comes up."

"Yep."

After Marc left, Jaimin turned to Frank. "Is he alright?"

"Yeah. Between the effects of the Ripper and the strong injections Doron has given him, 'ee's had the starch taken out of 'im. 'Ee just needs rest."

"Oh, but he will be, okay?"

Frank swung about to face her; his mouth curved with tenderness. "Yes, darlin', he's gonna be fine. 'Ee just needs to gain his strength back. We wouldn't be leavin' if Doron didn't feel he was ready. Doron has him on some sort of natural meds that hopefully will lessen the intoxication effect, as well as help him regain his strength," Frank added, as he turned his attention back to the controls.

"I don't know what would have happened to him if not for Doron."

"I do. Weda' lost him. Why 'ee was still alive when we found him, I don't know."

Lost in thought, Jaimin again turned her attention to the viewport and watched as darkness inched its way across the surface of Aden. By now they were so high that Aden's sun no longer had the strength to brighten the interior through the viewports. In fact, the sun looked simply like a small glowing ball against the blackness of space. Jaimin's sights shifted back to Aden. If she looked really hard, she could actually see a vaporous line of demarcation between daylight and nighttime stretching diagonally across the face of the planet. Somewhere on Aden's surface, daylight was steadily giving way to dusk. Her expression stilled and grew serious as the realization sunk in that this would be the last time she'd see home.

Her mind in turmoil, once again she wondered what she was doing. It wasn't like her to be so daring. What other choice did she have? That was just it, there were only two choices. One: stay there and marry Ahmed, who didn't want to marry her in the first place, and who most likely would end up taking a second wife. Or she could run. Now that raises yet another dilemma. Run to where? If she ran to her real parents, they were strangers, and worse, she could just barely speak their language. Their jubilancy not only scared her, it made her feel suffocated. Why couldn't she remember them? She wasn't a little baby in their arms at the time. Supposedly she was a nine-year-old child. Her memory of her real parents, and of being kidnapped should be vivid, yet none of it was clear.

Aannisah, not knowing the truth, had tried to encourage her to stay and marry Ahmed. *You can do it. Chin up and face the music.*

She couldn't do it. Just couldn't. By now Aannisah has read her letter and knows the truth about Ahmed. She also knows that she was kidnapped years ago and adopted by Hassan and Zari. Hopefully now Aannisah would understand.

Maybe it was best in more ways than one that she was leaving Aden behind. She needed time to sort out her thoughts. Time to come to grips with the fact she was never going to know who she really was. That's okay. She could make it on her own just fine. Years ago, she accepted the person she was. Oh, she knew she was different from the others. Her hair color for one. Her eyes were totally different, and even her skin tanned lighter.

"Frank, when you get a chance, I have a question."

"Darlin' fire away." With a shrug, he leaned back in the chair and swiveled it about to face her. "I ain't doin' nothun' but monitoring a bunch of blinkin' lights anyway. What's on yer mind, honey?"

Unconsciously her hands twisted together in her lap. "I don't know how to put this," she began. "But..." She inhaled a deep breath. "I don't want to go live with those people."

"I see." His eyes were gentle and contemplative. "Did you get a chance to listen to their message?"

She nodded. "I did."

"And...?"

"From their happy faces and excited tone of voices, I felt overwhelmed. Frank, I know you say they're my real parents. I don't question that. I don't remember them, and I don't feel the same excitement they do. They're strangers to me and it scares me to think I'll be dropped off to live with them."

Frank, bless his heart, was understanding as he set Jaimin's mind at ease. "Honey, nobody's goin' to just drop you off to live with people y' don't wanna live with. Y' got my word on that."

"Marc said—"

"'Ee ain't gonna force y' t' do nuthin' y' don't wanna do. I promise y'. Don't y' worry, darling, we'll work something out."

She released a breath of hope. "Thank you, Frank."

"Nuthin' to thank me for. Just the way it is."

CHAPTER EIGHTEEN

One week out of Port Jahara

"I'd like to make dinner tonight if that's okay," Jaimin said. With a laugh, she added, "I watched you make hamburgers, and I know I can make them."

"You just go right on ahead, darlin'. Hamburgers sounds fine with me."

Just then Marc entered the galley with his jacket slung over one shoulder. He'd been back in the cargo hold for the last hour, trying to figure out why the temperature was running way too cold back there. "What sounds fine, Frank?" he asked as he offered a nod in greeting to Jaimin and headed for the sink to wash up.

"Jaimin's offered to make burgers for dinner tonight. We had 'em the other night and she watched me make em."

Marc grinned. "Yeah, I could go for a burger. Sounds like Frank's been introducing you to good ol' fashioned American fast food." Suddenly he frowned. "So, where was I when you two were fixing burgers without me?"

Frank groaned. "In your own private hell."

"Yeah, you can say that again."

~ * ~

Marc turned off the faucet and reached for a towel, fully aware of Jaimin covertly watching him. Oh yeah...he'd been aware of her guarded glances ever since he was able to be up and about. If he thought it was cold in the cargo bay, it was nothing compared to the heat in the galley right now.

So just what the devil was he to do about it. Maybe Frank should have had a little talk with her as well. He'd been doing his part trying to stay clear of her for the past week. Not to say it had been easy, 'cause it hadn't.

Tossing the towel aside, he pitched his jacket onto a nearby wall hook, then turned to face her. She quickly looked away; her cheeks flushed.

Why is it she gets prettier every time he looks at her? Today she was wearing clothing that was anything, but Aden approved. Interesting, since he was used to seeing her in typical Adenian garb. Today she looked Terran. No, make that American with her platinum hair pulled back into a bouncy ponytail, wearing faded blue jeans and a pink T-shirt. She looked as pretty as a Christmas present just waiting to be opened.

Now it was his turn to stare. That is, until Frank deliberately cleared his throat.

Marc chuckled. With Frank as the self-appointed chaperone, it was going to be a long trip home.

He wondered where she got the clothes. Probably from her friend—*Dark Eyes*—the one who'd lured him backstage the night of the festival. What was her name? Anna? Aannisah? That was it, Aannisah. From what little he recalled; she somehow didn't seem quite as steeped in traditional Aden customs as Jaimin was.

"Grab a seat you two." Jaimin said. "I can't say these burgers are as good as yours, Frank, but maybe with a little practice..."

"Darlin', not to worry. They'll be just as good, if not better."

Marc took the first bite. "They' are better than yours, Frank. Good Job, Jaimin."

"Yes indeed," Frank replied as he popped a fry into his mouth. "Y' did good, girl."

Jaimin brought her plate to the table. "Thank you both."

Later that evening, Jaimin had retired to her cabin and Frank and Marc were sitting in the galley, nursing mugs of coffee.

"Thought y' should know what Jaimin shared with me today. I

didn't say anything earlier 'cause I kept hopin' she'd change 'er mind, but I asked her again this evening how she felt, and the answer was still the same."

"About what?" Marc asked as he looked up from staring into his coffee.

"She don't wanna go live with 'er real parents."

Dead silence.

"Yep' y heard me right."

"Why?"

"I'm not sure. She mentioned that their eagerness and excitement scared her, and that she didn't feel the same way. Plus, she can't even communicate with them—speak their language. I had 'er watch that video of them greetin' 'er. Set it to play in Adenian. Otherwise, she wouldn't understand one word they said. "

More silence.

"Anyway, I thought y' should know so y' can decide what yer gonna' do."

With a heavy sigh, Marc leaned back in the chair, cupping his hands behind his head. "I just told the Byers that I found her and bringing her back."

"I know."

"So, what am I supposed to do with her, Frank?"

"I dunno. She can't stay with me. She sure as 'ell can't stay with you."

Marc rubbed the back of his neck. "Unless someone has a better idea, the folks have plenty of room at their place, there's a couple of guests houses on the property. Hopefully one of them will appeal to her until she figures things out."

"Well, y'd better let yer folks and the Byers know whatever it is yer doin'."

"Yeah."

"So..." Frank continued, "I've been meanin' to ask y', that stuff Doron left for y', do y' feel like it's workin'?

"I don't feel loaded anymore if that's what you mean?"

"Good. Yep, that's what I mean. Hopefully, y'll be thinking with yer' head instead of what's below yer' belt. "

"I don't know what you're talking about."

"Y' think I ain't seen the looks you and that little gal have been stealing when y' think nobody's lookin'?"

Marc frowned and rose to his feet and began to turn away. "Just your imagination, Frank."

"Don't go just yet. I gotta tell y' somethin' else that I think you should know about."

With a huff, Marc sat back down. "Now what?"

"'Member when Nick first met Tressa?

"What about it?"

"Well, when he was zapped with a *Ripper* Tressa began feelin' everything he was feelin'. That's when they learned she's got creohen blood in 'er."

"Yeah, I remember. So, what's that have to do with anything?"

"I'll tell y'. When you were going through the worst of it, Jaimin was right there with you, feeling everythang—the pain, even aware of the demons y' were seein'. I watched it happen." Frank paused allowing that bit of news to sink in, then added "Someone in Jaimin's family might be creohen. Either that, or she's telepathic."

"So why are you telling me about it?"

"I'm tellin' y' because from what I understand, she may not read yer thoughts, but she sure as 'ell can read yer vibes."

"It's that obvious?"

At that, Frank huffed a laugh. "Yeah. Even though yer not actin' on it, Doron said it's still there for her to pick-up on."

"So, what am I supposed to do about it?"

"Don't know. I guess we could always lock 'er in her cabin for the duration."

"For the next eight weeks?" Marc muttered. He began to laugh. It had been a long time since he'd laughed. And it felt good.

"Sure, we'll just pass 'er meals under the door." Frank added between his own hoots of laughter.

~ * ~

The seven weeks that followed were unbelievably difficult, and passed incredibly slowly . Marc did his best to stay out of Jaimin's way and to keep a tight rein on his thoughts and feelings whenever she was around. It wasn't easy.

"Hot dog!" Frank announced. "Two more hours to Acacia. Think y' can last that long?"

Marc groaned. "Not if it goes as slow as the rest of this trip has."

"I take it y' let her folks know what's goin' on."

"I did," Marc replied, his attention glued now on the command console. Finally, he turned to face Frank. "They all want to meet us at the spaceport when we arrive."

"Well at least she'll be able to half-way communicate with them, thanks to that language course y' dug up on the ship's computer." Frank commented. "Do y' think the Byers are gonna stay at yer folks too?"

"I don't know. She's agreed to stay in one of the guest houses until she decides what she's going to do.

"Mom's having both houses aired out and cleaned, just in case her folks decide to stay in one of them for a while."

Frank nodded. "Well at least she'll have Rae, Tressa, Kira and Angela, not to mention all the babies, to help her adjust to this new world she's bein' thrown into."

"True. We'll be leaving hyperspace before long, Frank. You want to let her know that she needs to get everything packed and put away. Then when finished, have her come on up front."

"Will do."

~ * ~

By the time Jaimin descended the steps into the helm, Marc was monitoring controls, and verbal communications were on-going between Frank and Imperial's spaceport.

"How long, do you think, before we get there?" she asked.

"A little over an hour, darlin'. Won't be long now. Hey, I just realized yer speaking English. Good job.

"Thank you. I think it's starting to come back to me. The lessons have really helped."

"Well, you just keep up the good work, darlin' and nobody will ever know you spoke anythang different."

"Grab a seat, Jaimin." Marc said without looking away from the console. "We're going to be leaving hyperspace. You're going to feel a moment of dizziness, but it will be brief."

No sooner said than the onboard computer was announcing their upcoming departure from hyperspace followed by a countdown. As Marc cautioned, the wave of nausea came and went quickly.

"You, okay?" he asked.

"Yes."

"Good."

Gradually Acacia continued to grow larger until it completely engulfed the overhead screen as they entered orbit. It was another half-hour before a bark of static hailed a greeting. "Welcome to Acacia, *Antara*, please initiate your descent."

"Understood," Marc continued verbal contact, while Frank began entering the designated coordinates into the NAVCOMP. "Go ahead and take her on in, Frank."

"Yes sir, Captain."

Ever so slowly the inky blackness of space gave-way to the radiance of Acacia's luminous aura. Marc swiveled around to face Jaimin. "Don't be alarmed by the fire you're going to see out your viewport. It's all part of entering a planet's atmosphere. Nothing to worry about. Okay?"

Jaimin nodded.

~ * ~

No sooner had he turned back around than the *Antara* began to glow like a fanned ember with flames licking off the bow and the leading edge of both wings. An eerie orange flush filled the cabin as the firestorm outside swept across the viewports. At regular intervals a soft chime broke the silence signaling designated drops in elevation.

Reaching overhead, Marc made another adjustment to the controls, then relaxed for a moment. “You still okay back there? You’re awfully quiet.”

“Yes, I’m fine.”

He turned to face her, noting that her hands were stiffly folded in her lap, and her expression tense.

“Just a little bit longer, then it will pass. I promise.”

Other than that, one incident in which Frank had interrupted his amorous advances, the time on board ship with Jaimin went without a hitch. All communication and activities regarding Jaimin had been on a strict no-nonsense, non-personal level the entire time, which suited him just fine. It worked best that way for both. The way he saw it, this trip was meant to bring Miss Jenelle D’Anne Byers back to her parents and wind up twenty thousand credits richer for it.

~ * ~

Jaimin glanced up at the overhead monitor. Just as it was when they left Aden, Acacia now filled the entire screen, and from what she could tell they were heading into the nighttime side of the planet. Colonized areas were evident as bright clusters of light dotted the darkened surface.

Another crack of static preceded an audio message. “Welcome to Imperial, *Antara.*” The controller was female.

With cool formality, she began providing not only verbal clearance and landing coordinates, current temperature, weather conditions, and docking assignment. Once the essentials had been routinely dispatched, the interaction became more personal in breathy undertones. “Welcome home, Marc. Will I get to see you this trip? I missed you the last time you were home.”

"Yeah. Sorry about that, Kara. I had back-to-back contracts. When are you getting off work?"

"In five hours. Plan to stay for breakfast? We can spend the night making—"

"Honey, I'm not alone right now. Why don't you surprise me with what you have planned."

"Oh? You're not alone?"

Marc laughed. "No. Frank's with me on this trip, and I have a passenger on board as well."

"Oh, I didn't realize. Hi Frank."

"Hi there darlin."

"Oh dear..." She began to laugh. "Marc, I am so sorry."

"No worries."

"Anyway," she continued, "just make sure that—" she suddenly broke off mid-sentence. "Things are getting busy, Marc. I've got to go. Don't be late, okay?"

And he probably has a girl in every port strolled through Jaimin's mind. It was too bad the exchange was audio and not on the vid screen. She couldn't help being curious what this Kara looked like.

Jaimin quietly watched Marc guide the ship down through the various layers of unsettled air. Eventually he cut the speed, felt the response, booted the nose up and goosed the thrusters to slow their descent.

For Marc and Frank, it was the usual approach to Imperial's massive spaceport. For Jaimin, even at night, it was breathtaking. A vast dark ocean spread out beneath them for as far as she could see. Before long they were skimming over a flat plain. A range of mountains stood beyond. And all the while, at regular intervals, a soft chime continued signaling designated drops in elevation.

"See that bright-lit settlement up ahead, darlin'?" Frank said, drawing her attention to the master screen. "That-there is Imperial, Acacia's capital. That's where we're goin'."

"Oh, it looks like it's a big city."

"That it is. Just wait til y' meet the girls, they'll take y' shoppin'."

With a weary sigh, Marc patted his pocket for one of his smokes, found one and lit up. Long before they'd entered Acacia's orbit, the ship's main computer had already been in contact with Imperial. Basic identification, navigational data and clearance had all been electronically exchanged before Marc switched control back to manual. As they neared the spaceport, Jaimin could see in the distance, a circle of pulsing blue lights outlining a designated landing zone.

CHAPTER NINETEEN

Max, Delta, and the Byers were gathered at the fence that separated the tarmac from Port Imperial's main terminal. A distant high-pitched whine drew Max's attention. "I bet that's them now."

The ship was roughly a couple of miles across the spaceport, landing lights bathing the tarmac as it slowly advanced. Even at a distance *Antara* was impressive. Tiny, but bright strobe lights winked on the tip of each sweptback wing as they taxied behind a robotic drone.

Karissa Byers turned to her husband. "Oh Tom, I can't wait."

Tom laughed. "Neither can I, but I think we'll have to."

The closer Antara got, the louder the scream of her turbines as she continued to trail behind the robosphere.

"Shouldn't be too much longer," Max offered. "Soon as they dock and get shut down, we can go out there to greet them as they disembark.

The *Antara* followed the drone down a long, wide corridor where at last it was led into a flashing blue-lit circular pad.

~ * ~

Marc killed the forward drives. The pulsing of the proximity alarm sounded as the ground seemingly rose to meet them, and with a gentle thump the *Antara* settled onto her landing jacks. Even from inside the ship, the whine of her powerful turbines could be heard slowly descending.

Marc had no sooner depressed the key to lower the boarding ramp than he glanced up at the exterior vid-screen and watched headlights rushing across the tarmac.

"Looks like someone's coming to say hi," he announced.

He turned to face Jaimin. "Think you're ready?" At her hesitant look, he added, "Remember you're not leaving with them. You're just meeting them. That's all."

"That's right," Frank added. "You can do it."

The vehicle with both sets of parents pulled to a stop about thirty feet from the *Antara.* Marc was still securing the ship when he looked up and watched his dad leading the way across the burned and scarred tarmac.

"Want me to walk out there with y'?" Frank asked.

Jaimin nodded.

"Then, I say let's get the introductions over with, then y' can come back and gather yer things afterward.

"Alright." She turned to say goodbye to Marc, but he was still occupied shutting down and securing the ship.

He'd been distant ever since he'd fully recovered. Was she the cause? She appreciated the fact Frank had offered to escort her off the ship, but oh how she wanted Marc to be the one.

Frank palmed the main lock and stepped out first. The night air reeked of ozone and hot metal. Jaimin covered her ears at the descending whine of Antara's powerful turbines. Maybe to Marc and Frank it was just another day in the life of a pilot, but to Jaimin, the sights, the ear-piercing sounds, and the stench of a spaceport were an assault on her sheltered senses. She took-in a sweeping glance of her surroundings. *Antara's* bright floodlights illuminated the landing zone. Jaimin's eyes rose to the velvet backdrop of space where the very spiral of the Milky Way galaxy stretched across the night sky. Frank offered his hand. "Ready? I see yer folks comin'."

She'd barely heard him before she found herself being ushered down the ramp and toward the excited throng of people rushing toward them. By the time she arrived at the base of the ramp, the jubilant group of parents—all talking at once—had arrived to greet her.

Max quickly turned to Tom and Karissa. "First of all, I want to introduce Frank Reno. Frank was Marc's co-pilot on the trip. Frank, meet

Mister and Misses Tom Byers."

"Pleased to meet y'" Frank said, extending his hand in greeting. He then turned to Jaimin. "These people here are Marc's parents, Max and Delta Banner."

"Hello."

"Hello, Jaimin. And... then these two who have been waitin' for eleven long years," Max added, "are. your parents Tom and Karissa Byers."

"Hello kitten," her father said, using a favorite pet name and hoping she might remember it.

"Oh Jenelle," her mother whispered through tears. "You are so beautiful. May I hug you?"

"Momma," Jaimin murmured. She did remember them, and yet because of all the years of drugs and indoctrination, they somehow still felt like strangers.

"Marc should be joinin' us before too much longer," Frank piped up when there was a lull in the conversation. "He's securing the ship for the night."

He turned to Jaimin; "Darlin' is there anythang you want to bring with y' tonight? Otherwise, y' can always get yer things tomorrow."

"I think I'll just get my things tomorrow, if that's alright?"

Max spoke up. "Here he comes now."

All eyes turned to watch Marc make his way down the boarding ramp and come across the landing zone to join the group. Unable to look away, Jaimin watched him closely. She suspected his easy masculine grace covered up his low energy. Jaimin, however, literally felt. more than noticed the weakness lying beneath the surface.

With a curt nod he greeted the Byers, then turned to speak in low tones to Max. When he turned to leave, Tom Byers called out to him.

"Mister Banner...Karissa and I can't thank you enough for finding and bringing our daughter back to us. I understand that you went through a whole lot more than you ever anticipated."

"Just another Thursday," Marc countered.

"Well, I want you to know that I've already sent over the balance of what we owe you, plus two thousand extra for all the trouble you've had to go through.

"That wasn't necessary, sir."

"It's the least I can do."

"Then, thank you."

"No. Thank you. You brought our Janelle back to us."

Marc held Byer's gaze for a moment longer, then, "If you'll excuse me," he turned away

and headed over to Jaimin. "It's going to take time, but you're going to be alright." He said in a low voice for her ears only.

"Marc...Will I see you again?"

"Of course, you will, and Frank too."

"Marc, please. Don't leave just yet."

Lowering his head, Marc murmured in her ear. "You're going to be fine. Give it time."

When she didn't respond, he added. "I'll see you tomorrow. Okay?"

She glanced up at him. "Okay."

"Good," he said with an easy smile. "You can stay in the guest house for as long as you wish. Nobody uses it anyway."

His dark hair, longer than when she first met him, now clung to the back of his neck, brushing his collar. A lank of hair had fallen across his forehead and the bristles of a few days without shaving had darkened his face. He looked drained, weary. Well, what did she expect. he'd been through hell, and refused to take it easy on the trip back. Even with Frank willing to do what needed to be done, there was no stopping him.

"So, when you come back home," she asked, "do you stay in the house that your parents live in or one of the guest cottages?"

Marc laughed. She loved his laugh, and it had only been in the last few weeks that she had begun to hear him laugh. "Neither. I used to have a room in their house—that is, until they kicked me out."

"They kicked you out?" she repeated, her eyes wide with concern.

"Well maybe not." He smiled. "It was time."

"Oh."

Marc regarded her with gentle eyes. Suddenly he reached up and tenderly touched her cheek. Her hair fell over her shoulders in riotous waves of platinum silk. "They love you very much. Give them a chance."

"And" he added on a whisper, again for her ears only. "You're not Jaimin Ala Rashard anymore. You're Jenelle Byers. Remember that."

"Marc..." she responded, finding it hard to keep the tears from her voice. "Please...I don't want to say goodbye to you just yet."

"This isn't goodbye, Jenny," he whispered softly. "I'll see you tomorrow. How about I come by and give you a tour of the place? I'll bring the bike, and we can go for a ride. Would you like that?"

~ * ~

She nodded, and when she looked up into his face with her beautiful rainstorm eyes—the prettiest eyes he could ever remember seeing—he was a goner. Cupping her face in his hands, he pressed a kiss to her forehead, enfolded her in his arms and drew her against him. With his chin resting upon her head, he took a deep, calming breath and looked pointedly at the curious group of parents. All four sets of raised eyebrows and questioning eyes were focused on him.

Instantly, his rebellious side surfaced.

He didn't care what the hell they thought. Let them look and think what they damn-well please. He held her for a moment longer before boldly giving the top of her crown a slow and tender kiss. When at last he lifted his head, he gently set her away from him. "See you tomorrow, Jenny," he whispered as he turned away.

He stopped briefly to speak to the Byers one more time, and to thank his parents for their willingness to accommodate Jaimin for as long as she needed. He then turned for the main terminal, suspecting they were still watching with wide eyes and open mouths. Again, he didn't care. Let them think what they wanted.

"What the devil was that all about?" Frank groused, having caught up with Marc and keeping pace with him as they crossed the tarmac.

"I'm not sure myself," Marc casually replied as he continued his trek toward the terminal.

"Wull, y' damn well better figure it out. That was quite a little performance y' put on back there."

"Yeah...I know."

"So, after setting that little gal's heart to poundin', yer off now to spend the night *makin' it* with Kara?"

Without breaking stride, Marc turned to face him. "I don't see how that's any of your business, Frank, but to set your mind at ease, I've already called Kara and cancelled. I'm dead tired, and as soon as I secure the LZ with the port, I'm heading back for some much-needed sleep."

"Good. Cuz unless I miss my guess, that little gal's in love with y'."

"And which one might that be, Frank?"

Ignoring Marc's cocky response, Frank continued. "Dammit man, she's an innocent! Don't go usin' 'er, then stringin' her along like y' do all the others. Decide, one way or 'nother, and stick to it."

Having reached the spaceport Center of Operations, Marc turned to Frank before opening the door. "Goodnight Frank. I'll see you tomorrow to settle up for all your help and extra hard work."

"I don't need no settlin' up."

Marc laughed. "I know, Frank, but you have no idea how much I appreciated having you along, and everything you did."

~ * ~

Tom and Karissa came along to see the guest cottage that Janelle would be staying in. They had been invited to stay in the other cottage but turned it down saying they had reservations at the Imperial Marriott. Truth was, as much as they would have loved to have stayed, they felt it best to give Janelle a chance to adjust to her new life. Marc had already explained the situation to the Byers days before the *Antara* even entered Acacia's trajectory.

On the ride out to the Banner home, nothing was mentioned by anyone regarding Marc's amorous leave-taking. Not one word, despite their obvious shock and curiosity. Nevertheless, Jaimin was well aware of what they all must be thinking. With an inner smile, she was still thinking about him calling her...*Jenny*.

~ * ~

It wasn't large, but Jaimin found the guest cottage cozy. The interior was rustic. The décor so different from what she had been used to. She liked it. Somehow it felt right. The walls in the living room were off-white. Thick, colorful throw rugs covered wooden floors. A plush couch in tan leather, and two matching overstuffed chairs provided an inviting seating area. Tall, oblong windows embellished each side of the front door. A picture of a stunningly beautiful white horse hung above a fireplace.

The kitchen was a peaceful shade of yellow. White curtains hung from the big double window over the sink, and a quick peek in the cupboards and refer revealed that Misses Banner had even stocked them both with an assortment of food items. Four chairs surrounded a matching table, all made from some sort of wood. *Wood*...that was another thing she rarely saw, having lived in the desert. There was even a laundry room just off the kitchen. Shiny appliances were in both the laundry and kitchen. Appliances that, other than the coffee pot, she had no idea how to run.

As she advanced down a short hallway, she discovered two bedrooms at the back of the cottage. A large bath was located between the bedrooms, and it had both a tub and a shower. Misses Banner had even stocked the bathroom with personal supplies such as shampoo and cleansing gel, a toothbrush and paste to name a few. The walls of both bedrooms were done in a pale shade of blue. Both rooms were decorated alike with white bedding, rustic beds and matching nightstands and dressers. In one of the bedrooms a soft peach colored nightgown had been neatly laid across the foot of the bed for her use.

CHAPTER TWENTY

One week later

Jenelle was sitting in a big rocking chair on the front porch in her bare feet, sipping coffee. It was an absolutely beautiful morning, sunshine, blue sky, surrounded by lots of green. Green was everywhere. Green grass. Green trees. Green bushes and plants and flowers of every kind. There were even fragrant flowers growing in colorful pots decorating the porch.

She'd slept surprisingly well over the last week. This morning she had been up a couple of hours already, taken a shower, and was dressed in a new pair of faded blue jeans and a soft pink T-shirt with a slogan in burnished gold lettering across the front. Just one of several new outfits that she'd found hanging in the closet the day she'd moved in. Several pairs of shoes were lined up along the floor as well as even a pair of boots. All new.

She learned through Frank that Marc had turned down several job opportunities so that he could remain on Acacia with her. Life was good. She was happy—really happy for the first time she could ever remember. She enjoyed Marc's family, loved seeing the babies whenever they would come to visit. She had met his brothers, Clint and his family, Nick and Zeke and their families as well as Marc's sister, Rachel.

Mostly she was falling in love with Marc. Ever since that first morning when he came by and gave her a tour of the Banner land, there wasn't a day that he didn't come by for either a visit, or to take her for a trip on his bike, which usually included a picnic lunch.

"Hi there. I'm Tressa Banner, Marc's sister-in-law. I'm married to Marc's brother Nick."

Jenelle rose and greeted Tressa as she crossed the yard from the main house. "Yes, I remember meeting you."

"Well, it was such a busy night when we all came over to meet you, I'm not sure I would have remembered who was who."

They both laughed, and Jenelle confessed, "Marc does, indeed, have a large family. To be honest, I'm still trying to get used to my new name."

Tressa sat down on the step of the porch. "Don't worry, it will all fall into place before you even realize it."

"May I offer you coffee?" Jenelle asked.

"I'm good, thanks. Hey, I apologize for not coming the other day when Rae took you shopping. "

Tressa was very pregnant from the way her oversized shirt hugged her full stomach. Jenelle had only seen a pregnant woman one time that she could remember. On Aden, pregnant women were never seen in public.

Tressa noticed Jaimin's curiosity. "I'm eight months along with our third," she offered. "You might recall having seen our two boys that night when everyone was here."

Jenelle laughed. "Oh yes. I remember them. They kept you two very busy."

"The doctor says this one's another boy."

"Oh my...you'll have three busy little boys to chase after?"

Tressa gave a little shrug. "I figure if Delta, Marc's mom, could do it so could I. Marc and his brothers were not even her own. Their mother died shortly after Marc was born. Delta took on those three busy little boys with all the love and care as if they were her own.

"Oh...I didn't know she wasn't their real mom. How brave of her."

Tressa laughed, "Yes, and all under five at that. For the Banner family, three seems to be a magical number when it comes to boys. Even Marc's oldest brother has three boys. Younger than ours but promising to be havoc raisers just like the others.

"On Aden, three truly is a magical number. First, three basically means harmony, wisdom and understanding. It can also mean other things. For instance, in ritual, many actions must be repeated three times. There's a lot more, but this one I think is strange. On Aden a man can divorce his wife by simply saying the words 'I divorce you' three times."

That brought forth a peal of feminine laughter.

Jenelle glanced down at her new shirt and jeans, "I don't know who to thank for the beautiful clothes that were hanging in the closet. I assumed they were for me? If not, I apologize.

"Yes, Jenelle, they're meant for you. Before you arrived, Marc mentioned to Mom that all you had to wear were your clothes from Aden, so several of us gals went shopping. I hope you like them."

"Oh, I love them." She glanced down again at the T-shirt. "I am learning how to speak my new language, but I'm still struggling to read and write. What does this say?" she asked, pointing to the lettering sweeping across the front of her shirt.

Tressa smiled warmly. "It says *Stronger Every Day*. I personally picked that one out for you, Jenelle, because I know you're going to make those words come true."

"That's beautiful. Thank you."

"You're very welcome. We want you to enjoy the freedom of wearing the styles of this new life you're entering. If there is anything that I or any of us can do to help you adjust, just say the word."

"Thank you."

Tressa stood up. "Well, I think I hear a familiar rumble coming this way. I bet that's Marc. Mom says it's about the time he usually shows up."

Jenelle's heart skipped a beat as she heard the approaching bike getting closer until finally it emerged into view.

Tressa gave Marc a wave as she headed back to the main house.

Having pulled up in front of the cabin, Marc shut down the bike, set the kickstand and dismounted with a grin. "Miss Jenelle D'Anne Byers, would you do me the honor of allowing me to take you on another bike tour and picnic today?"

Jenelle's didn't know whether to laugh or throw her arms around him. Without fail, Marc showed up every day over the past week to take her on daily tours and picnics. She had seen almost every square foot of Banner acreage, from lush pine forests to pastureland, to a slow-moving river that ran through the property. Today he promised to take her to a lake that the family used for swimming parties.

At her hesitation he added, "If you prefer horses, we have those too."

"Oh...no, I love riding on your bike."

He laughed. "I remember when you hated it."

"That was a long time ago. Besides I'm wearing my bike clothes. See?" She did a quick twirl to show off. Feeling giddy and light-headed in his presence, she wanted to twirl around and around until she became dizzy and collapsed into a heap. The way she and Aannisah used to do as kids, but she kept it to only the one twirl.

Just watching her, Marc's wolf smile slowly became a seductive once-over. He especially liked the way the jeans hugged her hips and shapely legs. I like the T-shirt too."

"Thank you. Tressa picked it out for me. "Just let me put on a pair of shoes and I'll be ready to go," she said as she whirled around and disappeared inside the cabin. She looked young and fresh with her hair pulled back into a saucy ponytail.

While waiting, Marc remained standing next to his bike. Patting his pocket, he found a cigarette, lit up and leaned back to settle hipshot on the side of the seat.

Jenelle's heart was racing at hyperspeed as she tried to decide what shoes to put on. Marc Banner was a feast for feminine eyes. He looked so at ease on that big black motorcycle as he came riding up. He was clad in a pair of faded jeans, scuffed work boots and a dark blue shirt with rolled sleeves to his elbows.

He needed a shave, but maybe he'd decided to leave the shadow. It sort of went with his longer hair and especially the errant lock that always seemed to fall across his forehead.

Marc smiled as she stepped out onto the porch. "Boots" he said as he straightened away from the bike and crushed his cigarette beneath his heel. "Where'd you get the boots?"

"They were in the closet along with several changes of clothes. Tressa mentioned that you didn't want to see me in Adenian clothes or sandals any longer."

Marc feigned a look of confusion. "I said that?"

"In fact, you said it to me the night we arrived. You said for me to burn all my Adenian clothes. Make a party out of it."

Another feigned look, "I did?"

Jenelle laughed. "You know you did."

"Well, the one thing I do know for sure, you look stunning today," he said as he readjusted a blanket and picnic pac upon the bike. "That lake I mentioned yesterday would make a perfect spot for a picnic. Here, let me help you on."

A thrill of awareness rippled through her as their gazes met, only to be magnified when his hand captured her elbow to steady her as she swung a leg over the bike and settled onto the seat.

She watched him swing effortlessly onto the bike. "So, how far away is this lake?" she asked.

"Not far. Maybe forty-five minutes or so." He grinned. "Why? You in a hurry?"

She laughed. "Just curious. That's all."

"Once again, two things. Keep your..."

"I know. Keep my legs away from the exhaust pipes and lean into the curves with you."

"That's right."

Jenelle laughed. "You don't need to keep reminding me. This isn't the first time I've ridden with you."

"Then, hang on."

"Like this?" she asked, tightly wrapping her arms about him.

Marc grinned as he fired up the bike and felt her arms tighten even more "Yeah...just like that."

It was an awesome day for a bike ride. The sky was a bright blue, the sun warm, and a cool breeze moved through the trees as they progressed deeper into a forested area. Birds flitted from tree to tree.

Something darted across the road in front of them. "What was that?" she asked, looking over his shoulder.

"Just a *Glitchtail*. They're harmless."

"This is all Banner land?"

"Yes, ma'am."

"It's beautiful. I don't think I've ever seen so much green or so many birds."

He laughed. "Green's not a color you find in the desert."

After a while, they came to an area where the road straightened out for a stretch. "How you doing back there?"

"Fine."

"Okay if I open it up for a bit and dust her out? She's starting to complain. I can feel it."

"Yes."

"Okay then, hang on."

"I am."

Janelle's arms tightened as the bike began picking up speed, the throaty rumble rising to a thunderous roar.

Her heart racing, Janelle leaned forward against his back, loving the feel of the wind in her face. The sense of freedom and exhilaration was overwhelming as he continued accelerating, picking up speed. The wind tugged at her clothes and hair. The deep roar of the bike filled her ears, the vibration thrummed through her body. Every bump in the road, every curve and every turn was a physical sensation that she felt to the very core of her being. No wonder he liked riding his bike. She didn't have a word to describe it. Not even in Adenian. At last, he geared back down.

"Oh my..." Jenelle purred breathlessly.

"Yeah, I agree. Mind-bending, huh?"

He'd nearly let slip that it was the next best thing to sex, but at the last minute caught himself.

"Yes." She laughed. "Whatever mind bending is."

"The lake's just over that rise ahead. I don't know about you, but I'm getting hungry."

It turned out to be a good-sized lake surrounded by a grassy meadow at the edge of a forest. Beneath the trees, were three picnic tables with attached benches. Nestled in the trees behind the picnic tables was a small rustic looking cabin—a guest house perhaps. As Janelle glanced out into the lake, she noticed what appeared to be a deck anchored in the middle. In the center of the deck, stood a brightly colored sun-umbrella. The place was so beautiful. So peaceful, and so very different from anything she'd ever seen on Aden.

CHAPTER TWENTY-ONE

Marc guided the bike through tall grass, over to where the picnic tables were located. There, he cut the engine, set the kickstand, and dismounted. He then turned to help Jenelle.

Once again Jenelle felt a quiver of pleasure as his hands closed around her waist, and he lifted her off the bike as though she weighed nothing. It was so tempting to run her hands over his biceps, but better judgement had her resisting the urge. She looked up at him when he set her on her feet. “Ohhh...” She swayed her legs, unsteady after riding for over an hour.

Instantly, his hands returned to steady her. “I got you.”

“I don’t know what happened.”

Marc laughed. “Sometimes it just takes a minute to get your legs working again.”

“Oh Marc, this place is so pretty. Do you come here often?”

“Used to when I was younger. Nick, Clint, and I would come and spend a couple of nights here in the guest house, and fish off that raft during the day.”

Jenelle nodded. “When I think about it, I guess it’s kinda hard when you’re off-planet most of the time. So, is that a guest house?”

“It is. Hey, you didn’t happen to bring a swimsuit by any chance?”

Jenelle laughed. “No. Number One, I’m quite sure a swimsuit wasn’t on the list when your sisters kindly picked up a few things for me to wear. Why? Did you bring swim trunks?”

“No,” he said with a sexy grin, “but I don’t mind swimming in the buff if you...”

Janelle slid him a retiring look.

"What?" he asked innocently. "Bad idea?"

"What do you think?"

"Yeah. Bad idea. You can't fault a guy for asking."

Janelle knew he was just teasing, but she also knew that if had she agreed, he would be removing his clothes in a heartbeat. No modesty there.

"If you don't want to go for a swim, I say let's eat." he said as he removed their lunch from the back of the bike. "I'm curious to see what Annie packed for us today. He returned first with two blankets in his hands. "I leave the choice up to you. You can either spread these on the ground to sit on, or you can place them on the picnic benches and we can eat at a table. Either way. You decide."

She spread both blankets out on the grass. Overlapping them in the center. Slipping off her boots and socks, she lined her boots along the edge of the blankets, then sat down. It was so pretty and peaceful with the lake, the trees, and wildflowers everywhere. The air was fragrant with the sweet scent of moist green grass and the perfume of the wildflowers. A small furry animal scampered up a nearby tree. A flock of noisy little birds flitted from branch to branch overhead. It was all so very different from the hot desert world she had grown up in.

Marc joined her on the blankets, He reclined, stretching out his long legs as he supported himself on one elbow. At last, he opened the basket. "Hmm, two roasted *Koji* sandwiches, cookies, fruit and containers of some sort of juice."

"What is *Koji*?" she asked.

Marc laughed. "Well...You don't see them on Aden. That's for sure. Many ranchers here on Acacia raise them for meat. They are similar in taste to beef which is raised on Earth, and...not sure what to compare them with on Aden. Maybe a *Long-haired Desertbeast*."

"*Desertbeast*?" she repeated with a laugh. "What's a *Desertbeast*?"

He grinned. "Darned if I know. Here," he said as he handed one of the sandwiches

"Give it a try." Next, he asked, "*Novafruit* or a *Starbloom*?"

holding up both fruits for her selection.

"I think you'd better choose first, and I'll take what's left. I wouldn't know which one to pick. We don't have anything like either of those on Aden."

"They're both very good," he said, "Both native to Acacia."

Jenelle smiled. "You choose, and I'll take the other."

"Okay." He handed her one of the fruits. "This one is a *Starbloom*. You don't have to peel it. You just enjoy it as is."

The next half hour was spent eating as Marc shared a few hair-raising and laughable tales about he and his brothers. There were even a couple of stories about Frank that had her wiping tears of laughter from her eyes.

By now, they were both stretched out next to each other on their stomachs.

"What was that?" she asked, startled by a distant high-pitched howling sound.

"What?" he asked.

"That." she said as the howling came again.

Marc grinned. "That, Jenny, is a *Galaxian Screecher*."

"What's a Galax—"

"It's a small bird with a very loud voice. The males are a stunning shade of iridescent blue that flickers between blue and green in the sunlight. They're not dangerous or scary. They're just loud. That one is probably a half mile away."

"Really? It sounds so close."

He laughed. "Trust me. It's not."

~ * ~

A moment of silence passed during which he noticed the purple bruising on her wrist. "I don't remember doing this, but I must have since I doubt Frank put that on you. I'm damned sorry, Jenny."

Without thinking, he reached out and touched her wrist, marveling at the softness of her skin. "I hope you put ice on it." Her skin made him think of the velvety petals of a flower.

"I did," she replied.

Realizing what he was doing, he withdrew his hand, but not before seeing an answering *want* in her beautiful storm-gray eyes. Desire crashed through him like a thunderstorm. He could take her. If he pushed it just a little, he could have her. He knew that look, and he was no hero. so why was he torturing himself like this?

Take her. Make love to her. It's what you both want.

There was just one little problem. Would once be enough? Or would it only ignite a flame that couldn't be extinguished?

The thing was, he didn't want to hurt her. She had a life waiting for her when she returned to Earth with her parents. He didn't want her going to her new life wearing a huge stain on her conscience—all because he couldn't control himself.

He knew exactly what he was going to do. After the picnic and he takes her back to the cottage, he'd head for his ship and get good and drunk. Stinkin' loaded. That ought to do something, if not make him sick as a dog.

Jenelle softly cleared her throat. "So how long have you had your own ship?"

"The Antara? I don't know...I think I've had it about seven years now."

"I suppose you get used to seeing the stunning view outside your viewports. I don't think I could ever get used to it. It's...it's like magic."

"Magic? I'll show you magic." Maybe one of these times..." he went on.

"I'll take you up and show you Rydell's Comet. It passes within Acacia's range every month about this time."

Jenelle forced herself to breathe slowly as she listened.

Without thinking, he reached out and absently brushed a stray lock from her cheek.

"For most everyone," he went on, "it's no big deal—like seeing two Accacian suns rise and set every day. Not for me." He smiled as a memory crossed his mind. "I used to hop on my custom racing-bike and ride like the devil was after me, to see if I could beat it before it disappeared over the horizon." He rolled over onto his back. "Then after I got the *Antara*, I'd take it up beyond Acacia's orbit."

Suddenly his voice turned dreamy. "There's nothing, Jen, nothing more breathtaking, more sobering than to be above the glow of a planet's aura and find yourself in a race with a comet."

Her breath caught. With all that had transpired over the past weeks, Jenelle had only just begun to know Marc, and yet listening to him share this special memory nearly brought tears to her eyes. There was so much more to this man than she ever realized. So many levels.

"So," she asked, "do you ever win?"

"Nah," Slashing indentations shown beneath his cheekbones as he smiled at her. "Who knows...maybe one of these days."

He races a comet ...

Jenelle's heart melted. Other than when he cried over the loss of his friend, this was a new side to Marc and it tugged at her heart—this gentle, little boy side that he keeps well-hidden beneath a rough and often times cynical façade.

She would be leaving the Banners before long to go live with her parents. And when she does, it will take her a very long time, if ever, to get over Marc Banner. He'd rescued her from a marriage and life of bondage, and nearly lost his own life in the process. No, he hadn't told her that Ahmed was the one who attacked him. Frank had told her. Apparently, Marc eventually remembered Ahmed Farouk being the one behind the assault. Frank wanted to go after Ahmed, but Marc had said no. He was thankful he was alive, and just wanted to get the hell off Aden.

The conversation came to a lull. Marc's gaze swept over her mouth. Jenelle held her breath, afraid he was going to take her into his arms and kiss her, but even more than that, she was afraid that he might not.

"Jenny."

"Yes?"

He shook his head. "Nothing," he said as he rose to his feet and drew her up with him. "I just wanted to say your name."

"Oh..."

"It's a pretty name. Suits you."

"You think so?"

"I do," he whispered as he held out his arms in invitation.

Jaimin released a breathy sigh and willingly moved into the circle of Marc's embrace. Spreading her hands across his back, she burrowed her face into his shoulder.

"Jenny...," he sighed. And for a long, drawn-out moment he simply held her close, his hand moving soft as a whisper over her arms and shoulders. He could feel the heat of her body, smell the fresh soapy scent of her skin and hair. It was sensual and innocent all at the same time, and it was driving him over the edge.

Jenelle could hear the beating of his heart beneath her ear and felt her own heart pounding in response as he threaded his fingers through her hair. She drew in a deep breath and filled her senses with the faint scent of masculine cologne, of leather and motorcycle, and something else she couldn't name. It was the heady scent of man—*his scent*, and it stirred her desire all the more.

Her head fit perfectly in the hollow of his shoulder. "You know what?" he whispered, his mouth grazing her earlobe. "I think we'd better go for a little walk or something before things get out of hand."

She had no interest in going for a walk. In truth, she didn't want anything to tear her away from him. "Marc," she whispered, her voice shaky. "I don't want to go for walk. I don't want to do anything other than be here in your arms. Just like this."

Time hung suspended for a long moment, the only sounds, a gentle wind whispering through the trees, the soft twitters of a flock of tiny birds, and the lapping of the lake against the shore.

"Do you know what you've done to me, baby?" he asked in a deep voice laden with desire.

Jenelle didn't reply. She couldn't.

His hands slipped up her arms, bringing her even tighter against him. "You have any idea at all?"

"No," she whispered, as her heart slammed into her ribs. She wondered if it was anything close to what he was doing to her. Never had she known such feelings, such desires—even when she thought she was in love with Ahmed, she'd never felt anything like this.

"When your father first approached me," he murmured, his mouth still grazing her earlobe. "I was content with the way my life was going. I was doing exactly as I wanted and knew just what my future held. Then you came along and managed to bring everything, as I knew it, to a screeching halt." Lowering his head, Marc kissed her forehead. "Somehow you've turned everything I've ever believed-in into vapor."

"I didn't do anything, Marc."

"Yes, you did. Even if you didn't know it, you invaded my life and changed it."

"I don't know what you're talking—"

"That's the problem, Jenny," he whispered. "You're an innocent. You wouldn't know."

This time, he captured her mouth in a kiss that was demanding.

Lips parted and damp. Eyes closed. Jenelle had no idea how long she had been leaning into him, or even that he'd stopped kissing her. Ever so slowly she opened her eyes, fully expecting to find him silently laughing at her.

What she found, however, wasn't laughter. What she found was hooded sapphire eyes, lambent with need.

"Life was so simple before I met you. What is it that draws me to you?" With one finger, he tipped her chin up and searched her face. "What did you do? Did you cast some Adenian spell on me?"

Jenelle innocently passed her tongue over her lips. Foolish as it was, his predicable body tightened to unbearable readiness. If she only knew the thoughts raging through his mind right now, she wouldn't be still standing so pliant, so willing and trusting in his arms.

Marc's gaze, soft as a caress, his voice so seductive, it sent a shudder down her spine. Jenelle's senses lurched as his head descended, and he took her mouth again, flooding her senses with his kiss, his words, his masculine scent. The combination was so heady and so sensual, an odd lurching coiled in the pit of her stomach.

"You're driving me crazy," he groaned. The proof was a blatant hardness straining against her belly as he pressed her tighter against him.

When she was sure her legs were going to buckle, he swept her up weightlessly into his arms. In a daze, Jenelle wrapped her arms around his neck, closed her eyes and clung to him, aware that he was striding toward the blankets that were still spread upon the ground.

Marc knew it was crazy, knew he was treading on dangerous ground, but he couldn't seem to help himself as he lowered her to her feet, allowing her to slowly slide down the length of his body in the process, permitting her to feel the blatant differences in their anatomies. Blame it on a magic Adenian spell, or Acacia's double suns. Blame it on the madness that had been plaguing him from the moment he first laid eyes on her. Hell, it didn't make any difference. For all he knew, some mystical Goddess of Love was playing havoc with his mind. Under normal circumstances, he would have laughed at himself. He couldn't remember ever wanting a woman as badly as he wanted sweet Jenny right now.

"Marc..."

"Shhh...Let me take care of you."

This is not Ahmed, a small voice whispered. *This is Marc.*

Laying her down on the blankets, he followed her down, bracing splayed hands on either side of her head. His hands and lips were gentle, unhurried as sensations and emotions swept through her. As though being wrapped in a cocoon, she knew nothing but the sound of Marc's voice, nothing but the pleasure of his touch and kisses. And she wanted nothing more than to please him. As unbelievable as it was, Jenelle felt as though her mind was under someone else's control. Except for that one time when Frank interrupted them, she had never been so driven. Never had she known such thoughts. All she desired was to feel the hard length of his body pressed against hers, and to be able to please him. "Marc..." she moaned, unable to even think of what she wanted to say.

As desperately as she wanted him, the truth was, she knew absolutely nothing of what to do. Jenelle locked her arms around his neck and turned her face into the curve of his shoulder. "You might be disappointed," she whispered as lack of confidence taunted her from the edge.

She felt his smile against her temple. "You think so, huh?"

"I'm pretty sure," she answered. "I want to please you so much, but..."

He murmured something she didn't quite understand, and her insides clenched at the smoldering flame she saw in his eyes. His mouth found hers again, and the only sound was the pounding of her heart.

Ever so gently, he caressed her T-shirt off her, his mouth savoring each inch of her newly exposed flesh, his eyes conveying that he found her desirable. Next came her jeans, leaving her lying before him in simply her panties.

He then pulled his own shirt over his head and tossed it on the ground with her things. As though in worship, Jaimin ran her fingertips over Marc's chest and shoulders.

Alarms should have been going off. Every instinct should have been shouting for her to stop, to preserve her innocence, and yet it seemed *nobody was home*. "Marc, I feel sooo strange. I want...Oh, I don't know what I want."

Jenelle gloried in the shocking exploration of his gentle hands and mouth as he skimmed and laved her breasts, her ribs, her waist, and tightly clamped legs. When she could stand the ache of wanting no longer, she drew him closer, wrapping her arms and legs about him, convinced she would die if he didn't slake the desire he had aroused. "Please," she whispered.

Need rose swift and hot as Marc continued caressing her. She was sweet, so sweet, and he'd been wanting to make love to her for so long.

And yet...and yet now that he had his chance, something deep inside made him stop. It would be a major advantage taking—even for him if he followed through with what his body was screaming for him to do. Worse, it would once again make her a victim.

Letting her go was about the hardest thing he'd ever attempted in his life, but violating virgins was something he'd never done, never wanted to do, and he didn't intend to start now with innocent, trusting and sweet Jenelle.

Jenelle's eyes flew open when Marc broke the kiss and began pulling away. "What's wrong?" she whispered.

"Honey, I'm not the right guy for this. Someday you're going to meet Mister Right and you're going to want to marry him, have a family and the whole shebang."

He let out a long sigh when her arms slid around his neck. "No Marc... You are the right guy," she confessed as she lifted her head, her lips seeking his. "I need you, Marc. I don't want the whole shebang, whatever that is."

He hesitated for just a moment, then he was kissing her again, his mouth moving over hers gently, languidly, his tongue treasuring her lower lip. She was naked beneath him, and it was a heady sensation despite the fact that Jenelle didn't have the foggiest idea what she was getting into. She might not know it, but *he* knew it. He also knew that the lust that was driving her now wasn't hers. It was his, dammit. Her telepathic mind was feeling *his* lust as though it were her own.

She was an innocent victim, and like it or not, it was up to him to bring things to a halt before it was too late.

Marc tried to hold back, tried desperately to resist, but her lips were so sweet, her arms so inviting. He promised himself that each kiss would be the very last. Just one more and then he would let her go, help her get dressed and return home as quick as possible before things went any further. Just one more final time he kissed her. Jenelle moaned with pleasure, her arms drawing Marc closer, her body pressing into his.

She was too innocent to realize how she was affecting him—too naïve to know she was playing with fire when her tongue shyly touched his, then timidly entered his mouth.

Too late. No turning back now.

Desire rose hot and swift. "I've been going out of my mind with wanting you."

His voice was ragged, and in an onslaught of kisses and soothing words he coaxed her into relaxing, sweet-talked her into unclenching those sexy long legs. Then, as soft as a whisper, he touched her, a touch so gentle and so reverent it was barely perceptible. Jenelle held her breath, acute embarrassment warring with curiosity as he slowly, tenderly initiated her into the magical world of sensual awareness. Sighs turned to moans as Marc paced himself to her responses. Taking his time, he methodically strung her out until she was begging for release. Only then did he rise to his knees, never taking his eyes from her as he began, undoing the straining fly of his pants.

Jenelle could not look away as his muscled nudity was revealed. His tan line rode low on his hips, and she noticed an old scar just below his ribs. And then...and then when the fully aroused length of him was revealed, Jenelle looked away. Shocked. Embarrassed and yet curious.

Marc returned to her, his scent heaven as he bent to kiss her. "Jenny don't be afraid. Look at me, baby."

She opened her eyes to find him hovering over her, his hands on either side of her, bracing his weight. "We'll, take it real slow," he whispered.

Gentle pressure, a skillful hand and soft words. It was a killer combination that had Jenelle relaxing.

"That's it, honey," he whispered, as he moved into the cradle of her thighs and ever so carefully entered her delicate and incredibly tight passage.

Jenelle found herself gazing up into beautiful eyes that were hot with desire. She ached to tell him that she—" "Ohhh—"

"Marc," she whispered, "I don't know what to—how to..." Again, her breath caught.

"You're doing just fine, sweetheart."

"But I want to please you,"

"You already please me."

Jenelle was in so far over her head she never realized she was drowning until—

With a sharp inhale, she froze.

Marc stopped and rested his forehead against hers. Several long moments passed as he waited, hardly daring to breathe while allowing her to adjust. What was done, was done and there was no going back now.

His control was slipping fast. If she only knew how unsure he was of himself at this moment. "Jenny," he murmured unsteadily, "I know this hurts, and I'm so sorry, baby."

If only he knew what to tell her. But he didn't know. He knew nothing about what to expect or what to say to a virgin. If only he had the strength to withdraw.

Suddenly, Jenelle's hands were at his hips, wordlessly urging him on, and it was all it took. Slow and gentle, he made love to her. Never once breaking the pace he'd set. Jenelle forced her eyes open and found him watching her, his focus entirely on the rising surge between them.

What will he think of you tomorrow? A silent voice asked in the midst of it all. But the thought had hardly formed when Marc began picking up the pace. And then suddenly there was no more thinking. It was a little late for second thoughts anyway. When it hit, the spasm hit her both hard and by surprise as she cried out his name.

Marc followed close behind, his lips pressed to her throat.

For Jenelle, everything she had been reaching for suddenly came full circle with the power of his possession. At last, spent, and sated, she lay quietly in his arms.

Oh wow...Oh wow...

"You okay baby?"

She sighed. She had no idea.

In truth, Marc was just as stunned as she was. He'd only intended to kiss her one last time. But what had just happened was far beyond a kiss. He'd never been turned on so fast in his life.

~ * ~

Now what? He supposed the best thing to do now would be for him to apologize and get it over with. His apology would bring about one of two predicable responses. Either tears or fury. He was prepared for both.

"Jenny are you alright?" he asked again.

No response.

"I never intended for things to go this far," he said as he rose to his knees, hiked up his jeans, and fastened them.

He then shrugged into his shirt. The smoldering light in his eyes now thoroughly doused behind regret as he focused next on helping her get dressed.

Jaimin's eyes were glazed, her chest still rising and falling in the aftermath.

Time to wake her up sport. You can't take her back like this.

"Say something, Jenelle. Go ahead and scream at me. Hit me if you want. I deserve it."

In a fog, she looked up at him, her gaze clouded. "...What?"

He reached down and gently drew her to her feet. "I am sorry, Jenny. Do you want me to take you back? I will, if that's what you want."

She stood there a moment, stunned, and confused. A thousand bewildered thoughts flew through her mind. She ran her tongue over her swollen mouth, instantly aware of the warm, salty tang of his flesh on her lips. *What had she done?*

Feeling lower than the lowest reprobate, Marc watched her expression go through a myriad of changes. It took everything he had to keep from pulling her into his arms. But it would only bring about tears. He could handle her tears, but he deserved her fury, and he wondered just how long it would take for reality to set in, and for her to give him hell.

Heat flooded her cheeks as she approached the bike. "I want to go back. I need to leave. I need to go back. Now." she said on the verge of tears, her voice shaky.

"Okay."

With guilt and regret hanging like a dark cloud over him, Marc left the blankets and lunch pac on the ground and proceeded to help her get dressed.

Other than the throaty roar of his bike, the trip back was quiet. Blaming herself for what had happened, Jenelle kept as much distance as possible between herself and Marc. She was so embarrassed, so humiliated and ashamed by her wanton behavior. She hated having to even hang onto him. What must he think of her?

They'd no sooner pulled up in front of her cottage when Jenelle managed to get off the bike before Marc had a chance to assist her.

Marc reached for Jenelle's jacket that he'd tied down. "Here, let me walk you to the door," he said as he handed her the jacket.

"I think it best if you don't. I don't think you should come around me anymore either."

He stopped in his tracks. "O-kay. I guess that works," he muttered as he watched Jenelle enter the cottage and close the door without looking back.

Reality must have finally set in. With a heavy sigh, he swung his leg over his bike, freed the kickstand and fired the engine. There was another contract awaiting his decision to accept or decline. Guess he'd get back to them and take the job.

~ * ~

Later that afternoon.

"Frank? I gotta proposition for you."

"And what might that be?" Frank was in the middle of restocking supplies for Marc. Not that he had to, it was just a Frank thing, keeping busy as always.

"What would you say if I offered you a full-time position co-piloting the *Antara* with me*?"* I'll not only match what Nick and Zeke are paying, I'll up it.

"I dunno...that's a pretty hard proposition t' turn down."

"I meant it to be," Marc said.

"Wull then, you got yerself a co-pilot, Captain. So, whose gonna tell Nick and Zeke?"

Marc grinned. "I am."

"Since I'm stayin', I guess I'll hurry with the restockin' of things. Where we goin' this time?"

"Echo. Unless you got some loose ends to tie up here on Acacia, we'll be putting into space in about two hours."

"I ain't got no loose ends, but what's the hurry?"

"Just need to get going, that's all."

"I see..."

CHAPTER TWENTY-TWO

One month later

Jenelle's parents continued staying in Imperial but came to visit every day. And as the days passed, Jenelle had begun to feel more and more comfortable around them—even started to remember some of the memories they would share with her.

It had been over a month now since she last saw Marc. The days since had passed slowly and were spent waiting, hoping, and listening for the sound of his bike. Despite her impulsive words telling him not to come around her anymore, she prayed that he would stop by anyway. Unfortunately, it wasn't to be.

This morning she'd finally got up the courage to ask Delta about him. And her heart sank when Delta explained that Marc had taken on another assignment nearly a month ago and was no longer on Acacia.

"Didn't he tell you he was leaving?

"If he did, I didn't hear him."

"Oh Jenelle, I am so sorry. I thought you knew."

Jenelle looked away, hiding her forming tears. *He's no longer on Acacia.* Would she ever see him again? Just thinking of it set off a dropping feeling in the pit of her stomach—similar to going over a steep hill too fast.... only worse.

So, what did you expect? You told him to leave you alone. And he did. You were no more than a contract. Found. Returned and now on to the next bounty.

Was she the only one with a deep hole in her heart? She was so close to being sick to her stomach.

A knock at the door had Jenelle rushing to open it, once again hoping, praying...

"Hi kitten. Your mother and I brought lunch today," her father said as he came over the threshold with enough food packed into a box to feed an army. "We invited the Banners to join us."

"Oh, that was nice of you."

"We found the best little take-out," her mother added. "It was right around the corner from—Sweetheart! Honey, are you feeling, okay? I've noticed over the last few weeks you've been looking peaked. Now today, you really don't look well at all. Are you eating enough?"

Once again, fatigue and heartache washed over her as she forced a smile. "Oh Momma, it's nothing really. Today, I just—I just have a headache. That's all."

As if to mock her lie, she had to admit that she did indeed have a screaming headache.

Jenelle picked at her food while the others ate heartily. Oh, how she wanted to be left alone right now, but instead she managed to keep her smile pasted in place while two sets of parents continued conversing amid smiles and laughter.

Time to move on.

She'd been here nearly two months. There was no need to impose upon the Banners any longer. Her memories and love for her parents were slowly returning. Doron explained that once she was away from the Ala Rashards, and no longer under the influence of the mind-altering drugs that kept her numb to the truth, her memories and past life would slowly return.

Well, the memories of her past life were returning, she admitted. There was no need to put-off going home any longer. Later, that afternoon, before everyone left, Jenelle thanked Delta and Max for their warm hospitality and announced her decision to leave.

Delta accepted Janelle's extended hand with both of her own. "Honey, no thanks needed. It's been a pleasure having you here, getting to know both you and your parents. I'm sorry again, that Marc couldn't be here to see you off."

"It's okay. I understand. When assignments come up..." She

shrugged. "He has no choice."

"Well, that's partially true," Max said. "Bottom line, Marc should have at least stopped by to say goodbye before taking off like he did. I'm afraid he doesn't always play by the rules."

She smiled. "No. I suppose not."

"I am sorry Jenelle," Max continued, "Our son was raised better than that."

"It's okay Mister Banner. I understand. Truly, I do. Maybe it's best this way."

"Call me Max. I want you to know that Delta and I wish you the best of luck as you start your life all over again with your real mother and father this time."

"Thank you."

Tears gathered behind her eyes. She blinked and turned away so Max wouldn't notice. She cried so easily this past month, but especially today, after learning that Marc had left.

Max glanced over to the Byers. "We hope you will keep us posted now and then on how she's doing."

"We will."

"Max, would you give both Frank and Marc a message for me please?" Jenelle asked softly,

"Certainly."

"Please tell Frank that I will miss his friendship very much, and that I said goodbye."

"I'll let him know."

"And...would you tell Marc that I..."

Jenelle thought of him riding his bike hell-bent as if he owned the road. Thought of his anger and frightening strength as he lit-in to Ahmed that day. Thought of him holding her hand and begging her not to leave him when he was in such pain...and thought of his guilt, regret and heartfelt sadness twenty-some years after the death of his friend, Mitch.

Tell him that I've fallen in love with him—both the man as well as the boy. Tell him I...I will always be listening for his bike, and that I

will never ever forget him. And would you ask Frank to watch over him. He smokes too much and drinks too much. He doesn't eat right and...

Max good-naturedly waited.

Jenelle's shoulders rose and fell as she released a compressed breath. This was so difficult. Maybe Marc could leave without saying goodbye, but she couldn't. She swallowed the sob that threatened to surface. "Tell him ... please tell him I said goodbye," she added in a tiny voice.

"I'll tell him, honey."

That evening while Jenelle and her mother made the cottage sparkle as it had when Jenelle first moved in, her father spent the time making reservations for their return trip to Earth. She left the Banners that night with her parents to spend her last night on Acacia at the Imperial Marriott. Tomorrow they would leave Acacia, and she would never see Marc again. Never again.

How do you put your life back together once your heart has been shattered into a gazillion pieces? a silent voice asked.

He'd changed her permanently. Her life would never be put back together. She will go on missing him forever, always listening for the sound of his bike, and will never fall in love—ever—with anyone else.

~ * ~

Earth, Seattle
SeaPort Intergalactic Spaceport

It was mid-afternoon by the time their commercial starliner arrived at the space station that hovered high above Earth's orbit. From there they boarded a smaller commuter shuttle that would deliver them to the Spaceport.

Jenelle stared out the window as they glided over the tops of dozens of moored ships sitting in their designated landing pads. Soon they were gently banking into a turn. Geysers of dust coiled about them as they floated inches above the surface to their assigned location. Once there, it seemed as if the ground rose to meet them before the craft gently eased down onto its jacks.

Earlier, her mother mentioned that one of her best friends, Cassie Anderson, would be there to greet her at the spaceport. "I don't know if you will remember her, honey," Karissa said, "but she is excited to see you again and asked if she could meet us when we get in."

"Oh..."

Just then an announcement came over the speakers welcoming them to SeaPort, that their flight was on time, the Seattle skies were clear and sunny, and the temperature was a brisk thirty-three degrees.

"Here, honey, you're going to need something warmer than what you boarded with four weeks ago." Karissa said as she handed her daughter a warm full-length hooded coat with fur lining.

"Oh Mom, this is—Will I really need something this warm?"

"Yes, darling. You will. You've come from a desert planet and thirty-three degrees will seem unbearable, especially if there is a breeze of any kind. Here, let me help you put it on. I promise, you won't be sorry."

They merged with the exiting crowd off the shuttle. Jenelle was sandwiched between her father and her mother as they made their way down the gangway. Even with the protection of the heavy coat and hood, she could feel the bone-chilling cold seeping through the walls of the temporarily enclosed walkway that led from the gangway to the main terminal.

As they stepped into the warmth of the spaceport, her mother leaned forward, "I think I see Cassie now."

Jenelle looked up to see a young lady about her age with dark brown hair rushing forward to greet them. "Mister and Misses Byers, I have been so excited for this day."

She turned to Jenelle. "Hi Jenelle. I know you don't remember me. I'm Cassie Anderson. We used to be best of friends. I've missed you so much. I can't begin to tell you how excited I am to have you back."

"Hello..."

Jenelle started to extend her hand when Cassie quickly brought the handshaking to a halt. "No handshakes. I need a hug."

"Oh. Okay."

"What did you do to your hair?" Cassie exclaimed. "Did you bleach it platinum? It's so pretty."

"Cassie, honey," Karissa spoke up, "Jenelle was found living on a desert planet. The harsh sun bleached her hair over the years."

"Well, whatever. It's beautiful."

"Thank you."

Cassie stood back studying her. Finally with a compressed exhale she said. "I just can't believe you're back. I've missed you so much. Hey," she prattled on, "Do you by chance remember Danny McCall?"

"Who?"

"Danny McCall. He was the boy who used to walk you home from school every day. Surely you remember him."

"I'm sorry Cassie, but I really don't remember too much from my past." *And that includes you too,* a silent voice added.

At Jenelle's blank look, Cassie added, "Oh Jen, we have so much catching up to do. Plus, I want you to meet the rest of our friends again.

Once again Karissa stepped into the conversation and with a smile added, "The doctor said it will just take time, but her memory will slowly return,"

"Okay. So, in the meantime," Cassie added with a bright smile of her own, "we'll make new memories. Anyway, Danny's kept in touch with your parents over the years, always hoping for any news about you. He said he's never forgotten you. Just so you know, he's the one who let me know you'd been found. And he's going to be driving you home."

"Oh? How nice of him."

"Yes. Just wait until you see him. He's sooo handsome, Jen, plus he's in his final year of law school."

"How nice..."

Cassie, Jenelle, and her mother followed Tom Byers as they made their way to Baggage Recovery where he claimed their travel pacs.

"Mister and Misses Byers. Cassie."

Jenelle glanced up to see a tall young man working his way

through the crowd with a wave and a hundred-watt smile. *That must be our ride,* she thought. Even from a distance, there was an air of self-confidence about him as he wormed his way through the mass, offering apologies as he came through. Cassie was right, he was handsome. Several women did a double take as he passed by.

Cassie leaned forward and whispered, "There's Danny now. Oh, and look, he has roses."

Jenelle and Cassie continued watching him advance through the throng. Nice looking, yes, but he didn't look the least bit familiar. But then, she asked herself, how could he? Eleven years had passed since they supposedly knew each other. Eleven years ago, they were both kids.

"I'd forgotten how congested this place can get," he said as he greeted her dad with a handshake and her mother with the mention of her name and a gentle hug. He turned to Jenelle. "You must be Jenelle. I'm Daniel McCall." He flashed her a radiant smile. "Wow. Had I only known you were so beautiful, I'd have long ago gone looking for you myself. Here, these are for you," he said as he handed her the bouquet of fragrant red roses. "Although I must say, their beauty pales next to you."

"Thank you." Refraining from rolling her eyes, Jenelle humbly accepted the roses.

Daniel went on, "It's been a while, I know, and I don't expect you to remember, but we used to know each other at school."

Jenelle nodded; her mind completely blank on ever remembering the boy who supposedly walked her home from school every day.

At last, he turned to her father, "Tom, what do you say we get outta here?"

"I agree."

Daniel and her father led the way through the spaceport, stopping only when they got to the exit.

"Wait in here where its warm." Daniel said, "I'll run to get the LC."

Cassie sighed... "Isn't he just something else? And he has a new LC."

It was obvious Cassie was seriously smitten with Daniel McCall.

In truth, Jenelle supposed that women, young and old, would consider Daniel handsome. Who knows, maybe they'd even consider him better looking than Marc. Nevertheless, as far as she was concerned, there was no comparison. The difference was the same as likening a child's stuffed animal to a Lyrin Desert Cat.

They were so very different. Daniel was charming. Marc could be charming at times, yes, but most of the time he was just...Marc.

Daniel was clean-shaven and had perfectly styled hair. Marc was always in need of a shave, and if his hair isn't cut short as in past photos, it's tousled and usually hanging over his brow. Marc's sexy smile, however, would outshine Daniel's smile any day. No contest there.

There's a little matter of designer clothes. Marc's *designer clothes* entailed black jeans, work boots and generally a white T-shirt with rolled sleeves that exposed a "No Rules. No Regrets." tattoo.

Daniel drives a new car, and Jenelle would be willing to bet he's never gone over the speed limit in his life.

Marc races a comet.

"Just think..." Cassie said on another dreamy sigh, "he's going to be a lawyer. That's a wonderful career. Don't you think so too, Jenelle?"

"Yes. Yes, it is."

She'd had just about enough of Daniel McCall and how wonderful he was. Jaimin could easily see through Cassie. She was crazy about the guy. If it wouldn't be rude, she'd gladly give the bouquet of roses to Cassie.

CHAPTER TWENTY-THREE

Antara: Enroute from Echo to Lotus

"Y' got that music loud enough?"

Marc groaned. It was the one voice he least wanted to hear at the moment. "I happen to like it exactly the way it is."

"Sure y' do. It numbs yer brain along with the whiskey. Even Ruckus is hiding in the back." Frank stood in the open doorway to Marc's quarters, his coffee mug in hand, his pipe stuck between his teeth and the sweet aroma of pipe tobacco wafting in the air. "Is it necessary t' play it through-out the entire damn ship?"

No response.

"Y' know, y' wouldn't be feelin' so lousy if y'd at least taken the time to tell that little gal goodbye. Hell, y' were in such a damn hurry to put into space, even I never had the chance to say goodbye. Now y've gone and accepted a consignment to Lotus so who knows when we'll be back. She'll be gone by then."

"Yes, and I think you've said that at least fifty times already, Frank."

"Yeah, well I keep waitin' for it to sink in."

"And for me to do *what* about it?"

"That's up t' you."

"Thank you. We finally agree on something."

With a raised brow, Frank studied his captain before saying around the stem of his pipe, "Well, I can see yer disagreeable mood is even fouler than usual. Maybe we should make fer the next port so y' can remedy the cause."

Strained silence filled the cabin matching the sorrowful wail of the *power-guitar* crying out its despondent message. "And I suppose you think you know the cause?"

"Yer damn right I do. When yer drinkin' like this fer no good reason, we both know the cause."

Aware of Frank's judging eyes, Marc reached for the shot glass and raised it in a salute. Yes, he was drunk. Yes, his temper was short-fused, and as usual he was finding Frank's nosey opinion irritating. Swallowing the drink in one burning gulp, he defiantly wrist-wiped his mouth. "Go for it," he rasped. "You're so sure you've got it all figured out."

"Not a doubt in my mind. Hell, y've been skulking 'round here like a *rogue bull paka* ever since we left Acacia. Anyone with half a brain can figure it out. Y've gone nova over that little gal, and yer just too stubborn to own-up t' it."

Marc's eyes narrowed. "You're wrong, old man."

"Am I? Prove it. Go slake yer frustrations, and yer ill-temper along with it at the next port, so's we can get back to normal routine 'round here."

It was a dare. One that Frank knew full-well Marc would not accept. He started to turn for the corridor, then stopped. "And jist in case yer wonderin', alcohol ain't gonna cure what's eatin' away at yer guts right now."

"For your information. I wasn't wondering," Marc mumbled.

Hell, nobody had a better excuse to get roaring drunk than he did. Belligerently refilling the shot glass to the top for Frank's benefit, he wrapped his fingers around it and sat there staring into its amber depths.

Finally, with a heavy sigh he shoved the glass away and rose to his feet. As much as he hated admitting it, Frank was right. "So, is there any coffee left?"

"Just made a fresh pot."

"By the way," Marc muttered as Frank stepped aside to let him pass, "the alcohol helps."

"It only dulls the edges, son," Frank drawled in all seriousness. "Believe me, I know."

The heavy thud of Marc's boots echoed down the corridor as he made his way for the galley. He'd learned long ago not to take too seriously every baiting remark Frank made. This time, he told himself, Frank was wrong. Gone nova over Janelle. Hell, he'd settle down someday, when he was good and ready. In the meantime, he was damn good at what he did. No, the best thing that could have happened was for Jenelle to send him away. It was the very thing that gave him the courage to leave that day. Otherwise, he wasn't sure he would have had the strength to walk away from her. Besides, she deserved better. There's a Mister Perfect out there somewhere, just waiting for her to return—someone who would have more to offer than he does. But dammit, he didn't like the idea of her being in anyone else's arms. That was the kicker.

Frank followed him down to the galley. "Got somethun else y' need to hear.

Refusing to acknowledge Frank with more than a weary sigh, Marc poured a mug of coffee and slouched into a chair at the table.

"Max contacted us today," Frank went on. "Ahmed and a about four others showed up at the gates looking for Jenelle a couple of days ago."

That brought Marc's head up. "How would he have known to look for her there?"

"Dunno. She must have contacted someone and said where she was living. Her girlfriend, maybe?"

Marc cursed softly. "Aannisah. Jenelle mentioned something about wishing she could get a message to her mother, Zari, through Aannisah to let her know that she was all right." With a sigh, Marc leaned back in the chair. "I told her not to do it."

Frank continued. "Apparently when gate security notified Max, he instructed them not to allow Ahmed access onto the property. That's when trouble started. and I'm sorry to say John was killed. Two others injured.

"John? He'd been with us for years."

"I know."

"What about Ahmed? I hope somebody put him down."

"Apparently Clint happened to be at the folks, and both he and Max got involved in the showdown. Max got Ahmed with a clear shot. He was dead 'fore he hit the ground."

"Good. That S.O.B. got what he deserved."

~ * ~

"Look. There's Daniel now," Cassie announced as she pointed to the shiny black LC pulling up in the loading/unloading area. With Tom leading the way, they headed for the exit.

A blast of frigid air greeted them, nearly taking Jenelle's breath away when the outer door opened automatically.

Daniel was out of the vehicle and rushing around to open the doors as well as the carpet-lined trunk for their luggage. Tom sat in front with Daniel. Karissa, Jenelle, and Cassie sat behind. As soon as they were all settled on their heated leather seats, he pulled away. The LC was new with its clean, new scent of leather suffusing the inside.

"So..." her father spoke up. "Tell us about your job offer. Cassie mentioned you have a wonderful opportunity waiting for you when you graduate."

"Yes, I was offered a position at Sutcliffe, Johnson, and Bailey. They've offered to hold the position for me until I graduate in June."

"Oh my," Karissa said, getting into the conversation. "I bet that doesn't happen very often."

At that, Cassie spoke up. "No, it doesn't, Misses Byers. He's very fortunate."

Jenelle couldn't help but wonder if Cassie might be fitting into Daniel's future somewhere. From what she could tell, he would certainly make a good husband.

"Hey, what do you say we stop at Madden's and get a bite to eat? It's right on our way," Daniel said.

"Sounds good to me." Tom turned to Karissa, "That okay with you girls?"

Everyone agreed, including Jenelle. Although to be honest, the last thing she wanted to do was stop at some restaurant. She wasn't the least bit hungry. She was dead on her feet, and worst of all...was the deep ache in her heart. It was so hard to feel happy along with the others. All she wanted to do was get home—wherever that was—and crawl into bed.

"Danny, are you still good at *Grav-Tac-Toe?"* Cassie asked. "I remember how you were always entering tournaments and winning trophies and awards."

"Are you kidding? I haven't played that in years, Cas. That's child's play." He laughed, "I guess you could say I grew up."

Child's play, huh? a silent voice echoed as Jenelle's thoughts lingered on the man who races a comet on his motorcycle or takes his ship high above Acacia's aura and calls the view *magic*.

Feeling as though her strength was being sucked out of her, Jenelle turned with a heavy sigh to gaze out the window. Somewhere up there, somewhere beyond Earth's blue sky, was Acacia. Is it nighttime there, she wondered? Is Rydell's Comet speeding across the heavens tonight? Is Marc on his custom racing bike, or maybe in his ship, challenging the comet to another match?

Would she ever get over him? Ever? Probably not. How do you unlove someone? Is it even possible?

The Northwest's winter sun was just beginning to set by the time they reached the Byers home. As they approached, Jenelle couldn't help but be struck by the grandeur of the place. They turned off the main road to follow a long, curved driveway. The home was a large two-story structure that sat proudly on a knoll, surrounded by lush grounds with towering trees. The front of the home was dominated by a large, welcoming wrap-around porch with white columns and railings. It was so unlike, so opposite of everything she had known over the last eleven years.

"Going to be a cold one tonight, Tom," Daniel said as he hopped out of the LC to open the doors for the ladies.

Before she knew it, Jenelle was being whisked out of the vehicle by her father, ushered up the steps and into the house to be greeted by a rush of warm air and a cheerful housekeeper waiting at the open door.

"Welcome home, Mister and Misses Byers," the woman said as they hurried up the steps and inside the home. "It's good to have you back."

"Thank you, Tilly," Tom replied. "It's good to be back."

Tilly leveled her gaze on Jenelle as she came in with her parents. "This—this is our Jenelle? Oh my, honey you've grown into such a beautiful young lady."

Karissa stepped in after Jenelle. "Sweetheart, this is Tilly Martin. She's been with us for many years. She used to rock you to sleep when you were just a baby."

"Hello," Jenelle replied.

Karissa went on to explain to Tilly that Jenelle's memories of her past life were stolen from her, but that the doctor assured them that in time she would once again remember.

Tilly turned saddened eyes on Jenelle. "Oh, you poor darling. Just know that we all love you and are here to help you through this difficult adjustment."

"Thank you."

"So, are any of you hungry?" Tilly asked as she turned to the group. "If you are, I can..."

"Thank you, Tilly," Tom cut in. "We stopped to eat on the way out."

Karissa turned to Jenelle. "How about you, honey? You didn't eat anything at the restaurant."

At that point, Daniel stepped into the conversation. "Actually, I think Jenelle is worn out more than any of us realize."

"Yes, I agree." Tom said. "Karissa, darling, why don't you take Jenelle up and let her see her bedroom. I have a feeling she could use some alone-time about now. Am I right, kitten?"

On the verge of tears, Jenelle nodded, and drew in a shaky breath.

The next thing she knew she was wrapped in her father's arms, his jacket smelling vaguely familiar of aftershave and tobacco that touched hazy memories of a time long ago.

"Momma will show you to your room, honey," he said with a kiss on the top of her head. "we'll see you in the morning."

Jenelle nodded.

"Come with me darling," Karissa said, "I'll show you your room."

"We'll see you tomorrow, Jenelle." Daniel said as she followed her mother up a carpeted staircase, her legs feeling like jelly, the bouquet of roses still in her trembling hand.

"Yes..." Cassie chimed in. "I'll have some photos for you to see."

"Oh Jenelle, I can't tell you how ecstatic your father and I are to have you home where you belong. Here we are, honey. Here's your room." Karissa opened the door and switched on the light. With a soft laugh she added. "I apologize. I just couldn't change your room in all these years. I'm afraid it's exactly as it was when you were nine. Now that you're here, you can change and decorate it the way you want."

"It's alright, Momma, I don't mind."

So, this is what her room looked like back then. An old-fashioned canopy bed sat diagonally across one corner of the room. A pink and white patchwork quilt covered the bed with a matching canopy. White throw rugs lay neatly about a shiny wooden floor.

Jenelle stepped further into the room, noticing a line-up of dolls and stuffed animals decorating the bed. A doll house sat on the floor along the wall across from the bed. It was complete with miniature doll furniture. Jenelle approached it. Something about seeing it triggered a flash of memory, then it was gone.

"Your father made that for you, honey. You and I spent many hours making the curtains, covering the walls with paint, and the floors with carpet."

Jenelle nodded and made her way over to the bay window that had built-in seating. She imagined that many hours were also spent sitting on the pink and white cushions while looking out at the surrounding grounds. Now everything looked dark, cold, and frozen outside. Cassie said it had snowed a couple of days ago but melted the next day. Snow...what was snow, she wondered?

She glanced around the room once again. Nothing looked familiar, yet she was aware that there was a lot of love in this room. So much so that her mother had refused to change a thing just in case her little girl was found and returned.

"Momma," she said. "Thank you for the love you and Poppa have had for me, not only when I lived here, but over the years. You never gave up."

"No darling, we never did, and never would have. If Mister Banner had not found you...we would have begged him to keep looking."

Mister Banner...Just hearing his name left her weak with despondency.

"Honey, for now I suspect you'll find most everything you need in the closet or that cabinet against the wall. I had Tilly get all your nine-year-old things out of the closet and cabinet drawers and go shopping for a few new things for you."

"You and I will have to take a day and go shopping, so you can choose things that are to your liking. Now, you go ahead and change into something more comfortable while I make you a cup of hot cocoa."

Jenelle reached out and hugged her mother. "Thank you, Momma for everything. I might not remember my life back then. I know it was good to live here then, and it's good to be home now."

"Oh honey, you have no idea how good. Now go get ready, and I'll be right back with that cup of hot cocoa."

Jenelle changed into a soft, full-length nightgown that she found hanging in the closet, and was washing up in the connecting bathroom when her mother returned with her cocoa.

"I'm not staying, honey. I'm just going to leave this on the nightstand for you. Daddy and I will see you in the morning."

Another hug and Karissa headed for the door.

After her mother left, Jenelle turned down the lights, collected her mug of hot cocoa and made her way over to the window where she gazed into the moonless night beyond. Stars studded the sky, sparkling against the frozen blackness of space. Somewhere out there was Acacia. She found herself scanning the heavens for the brightest star, desperately searching for something—*someone*—already lost to her. She tried ignoring the empty, curling sensation in the pit of her stomach. Would it ever end, she wondered? Would she ever get over him? Ever? An eerie howl drifted on the frozen night air to seep through the windowpane. It sounded so lonely, so lost and so very sad.

Somewhere a million miles away—somewhere very special, Jenelle knew the call of the *Galaxian Screecher* echoed through the canopy of forest trees that surrounded an unforgettable lakeside. Tiny little birds darted from one tree to the next, singing their cheerful songs. Acacia's two suns would continue setting and rising as always, and a comet named Rydell would continue challenging the only man she could ever love. A million miles away, somewhere very magical, and very special, life was going on without her...

CHAPTER TWENTY-FOUR

Antara: Ten hours from Acacia.

"Frank, I'm going to drop you off at the spaceport. Clint will be meeting you to take you back to the house."

"Yer not comin'?"

"I got something I gotta do."

Frank had a pretty good idea what that *something* was. At least he hoped he was right.

~ * ~

Aspen Valley, Washington State

By now nearly three months had passed since that bitterly cold day when Jenelle first arrived home. Spring had begun chasing the cold away. Trees were starting to bud-out and spring bulbs had begun blooming. Instead of white and frozen, the land was turning green again.

Cassie came at least twice a week to get Jenelle. Shopping was the biggest attraction. It was with Cassie's encouragement that Jenelle one day made an appointment to have her platinum hair restored to its natural color of honey blonde. Afterward they ended up for a bite to eat at a local hamburger joint, a place where many of the young people their age hung out. With the help of a tutor that her parents had hired, Jenelle had not only learned to flawlessly speak her true language, but to read and write it as well.

Nearly every evening Daniel came by after class, and her mom would always have dinner ready when he got there. On weekends, he'd come by earlier in the day and they would go for a ride in his expensive LC. One day they drove up into the Cascades, where he took her to to a visitors center of a sleeping volcano called, Mt Rainier. On the way back, they stopped at an impressive ski lodge for dinner.

Yet, despite it all, despite everyone's love and attention, the void in Jenelle's heart had not healed. It wasn't *Mister Right* she wanted, or what he could provide. What her heart needed was Marc.

With a heavy sigh, Jenelle settled deeper into the overstuffed couch and pulled one of her mother's handmade quilts tighter about her. Daniel was kind, so caring. He was truly the *Mister Right* Marc spoke of. She should have been happy. Maybe if they grew up together, there might have even been a time when she would be planning to marry Daniel. He was going to be a lawyer, someone who could provide everything she could ever want. Only it wasn't Daniel she wanted.

Jenelle had no real interest in anything, just couldn't get caught up in anything. Never again would she laugh at his cocky and sarcastic comebacks to Frank or see the tender side that he hid so well. Memories were hard to let go, like the sadness in his eyes and voice when he said, *I should have been the one to die.* She doubted he even knew he was crying that day, let alone that she held him and cried with him. There were so many levels to Marc Banner, and she had only just begun to see them. His eyes spoke volumes when he was passionate about something. His bike for instance. He loved his bike, and she missed riding with him. Missed the wind blowing through her hair. Missed the thrill of hanging on to him for dear life when he'd turn the bike loose on a straight stretch.

She recalled how his eyes lit up as he told her about the comet, Rydell. Like an excited kid, he was eager to take her up above Acacia that very night to show her the comet up close. Maybe even race it.

Sadly, it never happened. He left that very afternoon. Walked out of her life—all because she had told him not to come around anymore.

It was no wonder he never came back, never said goodbye, or wished her good luck. She had no one to blame but herself.

The sound of an approaching car interrupted her thoughts. Daniel was here. Her mom had made his favorite meal—old fashioned meatloaf, baked potatoes, and seasoned green beans for dinner. Apple pie for dessert.

Next came a familiar knock. With a sigh, Jenelle forced herself to get up off the couch and answer the door.

"Hi gorgeous." Leaning forward Daniel gave her a quick peck on her cheek. "Hmm, something sure smells good."

"Momma's been busy. Here," she said. "Let me take your jacket."

Daniel went on, "I don't know about anyone else, but I'm starved."

"Well, that's good to hear." Karissa said as she entered the dining room with a platter of baked potatoes. "Jenelle, honey, would you mind bringing in the dinner rolls?"

"Certainly."

She hurried into the kitchen for the rolls and anything else that she could bring in.

While Jenelle and her mother got things on the table, Daniel sat in the living room visiting with Tom. By the time the men were being called for dinner, they had discussed everything from the drop in stocks to the cost of living these days.

~ * ~

SeaPort Intergalactic Spaceport

Thank God the *Antara* was just small enough that it was allowed to land at SeaPort without having to leave it at the space station and take a commuter the rest of the way in. He was just setting the ship down on its jacks when the customary announcement came through welcoming *Antara,* and announcing that the weather was sunny and a mild seventy-two degrees.

At least it was a nice day, he thought as he secured the ship, then turned for the cargo bay and his bike. Now to find Aspen Valley, wherever that was. All he knew was that it was somewhere northeast of SeaPort.

On the way, he spotted a small combination convenience store/fueling station. The place was like a scene right out of an old western movie. Frank would have been right at home here.

Two old timers, sitting on a wooden bench under a large covered porch watched with interest as he pulled in and stopped directly in front of them.

"Whatcha riding there, son?" one of them asked.

Leaving the bike loping at an idle, Marc straddled the it and planted his booted feet. "A ninety-four Harley."

"I told you, Steve," the other man piped up. "I knew I heard a Harley coming. Can't miss that iconic rumble."

"Yep, can't tell you when I last heard one. Got yourself a real beauty there mister."

"Thanks. I'm looking for the Byers place. Know where it is?"

"You're almost there. Stay on this road until you get to Joneses Dairy. Then hang a left at Junction Eighteen and go about another quarter mile. The Byers place is on your right. You can't miss it."

"Thanks."

~ * ~

The table had been cleared and Karissa was just bringing in the pie when suddenly a familiar rumble could be heard in the distance and getting louder.

"What is *that*?" Daniel asked, frowning as though he smelled something bad.

Jenelle's stomach did a flipflop. She'd know that sound anywhere. *Marc.*

Daniel rose from the table when the rumbling began gearing down to turn into the driveway. Eventually the noise stopped in front of the house. Daniel was at the open door as Marc was mounting the steps onto the massive porch.

"May I help you?" Daniel asked, all business as he gave Marc an insulting once-over.

"Jenny around?"

"Who? You mean Jenelle?"

"No. I mean Jenny."

"Who, may I ask, wants to know?"

"Me."

Like two dogs sizing one another up before the fight gets started, the tension between Marc and Daniel was thick.

"Marc." Jenelle was wedging herself between the two men. "Marc, what are you doing here? Please, please come in."

"Jenny, I hardly recognize you. I like your hair. That your natural color?"

Daniel turned astonished eyes upon Jenelle. "You *know* this guy?" he asked as though she'd just invited some scruffy derelict into her house.

Purposely adding fuel to the fire, Marc flashed him a smile as he followed Jenelle inside. He had the guy figured out immediately. Either family or boyfriend. Well-dressed, right down to his brown cardigan sweater and shiny new loafers. Far as Marc was concerned the guy was a conceited jerk who thought he was better than others. He'd met too many just like him over the years.

However, now that he'd been invited in and the door was shut behind him, Marc couldn't help maintaining his best irritating smile. At last, he turned to face the snob. "You know, come to think of it, Jenny may have mentioned you once," he lied. "Said your name was—He snapped his fingers and managed a thoughtful frown, "let me think...Digby? No... Delbert! That was it, Delbert."

Daniel bristled.

Still standing between them, Jenelle wanted to hide. Eyes sparkling with mirth, Marc continued to grin at Daniel over the top of her head. "Now I have a face to put with the name," he drawled.

"Marc, this is Daniel McCall. We were kids together. Daniel, Marc Banner. He's the one who rescued me."

"Just doin' what I do best," Marc replied smoothly. Still smiling.

Neither man acknowledged nor offered their hand in greeting.

Jenelle cringed. This had to stop before things got out of hand. Daniel was angry enough to say something he'd regret. Marc looked as though all he needed was an excuse.

Karissa was in the dining room, staring open-mouthed at the unlikely threesome gathered at the front door. Tom, on the other hand, rose from his chair with a grin, and approached Marc with a welcoming handshake. "Marc Banner. What a nice surprise. What brings you here, if I might ask?"

"Just happened to be in the area, Tom," he lied. "Thought I'd stop by to see how Jenny's doing."

"Well, come join us. We're about to break into homemade apple pie.

"Apple pie, huh? My favorite."

Daniel looked completely stunned when Marc calmly took the seat next to Jenelle. The only place left was across the table and down next to Tom.

During a quiet moment of pie and coffee, Daniel possessively brought up a few memories, "Jenelle, remember when we used to play Grav-Tac-Toe? You were good at it as I recall. "

Marc was getting the picture. Jerkface wasn't family. He was her damn boyfriend. Well...that's fine, he had his own list of *remember whens* to casually toss out. So, what if they weren't true. They'd be good for a laugh just watching *Delbert's* face turn red with fury.

"So...you know how to play Grav-Tac-Toe?" he asked in an upbeat tone. I used to play that with my brothers all the time."

"Yes," Daniel replied, "I've grown up since those days."

Karissa spoke up, 'Daniel's won many trophies and awards in competitions."

"No shit."

Janelle choked on her coffee and coughed until she had to get up and leave the table with Misses Byers trailing behind.

Oh man, this was going to be fun. "Yeah..." Marc went on, as if reliving a memory. "I remember when things would get boring onboard ship, Jenny and I would play Grav-Tac-Toe. The winner would get to put on a Nate Jennings collection of hits, get to choose which song to start off with first, and we'd dance til' we dropped."

Dead silence.

"Yep. We had a good ol' time, Jenny and I... I have to say, Grav-Tac-Toe sure took the doldrums out of ship life." He leaned back in the chair and with a wink added, "I never did tell her, but I would often let her win just so we could get on with the fun stuff."

Jenelle and her mother finally returned. One glance from Jenny told him if looks could kill, he was already dead.

"By the way Misses Byers," he said as he patted his belly, "that was the best apple pie I've ever had."

"Thank you, Marc." Her voice was a bit shaky as she continued assisting Jenelle.

Delbert's face was beat red. But as they say...*C'est la Vie.*

Tom was the only one grinning, his eyes sparkling. He knew it was a bunch of crock.

~ * ~

As soon as Jenelle collected herself, Daniel rose from his chair. "I'd better be going. I have a test tomorrow. With a coy nod toward the living room, he signaled for Jenelle to see him to the door.

"Nice meeting you Delb- uh Dan."

"Daniel, I am so very sorry," she whispered. "You don't believe that story, I hope."

"Of course not. But what's he doing here?"

"I don't know."

In silence, Daniel looked away. "Is there something between you two? Because if there is, I refuse to compete against vermin like him. He's not your type, Jenelle. He's an uncouth low life. You deserve better than the likes of him."

And in truth, Marc did indeed look like hell. He was in need of a shave, and his hair was in serious need of a cut—even more than usual. But it was the emptiness in his eyes that caught her attention.

Tell him the truth. He deserves to know where he stands.

Her silence said it all. After a long, drawn-out moment he whispered. "I see..."

"Daniel, I know I should have said something much sooner, but honestly I never expected to see him again."

"So, what are you saying, Jenelle, is that since you didn't expect to see him again, I was second best? Well, I feel sorry for you because from what I can see, it's only one-sided." With a heavy sigh, he added. "I wish you much happiness, Jenelle Byers."

With that he opened the door and walked out of her life.

When she returned to the dining room, her mother was clearing the table and Marc and her father were still at the table, deep in conversation. Antique cars to be exact.

"Kitten, why don't you take Marc out to see my collection."

She was about to turn him down, complaining of a headache, when Marc rose from his chair. "I'd like to see that T-bird."

Jenelle cleared her throat. "Follow me."

"As soon as the door closed behind them and they were crossing the porch, she turned on him. "Why?"

"Why what?" he asked, feigning innocence.

"I've never been so embarrassed in my life. Why did you lie about us playing that stupid game? *Dancing until we dropped*? Letting me win so we could get on with the *fun stuff*? What were you thinking?"

Marc shrugged. "It was just a story, Jenny. Nobody believed it."

"Well, Daniel believed it. Isn't that what you intended? Plus, you lied about me remembering him, when the truth is I didn't remember him at all. To say nothing of calling him Delbert—*Delbert*!"

Marc couldn't help grinning. "Made him mad, huh?"

"You said it purposely for that reason."

"I could have called him *Slick*. He's going to be a lawyer, isn't he?"

"You're not funny. How could you? What were you trying to do? Prove just how right his impression is of you? You couldn't have been cruder if you'd tried."

Marc smiled. "Oh yes. I could have been far, far more crude, but the shock on your mom's face stopped me from taking it further." Quite pleased with himself, he bent his head, lit up a cigarette and inhaled slowly. "Had to do something to get even. I'm telling you, Jenny, when he opened the door and looked at me as if I was some lower life-form who just crawled out from under a rock, I wanted to take-him-on so bad. But that's when you arrived."

"Well, you're a fine one to get upset over name calling. You, who's always using insulting and derogatory names to refer to people."

With a slight frown, Marc feigned a confused look. "I do that?"

She ignored him. "Daniel is a nice guy, he would never..."

"Yeah, he's a real saint." Marc closed the distance between them, taking her into his arms. "Jenny, *Slick's* not the one for you."

The tears started. "Oh? Am I to believe *you* are?"

"No. You deserve better than either of us, Jen."

"Why did you come here, Marc? You did *not* just happen to be in the area. Another lie."

"No. I came because I had a delivery to make anyway," he lied again, "and I thought I'd drop by to see how you're doing before I head back."

"Oh yeah? So where was your delivery?"

He hesitated briefly. "L.A."

"Los Angeles, huh...." Well, that's hardly in the area of Aspen Valley."

Marc laughed. "Jenny, if it's on Earth, then *anywhere* is in *the area*."

"Well, now you know. I'm doing just fine."

They'd reached the large barn where her father kept his classic cars. Jenelle unlocked the door, stepped inside, and switched on the lights.

Crushing his cigarette in a small ashtray just outside the barn, Marc followed her inside. Fifty-some shiny, fully restored American classics glistened beneath the bright lights. "...Whoa," he breathed as he slowly scanned the interior. "Tom said he's been collecting these for going on thirty years."

"Yes, that's what I understand."

Silence fell as Marc began wandering in awe down one of the aisles that separated three rows of beautifully restored American cars. The first to catch his eye was a gleaming, turquoise, and white hardtop Nineteen-Fifty-Seven Chevy with shiny spoked wheels. "Sweet," he whispered as he stood gazing at it in stunned silence.

Next was a jet-black Nineteen-Sixty-Seven Corvette. And it was only the beginning. There were so many cars. All in showroom condition. At last, he turned to Jenelle. "These are beautiful," he said in complete reverence.

"Yes, and I understand that Dad has had them all in one car show or another over the years."

"I've only seen pictures of these babies." Lifting his head, he quickly scanned the rows. "Wonder where that T-bird is?" He grinned. Also, your dad mentioned a Dodge Charger. Gotta see that too."

"The T-bird is about fifth down in the third row," Tom said as he came through the entrance.

"That one's my favorite out of them all," Jenelle said. With a laugh she added, "I'm a T-bird girl, and as soon as I learn how to drive, Dad said he'd let me and Cassie take it for a little spin."

"That's right, kitten, that's your car. The Dodge is just down from the bird." Tom added.

Marc made his way over to the third row, stopping before the white Nineteen-Fifty-Seven Thunderbird hardtop convertible. Tom followed him over. "It was pure junk when I bought it. Now look at her. Just like the day she came off the assembly line."

"Awesome. I was just telling Jenny I've only seen pictures of these cars. Only pictures."

"Yes, nowadays they're next to impossible to find in any condition, let alone restored."

In awe, Marc slowly walked completely around the bird. The interior was done in flashy red and white tuck and roll leather. Same with the dash. "Whew..." Marc released a breathy whistle. "What a beauty."

From there they moved on down to the bright orange Nineteen-Sixty-Eight Dodge Charger.

For Marc it was another moment of silent reverence as he quietly looked over the Charger. "Mopar," he whispered in pure awe. "Straight out of the Muscle Car Era."

"I see you know about muscle cars."

Marc grinned. "Yeah, just enough to be dangerous, Tom." He slowly made his way down the side of the Charger, peering inside the windows as he went. "Beautiful. Just beautiful."

"Go ahead," Tom said, "open her up and see the inside."

Marc opened the driver's door, and marveled at the black interior including leather bucket seats When at last he closed the door he couldn't help but note the solid, heavy sound when it clicked shut. "You just don't hear that sound these days," he said.

"I agree," Tom responded. "Like I say, they don't make them like they used to anymore."

Glancing down Marc checked out the wheels. "Whoa...Even Crager mags." He turned to Tom. "So, what's this baby got under the hood?"

Tom grinned. "That one there has a four-forty Hemi with a four-barrel carb."

Marc released a breathy whistle. "Bet this baby walks."

Tom laughed. "That it does." With that, Tom turned to Jenelle. Kitten, your mom and I are heading to town to get in some last-minute shopping before a sale goes off. Anyway, don't forget to lock up when you leave."

"I won't." Jenelle walked him to the door and stood there as they pulled away.

"I suppose I should get going too," Marc said, as he came up beside her and began shrugging into his leather jacket.

"You're leaving too?"

"Gotta vacate the landing pad in about three hours or get charged for another day "

"Oh."

Marc paused. "I'm sorry I left that day without saying goodbye."

Ignoring his apology, Jenelle turned to face him. "Take me with you," she whispered brokenly.

"What?'

"Take me with you, Marc."

"Jenny, you haven't even had a chance yet to know what you want out of your new life yet. One of these days you're going to be snatched up so fast, you'll forget all about me."

Just saying the words jolted the very heart he never even realized he had. With a sigh, he took her into his arms and drew her close. "Baby, I'm no good for you. It would never work. You'd never be happy with me."

Oh yes, she would. Her senses were filled with Marc. The way he held her, the sound of his voice, the way he smelled... of leather and smoke and motorcycle.

At last, she stepped out of his arms and backed away. "Why did you come here?"

"Why did I come here?" With his mind in turmoil, Marc hesitated, unable to voice the words he knew she wanted to hear. *I came because I... because I'm so damn sorry for that day at the lake. I never—never meant to hurt you. I came because I regret having left you like I did. I love you more than life itself and I came because I just needed to see you and hear your voice just one last time.*

Arms folded and a set look on her face, Jenelle waited for an answer.

"Like I explained earlier, I was in the area, and I just needed to see for myself that you're doing okay."

"Well, don't worry about me. As you can see, I'm doing just fine. You can go on back to your life now."

"Yes, you've got a good life ahead of you." he agreed "Well...I guess I should be going. Be sure to tell your father that I said thanks for letting me see his cars, I had one hell of a good time tonight getting to see those classics."

No response.

"Well..." And without another word, he turned and headed for his bike.

It was better this way, he told himself. At least now when he thought of her, he would be able to think of her safe and doing well, surrounded by loving parents and friends. It was a life that she deserved.

~ * ~

Jenelle remained silently standing outside the building as Marc Banner walked out of her life, taking her heart with him for the second time. She knew she shouldn't watch him leave. Watching would only make it worse. Yet, he was almost to his bike, and she just couldn't look away. Unable to stop the tears, she blindly watched as he mounted and fired up the bike. Without so much as a wave or a backward glance, he started down the drive. Jenelle swallowed hard and waited until his taillights disappeared around a bend in the road. Even then, she continued listening as that familiar deep rumble got farther and farther away—until she no longer could hear it.

He's gone.

Out of the ensuing silence came a quiet inner voice. *Let him go. You have so much more waiting for you here. A life that was stolen from you eleven years ago. A beautiful future awaits you. Let him go.*

What more could she have done? She wasn't a begging kind of person. Never was one to force herself upon anyone—especially if she wasn't wanted. It just wasn't her.

Fine. Let him go. Maybe Daniel was right. Maybe her love for Marc was only one-sided. Her side. To Marc Banner maybe she was simply a contract. He'd hunted, found, and delivered her for a price. Simple as that. "I hate you, Marc Banner."

The words weren't spoken in anger, they were whispered in sorrow. She inhaled a trembling breath and proceeded to wipe the tears away.

The butterflies were back, coiling in the pit of her stomach again. Same as when he'd left before. How long would it hurt this time, she wondered? Would it take as long for the numbness to set-in as it did the first time?

Her heart had only just begun to heal. “Now what?” she whispered brokenly. How does one go on living when the only person that your heart beats for is gone?

In her wildest dreams she never thought she’d ever see him again. Somehow, she’d managed to resign herself to the fact that Marc Banner had been reduced to only a memory. She’d even begun to accept her new life without him.

Now she didn’t know if she had the courage or the strength to go through it all over again. It would be harder this time. So much harder. This time it wasn’t just past memories of being on his ship, of caring for him when he needed her most, crying with him, riding on his bike, or finding love with him at the lake. Now she had new memories to try to forget. Memories of him being here at her home. The place echoed now with the sound of his voice and laughter. Even inside this very building, she could still hear his excitement and whispered approvals of her father’s cars. It will be so much harder this time. So very much harder.

With a heavy sigh and trembling fingers, she took another swipe at her damp cheeks and decided she just couldn’t deal with it tonight. If only she could talk to Aannisah. She’d know what to do. She’d know how to deal with it.

Tomorrow, Jenelle decided...Tomorrow she’ll call Cassie. Maybe they could go do something fun. Yes... that’s what she’ll do. She’ll call Cassie.

CHAPTER TWWENTY-FIVE

Jenelle was ready to lock up the building when suddenly—There. Standing stock still, she cautiously listened. There it was again. That familiar sound, echoing in the distant night air. As if drifting on the waves of the wind, the sound was so distant that it softly swelled one moment, then died to a whisper the next. It always returned sounding a bit closer each time.

Remaining just outside the entrance of the building, Jenelle held her breath and listened. She had no idea how much time had passed since Marc had left, but she knew of no one else in the area who rode a motorcycle, let alone one that sounded like that.

Before long the bike began gearing down, and gearing down until the beam of a single headlight turned off the main road and flickered across a border of yellow daffodils as it came down the long driveway.

Marc... Jenelle ducked back into the building. She could only imagine how bloodshot her eyes were.

The loud rumble stopped just outside the building, and when she heard him shut it down, Jenelle quickly hurried down one of the aisles, pretending interest in a big shiny red boat of a car.

"Jenny?"

"Oh..." she said without turning around. "You're back. Did you forget something?" she asked with cool curiosity.

Marc cleared his throat. "Yeah. Got as far as Junction Eighteen when it hit me..."

"Oh. Well, it's a good thing you remembered before going much further," she replied as though discussing the weather, yet still feigning interest in the big red car.

"Dammit, Jenny," he said in a heated rush of words. With a

helpless gesture, he added, "Truth is, I got to thinking about you ending up with *Slick.* Just can't see you happy with that guy. That court clown is an arrogant, conceited, S.O.B. He'd have you signing some damn pre-nuptial contract outlining your duties as his wife and have his name on everything else in his favor before the ink's even dry on the marriage license."

"What do you care?" she retorted. "Besides, who said anything about marriage?"

She swiped at her cheeks one more time before turning around and coming forward—red face, red eyes, and all. "Daniel won't be back, Marc."

"Good." He stepped forward, "That's good, 'cause a couple of times there, I was ready to beat the crap out of him."

She stepped back. "Yes, that was all too obvious."

For now, Delbert won't be back. So, what are you going to do, sport? You going to take her with you?

For the first time in his cocky, hedonistic and self-absorbed life, he—Marc Banner—who was always quick with smart ass, easy comebacks was suddenly lost for direction. Lost for words. "Jenny..."

"I wouldn't have married him anyway," she said, lifting her head to glance up at him. "He was just a friend. That's all."

So, what are you going to do pal? Came the silent inner voice. *You want Slick worming his way back into her life after you leave? You know he will.*

"Jenny..." he began again. "Did—you really mean it when you asked to go with me?"

Again, she looked up at him. "Why?"

"If I were to take you with me, do you know what you'd be getting yourself into? There's a lot about me you don't know, and it's not all good."

The *little boy* insecurities were surfacing. Jenelle held her breath for only an instant before responding. "I wouldn't have asked otherwise."

He turned his back and moved toward the open door. Sliding his hands, palms out, into his back pockets he remained there, staring out into the darkness. When he turned back to her, he looked more insecure and vulnerable than she'd ever seen him. She wanted to cover his stubbled face with kisses, but she restrained herself.

"I'm terrible to live with, Jenny. I can be a regular ass without even trying."

"That's true. I've seen you in action. More than once."

"I'm crude."

"Yes. That you are."

"Foul-mouthed."

"That too."

He paused. "I'm on shaky ground here, baby. I've never done this before. You don't suppose we could just take off, could we—if we do this—that is? Do we have to tell Tom and Karissa? They won't like it. Hell, they just got you back. I noticed your dad's gun collection in the den, Jenny. I'm sure it was on purpose that he steered me into the den, supposedly to show me his car awards and trophies."

Jenelle laughed. "I know my dad likes you, Marc."

"Uh huh. Especially after my little performance at the table tonight, for which I'm sorry."

"He's never invited Daniel to see his cars. I *know* because Daniel mentioned it a while back."

"No sh—He hasn't?"

"As for Mom, you might be a bit rough around the edges for her right now, but give her time."

Drawing her into his arms, Marc tucked her head beneath his chin and thought about the risk of losing her if he were to leave her behind—thought about the dangers by just being with him if he were to take her.

"If—and I mean *if* you come with me," he said as though coming to a very difficult decision. "The very first thing I'd do is to take you off the market."

Jenelle frowned. "Market?"

"Yeah. We'd make it official."

At her look of confusion, he added, "you know...Put a ring on it?"

Silence.

"*Get Hitched?... Married*? What the devil do they call it on Aden?"

"Married. They call it married, Marc, and you don't have to marry me. I know you're not the marrying kind and I'm not asking for that. I just want to be with you. That's all. No strings attached."

"There you go," he drawled. "Trying to sully my reputation that I've worked so hard to keep spotless."

"Marc, it's just that I don't want you to ever feel I'm tying you down. You'd be free to do what you want, and—"

"That's another thing you don't know about me. I'm a selfish S.O.B. Three things I don't share or loan out...Ever. My gun. My bike, or my woman. If you come with me*...your mine.*

"Then, I wouldn't have it any other way."

He gently sifted his fingers through her hair until he reached the ends. "Spun from stardust," he murmured softly.

"I love you, Marc Banner." Rising on her tiptoes, Jenelle pressed her open mouth to his and felt her knees weaken when suddenly she was drawn tighter into his embrace.

Gently working his hands beneath her coat, he cupped her bottom, drawing her firmly against him. "Mmm ...There. That's much better."

She pressed her face into the warmth of his neck and breathed in his essence *Marc...*

He pulled back, his eyes intense. "I don't have much to offer. All I have is my ship and my bike. Other than that, I don't have a pot to..."

Jenelle pressed her fingers over his lips. "It's alright. I don't care. We can live on your ship if we need to."

He kissed her fingers. "Frank lives there too. Just the three of us? Yeah, I can just picture it. Real cozy."

With a compressed breath he added, "It isn't that I don't have credits. I've been setting aside credits for a long time. I'm not destitute. I just don't have a suitable roof to put over our heads right now."

"Well, maybe we could stay in the cottage I stayed in until something better comes along.

"Yeah, that might work for a while. You know how I make a living, Jen. I'll be away a lot of the time, but you'd be close to Mom and my sisters."

She laughed. "Oh no you don't. Once we're married, I'm not turning you lose to hunt down someone else's daughter. No way. You see, I'm selfish too."

"What are you talking about? Surely, you're not planning to come with me?"

"Oh, but surely I am."

"Baby, you.ve got me so tangled-up inside I can't even think straight," he murmured brokenly, his voice muffled against her hair. "To be honest, I've never been so scared as I am right now. Because of what I do for a living," he went on, "your life will be at risk just by being on board my ship. If anything were to happen to you..."

"Then, maybe it's time for you to get out of the search and recovery business."

The realization of losing her surged through him with stark reality. He gazed deeply into her eyes and said the words she never thought she would ever hear. In truth, they were words he'd never said to any other woman for that matter, "I love you so damn much, it hurts."

CHAPTER TWENTY-SIX

They were going home. Back to Acacia.

They were married two months ago by Pastor Edwards, a family friend of the Byers. It had been a warm, sunshiny summer day. The small ceremony was held in the Byer's beautifully groomed back yard, amid towering fir trees and pots of fragrant roses. Just family and close friends in attendance: The Byers, the entire Banner clan, Zeke and his family, and Frank of course. Aannisah had been brought out from Aden to be Maid of Honor—and ended up deciding to remain on Acacia. Cassie was her only other bridesmaid, who by now was engaged to Daniel. Unfortunately, Daniel couldn't make the wedding.

Nick and Clint stood up with Marc. What a handsome sight those three brothers made, each in a black tux. Marc and Nick looked so much alike standing next to each other, you'd think they were twins. Marc had gotten a fresh haircut. and was looking as nervous as a fish out of water, while Nick was grinning watching Tom walk Jenelle down the aisle.

After the ceremony, Marc completely rattled Karissa by a combination of calling her "Mom," kissing her on the cheek and enfolding her in a hug that literally lifted her off the ground. In response, everyone cheered and raised glasses of champagne in salute.

Besides offering to furnish a complete houseful of new furniture whenever they are ready, Tom had gifted the newlyweds with the Fifty-Seven T-bird for Jenelle, and the Sixty-Eight Dodge Charger RT for Marc. Max offered Marc a chance to go into business with him. It entailed half of his established and lucrative commercial transport corporation, and it was a chance for Marc to get out of search and recovery. Plus, as a wedding gift, Max and Delta had presented the couple with one-hundred acres of prime Banner acreage of their choosing.

Without even thinking about it, Marc and Jenny knew exactly what parcel they were going to choose. There was a gentle knoll on a particular portion of acreage where a house could be built overlooking a very special, very magical lakeside, where the haunting sound of the *Galaxian Screecher* could be heard drifting through the cool, shady forest that surrounds the lake.

Two days after the wedding they took off, amid tears and promises to return in time for Marc and Tom to get the RT ready for an upcoming car show.

Marc rented a sporty rental for the trip to the spaceport. Nick had already deposited Marc's bike to *Antara's* hold for him. He also caged Ruckus and hauled him back to Acacia for Delta to care for until the couple returned.

Marc had his own wedding surprise for Jenny. He made a stop in Seattle where they spent the next four days locked behind closed doors in a luxurious hotel. Hungry only for each other, they refused room service for anything other than clean towels, sheets, and an occasional meal now and then.

There were times when they were lying together sated, their damp bodies cooling, that Jenelle would see a hint of uncertainty behind the love in Marc's deep sapphire eyes. Yes, what he did for a living was dangerous, and he worried about her. In his mind, just being married to her, let alone having her onboard the *Antara* with him, put her life in danger and it scared him.

He hadn't yet said that he would accept his father's offer to go into business with him. Hopefully the day would come when he'd realize that it was a generous offer that would allow him to remain home. Until then, she vowed to continue smoothing those worry lines from his brow and smother him in a thousand kisses until he hauled her into his arms and conquered her with gentle and passionate love.

Port Imperial ACACIA

Four hours and they'd be landing at Imperial.

"Computer's registering high stratosphereic winds up ahead," Marc said. "It might get a bit rough."

Just then the ship lifted, dropped, then veered off course as a sudden gust of wind came out of nowhere. Marc tapped in the correction, then swore under his breath when, moments later, the wind suddenly shifted, requiring yet another correction.

It wasn't all that long ago Jenny would have been clinging, white-knuckled, to the edges of her seat. Now she simply settled deeper into the co-pilot's seat. With a sigh, she drew her legs up and rested her chin on her knees. Her eyes were drawn to Marc as he fought his way down through the various layers of unstable air. Eventually he cut the speed, felt the response and booted the nose up to slow their descent.

He was wearing his usual black pants and a white short-sleeved T-shirt that stretched across his chest and biceps. Worshipping him when he wasn't noticing, had become her favorite pastime over the past two months. She loved every facet of this man, from the grief-stricken ten-year old, to the chivalrous *knight* who came to her rescue when Ahmed would have raped her...to the nervous and insecure bridegroom who looked as though he wanted to cut and run. Jenelle distinctly recalled Nick subtly saying something out of the corner of his mouth that must have settled Marc. At least he was still standing there by the time she and her father made it down the aisle.

Over the past two months Marc had taken the time to teach Jenelle a few basics in piloting the *Antara*. It all started out with him quickly and unexpectedly handing over the controls while he ran back to the galley. Ignoring her panicked protest, he hurried back with a couple of drinks from the *froster*.

"Hey...you did good," he'd said, his voice laden with inflated praise as he handed her a glass.

Jenelle sent him a dirty look. "Don't you *ever* do that again."

Other than teaching her a few important beginning steps in piloting, time was spent sheltered in the captain's quarters with the ship on auto-pilot. He was so gentle with her, always pacing himself to her responses. Jenelle had no idea that it was possible to love someone as much as she loved this man.

At the moment Marc was monitoring the controls when... "Sonofa..."

"What?" Jenelle rushed forward. "What's wrong?"

Marc pointed to the rear vid-screen. "Look what's challenging us to a race."

"Is that...?"

"Yes! Want to race it?"

"If it catches up with us, it won't run into us, will it?"

Marc laughed. "No. I know it doesn't look like it, but it's over six million kilometers straight up from us. That's close if you're talking astrophysics, but it's still very far away. The only thing it can do is pass us up. So, shall we give it a run? Time's a wasting."

"Let's do it!"

"Okay then..." He began quickly punching keys and adjusting controls. "I'm going to need you to remain in Frank's spot and strap in. I want you to monitor a couple of things for me. Think you can do that?"

"Yes. If it's something I know how to do."

"It is. You remember me teaching you about this panel, right?"

"Yes."

"We'll race until..." he pointed to a display on the console. "Until it says Five, two, zero, zero, eight, five. That number marks the finish line for us. We've got a tiny bit of an advantage in lead. And I mean a tiny bit." He grinned. "It's called a handicap."

"What happens if we go beyond the finish line?" she asked cautiously.

"Nothing will happen. Rydell will remain in its orbit high above us, and we'd still be orbiting Acacia, just like we are now."

"Oh..."

Leaning across the small distance between them, he pointed to another bank of red-lit indicators on an overhead facia. "As soon as these turn green, you let me know. Okay?"

"Okay," she said, studying the panel before her.

Marc adjusted her safety harness. "You'll want this good and tight. It's going to be rough." He settled back into his seat. "Ready?"

"I think so."

"Good. We gotta hurry."

With that Marc slid a control forward. The *Antara* responded. Shuddering violently, and with a thunderous roar, it began picking up speed under full emergency power. The noise was deafening. Jenelle was instantly pinned back in her seat. Interior lights flickered, red-lit indicators pulsed their silent warnings, and a host of klaxons were triggered by the brutal demand. The vibrations of the rising torque threatened to snap every bolt and rivet in *Antara's* frame, and yet Marc ruthlessly held to his purpose. "Come on, baby. You can do it. Come on...come on."

"Warning! This ship is not designed to accelerate above—"

"Yes, it is." Marc shouted as he shut the message down.

"Acceleration panels have been calibrated, Marc." Jenelle called-out, her voice raised against the scream of straining drives. "All lights are green."

It was tangible—the sense of determination that filled the air. Marc's fingers danced across the console, chimes proclaimed the completion of procedures, and red-lit indicators pulsed their responses.

"Warning. Risk factor..." Again, Marc shut down the voice that was calmly detailing the dire consequences of their present course of action.

"Jenny, how close are we to the finish?" he shouted over the klaxons and rattling vibrations.

"It's at five, two, zero, zero, eight, three." Janelle shouted back.

"We're almost there. Come on baby, you can do it. Come on."

Jenelle glanced up at the ceiling viewport just as the tip of Rydell's fiery nose came within site. Even though the comet was millions of kilometers above them, they appeared to be racing neck and neck...with the comet seemingly gaining.

"Now. What's the numbers now, Jen?"

"Five, two, zero, zero, eight, four... Five. We're at the Finish Line,

Marc."

"We did it!" he shouted above the combined roar of laboring drives and pulsing klaxons.

Five seconds later Rydell edged ahead, its fiery tail trailing behind. In the time it took for *Antara's* thrust to decrease, and the pressure of the G-forces to lift, high overhead Rydell was burning passed them.

"We did it, Jen! Can you believe it? We did it. And with five seconds to spare."

Unable to contain his excitement, Marc unsnapped her harness, dragged her from the seat into his arms and thoroughly kissed her. The joy on his face nearly brought tears to her eyes. Once again, the boy in him had emerged.

Yes, it was just a silly race. Not the same as racing two vehicles, or two racing-bikes against each other. There was a huge gap separating *Antara* from the comet, but to Marc it was everything he'd waited years for. Yes, he'd set the rules of the race. Yes, he'd decided on the finish line, and even gave himself a tiny handicap. Yet tempted as he might have been, he did not slip *Antara* into hyperdrive to make sure he won. That would have been cheating.

For a moment they simply stood in stunned silence, as *Antara's* tortured drives kept up a steady descending moan. High above, Rydell's fiery tail continued to pass over them.

"Wow." Marc breathed. "Nice *Welcome Home*, huh?"

"People won't believe us, Marc. They won't believe you raced Rydell, let alone won."

"Who cares?" he replied dismissively "Far as I'm concerned, it's just between you, me and Rydell."

He captured her hand and placed a slow and sensuous kiss to her open palm. Just that simple act had her blinking back tears and she felt in her heart that Marc Banner had finally come to terms with himself and the decisions that yet lay ahead.

He smiled, and once again those slashing indentations formed beneath his cheekbones as he murmured in a lazy, sexy voice. "Misses

Banner, we've got about two hours before arriving at Imperial. What do you say I put this bird on *Auto* and we go back and celebrate. I might have a scar or two you haven't seen yet."

Jenelle laughed, "I'd love to see your scars, Mister Banner."

~ * ~

Port Imperial

It was nighttime and they were coming in low, skimming over a dark landscape. He'd already been in touch with the spaceport, and it was just a matter of time before he'd be killing the ship's forward motion and firing the reverse thrusters to slow their descent.. The comset chimed and Marc reached overhead to flick it on. "Banner, here."

"Marc Banner. I understand congratulations are in order." The voice and image belonged to a heavy-set, middle-aged woman with brassy blonde hair and laugh lines framing her eyes.

"Hi Shara. Word gets around, I see."

"You better believe it. Especially when the last of the Banner boys gets pulled off the market." She laughed boisterously. "Believe me, the tears have been flowing long and hard from all the broken-hearted hopefuls around here."

Marc grinned. "Awe… Such a shame."

"So, who's the lucky gal? Anyone I know? She must be something special to rope you."

Marc laughed. "She is.. She's not from around here, but I promise I'll bring her by so you can meet her."

"You'd better. That's all I can say. Hon, the robosphere should be pulling up any moment now. You know what to do from there."

"Thanks.." With that, the vid-screen went black.

"Marc?" Jenelle spoke up, "are they expecting us at a certain time? I mean, is someone going to be waiting for us at the terminal?"

"No. Why?"

"Well, I was just thinking maybe after you get the ship settled, we could grab a couple blankets, take the bike and head for the lake to spend the night in that little guest cottage out there. If nobody's waiting for us at the spaceport, then nobody will miss us if we don't make it home until sometime tomorrow. And if they should ask, we can always say we had an unexpected layover."

Obviously reading more than she did into her innocent choice of words, a lazy, knowing smile touched the corners of his mouth as he remained focused on trailing the robosphere into their assigned berth.

With a jolt, Antara settled onto her jacks. A soft chime sounded, and a bank of tiny lights winked from the command console in response. The declining howl of Antara's powerful drives resonated throughout the helm as Jenelle calmly remained seated, awaiting Marc's thoughts about going to the lake.

Finally he swiveled around to face her; his look suggestive, lusty as he studied her for a long, tense moment. "The lake… Yeah…That can be arranged." he drawled.

Normally, it is a thirty minute process to shut down and secure the ship. Tonight, however, Marc cut the time in half by skipping a few chosen procedures. "This way, Misses Banner," he purred as he took her by the hand and headed for the hold where his bike awaited.

"Layover, huh…" he murmured softly, still quietly pondering the term as he released the cargo ties tethering the Harley to the bulkhead. "Hmm … and here all this time, I thought layover meant something entirely different."

His candid one-liner was a direct blend of childlike innocence and the intense, white-hot passion of a man… her man.

Jenelle D'Ann Banner was finally home. And it felt good.

Banner's Bonus
Banner's Series Book One

CHAPTER ONE

Earth Date: 2105 Port Ireland
Terra Four 70 A.C. (After Colonization)

"Listen, Garrett, I don't give a rebel's damn what game or whose bed you have to drag him out of, *just get Banner.* You hear me?"

Standing behind his massive desk and bracing his weight upon the knuckles of firmly planted fists, Jonathan Loring's voice could be heard in the main hallway of LorTech's Central Control.

Lending him distinction, Loring's dark hair was dusted with gray at the temples. Though generally good-natured and quick to find humor, a frown now creased his brow.

"According to his itinerary," Loring continued with less volume, "he should have arrived in port sometime this afternoon."

Dan Garrett's shoulders slumped. "He's here all right, Mr. Loring, but it's been over two hours since I last saw him. He had just finished unloading a large shipment and said something about heading to the Star Cruiser. Sir, I'll never find him in that place...providing he's even still there."

"Look, I don't give a damn where he—"

"I'll get him," Garrett quickly cut in. "I'll find him for you, Mr. Loring."

The Star Cruiser was noisy and crowded. The atmosphere was a mixture of music, loud voices, laughter and a heavy blanket of smoke.

A wide variety of people mingled together. Some were long-haul freighters, eagerly celebrating the end of an eighteen-month run. Then there were the miners—*diggers,* as they were called—just in from the asteroids and anxious to set their fantasies into motion, most of which had been months in the making. Still others, like Nick Banner, were there merely to celebrate the payout of a six-week cargo run.

Like so many other freelance cargo pilots, Banner was the owner and sole operator of a small cargo ship. With cargo runs being long and lonely, it was common for some pilots to take a woman aboard. In essence, she needed a lift to his destination, and in exchange she offered her companionship with all its connotations. Nick Banner wasn't interested in that kind of arrangement. Six weeks in space can be a big mistake when stuck with someone you don't happen to get along with. He'd tried it once—shortly after he'd acquired the *Victorious.* It turned into a catastrophe and from then on he resolved to limit his women to port only.

Terra Four's port taverns, and the love-starved crewmen who frequented them, were no different now than they were on Earth a little over two centuries ago when the tall sailing ships would come to port.

Just as it was then, an easy lay could always be found hanging around the port bars. Banner, however, had never known a time when he wasn't surrounded by women vying for his attention. He had never once paid for a woman's favors, and being with the same one for more than a couple of days didn't happen to be his idea of a good time.

He was barely twenty-one when he fell hopelessly in love with Linnae. So crazy in love, he turned his back on all the others, even walked away from the gaming tables and asked her to marry him. Blind to everything, he closed his mind to the ugly rumors going around about her.

"She's a whore, Nick. Dammit man, open your eyes; she's using you. Why can't you see that?"

More than once Nick's fist had split his older brother's lip for those very words. Even his friend, Zeke, had tried to dissuade him, but to no avail. Stubborn and hardheaded as they come, he had defended Linnae's honor right down to the bitter end, when he'd shown up unannounced one evening. As the door opened, Nick simply stood there watching in mute shock while another man in the background scrambled about for his clothing.

Drunk and giggling, Linnae tried to coax Nick to join the fun, but he turned away without a backward glance. And in many ways was still on the run.

He left home shortly thereafter. Setting out for a small, untamed world called Echo, he spent the better part of two years burying his heartache and anger in hard labor and life-threatening assignments. If nothing else, those years had taught him the meaning of being tough and living hard. He also earned damned good credits for his endeavors, and when he returned to civilization it was with a determination to live again.

The first thing he had done was place a hefty down payment on a small cargo ship, already christened the *Victorious.* Not long after that he formed a partnership with a drinking companion, Quint Kendyl. It was a business venture that entailed using Quint's connections and Nick's ship to make short runs for a local courier. Eventually, however, the partnership failed due to conflict of interests between the two men.

Looking for bigger and better brought Nick to Terra Four when, operating under the name of Banner Enterprises, he picked up a variety of freight and mail runs within the sector. By now he was over Linnae, though the scar of her betrayal ran deep. Vowing no one would ever own his heart again, he regarded women as nothing more than playthings—entertaining diversions to be enjoyed and left behind.

Nick Banner had been branded a hard case back then. Come payday he could usually be found bucking roulette at one of the local port dives, where he drank everyone under the table, fought half the security force with his bare fists, and generally wound up passed out in some woman's bed.

But that was *then.* Miraculously recognizing Nick's ingrained honesty and reputation as a hard worker, a man named Linc Sheldon took Nick under his wing. It was Sheldon who, in time, introduced Nick to Jonathan Loring.

~ * ~

Dan Garrett entered the doors of the dimly lit Star Cruiser. To his left, a brawl had broken out in the corner, and two men seated at a nearby table were taking bets on the winner. To Garrett's right, a group of inebriated coworkers were starting the next game of *"Bounty"*.

"Hey, Garret, come on over. You wanna get in on this? We've got room for one more." James Cleary had a stupid grin plastered on his face and eyes at half-mast. Four others in the same condition were poured into their chairs around the game table—full mugs of ale within easy reach. One of them absently shuffled a deck of cards while the others had already positioned their pawns on the holograph game board.

"Not tonight, Cleary. I'm looking for Banner. Have you seen him around?"

"Not more than thirty minutes ago," Cleary answered.

"'Ee's 'ere...somewhere," one of the other men spoke up. "Lucky devil had two blondes hangin' on 'im." The man grinned then added, "Both of 'em clinging to 'im like *shateries."* With that, the men at the table burst into a round of raucous laughter. It seemed the *shateri* was always the brunt of someone's joke. The small fur-bearing animal, found along the southern coastline of Terra Four's main continent, was not only known for its luxurious fur but was also notorious for its enthusiasm for procreation.

Garrett couldn't help but grin; their laughter was contagious. "Thanks, fellas. If you happen to see him again, tell him I'm looking for him."

Dan Garrett continued making his way through the crowd, his eyes intently sifting through a murky sea of smoke and faces. Finally, he climbed a set of wide stairs that led to a mezzanine from which he could survey the entire main floor. The mezzanine was an extension of the bar, a balcony furnished with tables and chairs that completely encircled the room.

Finding an empty table near the balustrade, Garrett claimed it, and from his perch began methodically scanning the entire main level. Behind him several drunk and boisterous crewmen were engaged in singing a bawdy song. All around, people were drinking and laughing, either burying their fears and troubles or celebrating their good fortune.

Banner, who seemed to rarely have fears or troubles to bury, was drinking to his luck when Garrett's eyes finally locked onto him. Seated at a game table on the opposite side of the room and true to form, Nick

Banner was casually sprawled in his chair—all six-foot-four of him. From the smug grin tugging at the corners of his mouth and the stack of game chips at his elbow, there was little doubt who was winning.

There was an unconscious grace about Nick Banner. He always seemed to turn heads. In all honesty, Garrett was secretly envious of Banner's magnetism and innate ability to attract women. Though they were traits he yearned to possess himself, he had resigned long ago to the fact that he simply didn't have it and never would.

Even the faded, scarred leathers that Banner wore would have looked shoddy on anyone else. But with his dark hair and hard, lean body, the well-worn attire lent a primitively appealing air of danger.

~ * ~

Reaching for his mug of ale, Nick laid the winning cards on the table. He liked winning, but cleaning up on a table of drunken comrades wasn't much of a challenge, not to mention that it grated on his sense of fair play. It was time to call it quits. "Gentlemen, I believe this completes the game, and it looks like I win." He grinned and added, "Again."

A stunning brunette now stood at his back, both hands draped possessively over his shoulders as though she might lose him to another should she dare to let go. Leaning down, she whispered something in his ear that brought forth a crooked grin as he downed his last swallow of brew.

"Fellas, what can I say? I hate to win and run, but worse yet, I hate keeping a lady waiting. Here," he said, separating half of his winnings and tossing the coins back onto the table. "The drinks are on me." With that, the table burst into a round of boisterous cheers and Nick rose to escort his luscious companion to the nearest exit.

He no sooner began guiding her, his hand at the small of her back when, "Hey, Nick! Wait up!"

Banner turned to see Dan Garrett elbowing his way through the crowd.

"Garrett. What's up?"

"Loring wants to see you."

"Tell him I'll drop by first thing in the morning." He turned and resumed guiding his companion toward the exit.

"Nick. He means to see you. *Now.*"

Groaning inwardly, Nick stopped short, turning to Garrett in exasperation. "And it just *can't* wait until tomorrow."

It was clear from the look on Garrett's face that he was painfully aware of his ill-timing. "Sorry, Nick, but no it can't. I wish I could tell you what it's all about, but I'm sure it's important."

With a heavy sigh of regret, Nick turned to the girl. Tightening his hold on her, he drew her nearby. "Baby..." he began, capturing her chin in a hold that was both gentle and possessive at the same time.

"Gina," she corrected. "My name's Gina."

Nick grinned. "Gina, honey..." Nuzzling against her ear he murmured something that made the woman glow, then punctuated it with a lusty kiss.

At last he turned to Garrett. "Let's get out of here 'fore I change my mind."

A landcraft waited outside the Star Cruiser for the 30-minute ride from Port Ireland to the headquarters of LorTech Equipment. The sleek, low-slung vehicle was a sporty two-seater model. Her shiny black exterior said she was new; the logo on her doors said she belonged to LorTech.

"Well, I see Jonathan finally broke down and replaced one of those tired vehicles. How long have you had this?" Nick asked, running an appreciative eye over the smart new rig.

"About three months now," Garrett answered, fishing a remote from his pocket and entering a code. In response, both doors disengaged and slid silently backward to disappear into the rear quarter panel on each side.

With a low whistle, Nick climbed in and continued his appraisal from the inside. The complex dash was a mini cockpit, loaded with options ranging from a host of digital readouts to a small rear display monitor. "N i c e," he drawled approvingly as the control console snapped to life the instant Garrett's weight settled into the driver's seat.

Owned by Jonathan Loring, LorTech was a fast-growing research equipment company presently booming with a recent contract to supply equipment to Echo, a small and relatively unexplored rim world.

It was nighttime, and traffic was heavy at first but thinned progressively the farther they traveled from the city. Soon, the landcraft picked up speed and the landscape began whisking by in a blur. Both men remained silent, each deep in his own thoughts.

The environment was particularly dreary, consisting mainly of processing plants and warehouses. Then the scenery gradually changed. The buildings became taller and seemed to stretch farther apart. Some had tanks attached to them. Others had pipes that ran from one building to the next. Eerie puffs of vapor rose from their stacks, illuminated by the surrounding floodlights.

Terra Four was a Class E planet, located within the Sector Five System. Its distance from Earth measured in time was roughly six weeks. Before *Stellar drive,* it had taken years to reach the Sector Five System.

First discovered around the turn of the century by an unmanned probe during Earth's so called "Race for Space" era, Terra Four was the fourth of five planets that were named for their likeness to Earth. Colonization didn't occur, however, until almost thirty-five years later.

The first settlement formed was a tiny mining colony, Port New America, nestled high in the Cascades, Terra Four's northernmost mountains. Eventually more colonists arrived; more settlements sprouted up, and with them various forms of livelihood developed. Ultimately, through economic evolution many small mining towns combined to create thriving cities. Port Ireland grew to become the largest and most advanced city on Terra Four.

Pulling up to LorTech's outside gates, Garrett flashed the required credentials to the guard, and they were waived on through.

As Nick palmed the security lock at the main entrance to the massive complex, a hidden scanner began crosschecking his palm print, retinal and voice patterns with his stated identity. "Come on...*come on,"* he muttered, releasing an impatient sigh as they waited. As if prompted by his frustration, a green light snapped to life on a small panel and the lock on the door clicked open. Nick wasted no time barging through. Garrett followed at his heels, trying to keep up with Banner's lengthy stride.

Taking the steps three at a time, Nick hastily made his way up a flight of stairs and down a long carpeted hallway until they finally came to a door with "Jonathan T. Loring, President" inscribed on it.

"Hi, Lizzy," he muttered, striding through the reception area toward the inner office.

"Nick. Wait! Let me tell him you're—"

"It's okay darlin', I know my way in."

"Yes, but—"

Skipping formalities, Nick hit the pressure-plate and barged in as the door opened into Jonathan's spacious office. Loring's back was turned as he stood before a floor to ceiling glass wall overlooking the compound.

"Ah, Nick!" he said, whirling around. "Thank God, he found you."

"Yeah. Your timing's impeccable, Jon."

"Have a seat. *Please,"* Jonathan said, indicating one of two leather chairs in front of his desk. At the same time, he turned to Garrett, thanking and perfunctorily dismissing him.

Nick sank into a comfortable chair, planting one booted foot across the opposite thigh. "So, what's going on?"

Taking his seat, Jonathan lifted an envelope off his desk and wordlessly handed it to Nick.

Accepting the note, Nick held eye contact with his friend, assessing the indisputable mixture of terror and anger in the man's eyes. At last, he withdrew the note from its envelope and began reading.

Mr. Loring, I overheard part of a conversation that could cost my life as well as those in my family. For that reason, I choose not to reveal myself, but I want you to know that your daughter's life may be in danger. I wish I had heard more, but I strongly suspect "The Leader" is behind this.

Without comment, Nick patted his pockets, found a cigarette, lit it, and blew a lazy stream of smoke toward the ceiling where it was instantly ushered into the nearest vent. "I seem to be missing a few lines here, Jon. Maybe you'd better take this from the top. And who the devil's *The Leader?"*

Staring at Nick with blank eyes, Loring began. "That's just it; I'm not sure. There are several possibilities. Rumor has it there are at least two mega-corps that want total possession of Echo."

Maintaining eye contact with Loring, Nick took a slow drag from his cigarette. "Just exactly who are these two corporations?"

Loring hesitated. "Hell, it's a rumor, Nick. Your guess is as good as mine."

"Then *guess,* dammit!"

A long moment of silence passed before Loring reluctantly offered a name. "Frontier Enterprises could be one."

"And?"

"These are just guesses, Nick. There's no way of—"

"And?" he persisted.

"Possibly...Chase Explorations."

Nick examined his cigarette intently, deep in thought as he watched smoke curl off the tip. "Chase Explorations," he mused. "Aren't they based out of Paragon? What the devil are they doing clear out here, messin' around with a small rim world like Echo?"

"Howard Chase has become greedy over the years," Loring explained, dragging his hand through his thick hair. "His company has grown, but at the expense of others."

"So, you figure Chase is *The Leader?"*

Loring shrugged. "It's possible. They've certainly managed to cut down most everyone in their way. It's known they want control of Echo, and LorTech is one of the few left in their path."

"Making *you* their target now. Right?" Not waiting for an answer, Nick lifted the note for emphasis. "Does *she* know about this?"

"Hell no. And that's the way it stays...at least until I can get her out of here. Knowing Tressa, she would refuse to leave."

Reading the note over again, Nick winced against up-trailing smoke as the cigarette dangled from his mouth. "So, what is it you want from me?"

Jonathan dragged in a deep breath, letting it out slowly. "Nick," he began, "I need you to take Tressa off-planet for me. Surely you know of some place where she will be safe until we find out what the hell this is all about."

One dark brow arched. "Me? I appreciate your confidence, but it's a bit out of my line, wouldn't you say? Sounds like you need a hired gun. Not some randy cargo pilot traipsing all over the galaxy trying to find a safe place to stash—"

"Dammit, Nick, you're a hell of a lot more than just a cargo pilot and we both know it. Besides," he added, "I don't need a hired gun. I'm not asking you to assassinate anyone. All I'm asking is that you get my daughter out of here until I can get to the bottom of this." Loring's voice eased off, betraying the depth of his feelings. "Believe me, if I thought there was anyone else..." He left the sentence hanging.

Nick calmly leaned forward, depositing a lump of ash into the ashtray on Loring's desk. "I'm not sure I'm your man for this, Jon," he said quietly. "Besides, I still have two deliveries yet to make. I can't just take off."

"I understand your position, Nick. Go ahead and make those deliveries. She wouldn't be a problem. I just need her out of here, that's all."

Nick tensed, shifting uncomfortably in the chair. Glancing away, he smiled in polite restraint. "We're talking about a chunk of time here," he said, his eyes cutting back to Loring. "You aware of that?"

Three hellishly long weeks at the least, a silent voice echoed.

A frown creased Loring's brow and his gaze darkened as he slowly rose and moved from behind his desk. There was no misreading the grim look on his face as he came around to settle hip-shot upon the front corner of his desk. "Make no mistake," he began slowly, his tone laden with warning. "I know full well what I'm asking of you. Just as you do."

Loring's grave expression eased. "Besides, you seem to forget, I've always seen more in you than you see in yourself. If I didn't, believe me, I'd never entrust Tressie into your care for a single minute."

Deep in thought for a long span of silence Nick stared at the smoke curling up from his cigarette.

"Dammit, Nick, this is my daughter!"

"And I'm telling you, you've got the wrong man." With his beautiful daughter, Loring didn't know how wrong.

"But you're the only one I trust. I know what you're thinking," he added, "and it might help to know that she's already spoken for."

Nick's eyes lifted to meet Loring's. "Oh yeah? Anyone I know?"

"He's new around here. Name's Sinclair. Look, I'm not saying it would be easy. You'll need to let her know who's boss right from the start. After that, she'll settle right in for you.

"Oh, and those rumors you may have heard," he added, "Tressa has not inherited her mother's gift. Thank God."

Nick shot him a puzzled look but said nothing. It had been eight years since he had first walked through the doors of LorTech Equipment. Tressa was just a kid then. With her off to boarding school most of the time, their initial introduction had never progressed much beyond a nodding acquaintance. It had only been in the last six months that he remembered seeing more of her around the complex. She had definitely grown up. And along with it, her personality had changed from giggly to politely aloof.

He had heard of Jonathan's desire for Tressa to work at his side, so whether her aloof indifference was due to shyness, conceit or professionalism, it was hard to tell. At any rate, he had never lost any sleep over it. Spoken for or not, she was *Loring's daughter* and *that* made her off limits under all circumstances—even if he was interested. Which he wasn't.

Now here he was, doomed to baby-sit this spoiled, liberated woman/child for however long it took. Worse yet, he would have to still be on speaking terms with her by the time they arrived at their destination—wherever the hell that was.

"Well?" Jonathan asked with an edge of desperation.

Doubt laced with irritation coursed through Nick. Leaning back, he unconsciously studied Loring, wishing like hell he could come up with some alternative. At last, he released a compressed sigh. "So, when do we leave?"

Relief flooded Loring's face. "You'll do it then?"

"Under the circumstances I don't have a hell of a choice. I'll take her to Acacia. It's roughly a three-week flight from here. That should buy you a little time. Delta will enjoy the company, and after I see Tressa safe, I'll do what I can to help."

"I'm thinking that it might not hurt for you to stay off-planet for a while yourself. If that electro blade had gone much deeper..."

Nick's entire left side still ached, a pain he had successfully been ignoring until Jon brought up the subject. For a brief moment he reflected on the night he'd been attacked. *He had just finished loading a shipment into the hold. Turning to key-in the security, he had detected movement in the shadows and a glint off something metallic. He vaguely remembered whirling to ward off the attack, but too late to evade the thrust. Gut-wrenching pain began in his lower back and ripped up his side as he went down.* In that clouded moment, he had recognized one man: his ex-partner, Quint Kendyl.

The pain kept him semiconscious as he lay face down on the scarred surface of the landing zone. And although he had been unable to distinguish little more than the grating edge of voices, there was no doubting the distinctive boots of the man who stood before him. "Kendyl" was the last thought that registered as he slipped into unconsciousness.

"Are you listening to what I'm saying?" Loring broke in.

Without comment Nick leaned forward to deposit another lump of ash into the ashtray.

"I was saying...that if—"

"Yeah, I heard you," Nick mumbled. "I'll deal with it in my own way, Jon. I won't hide, if that's what you're suggesting."

Silence passed as Nick contemplated the plan. "I'm going to be up-front with you. No matter how careful we are, there's no guarantee that Acacia's going to be a safe haven. It's not common knowledge I'm from Acacia, but if someone gets to nosing around, it's on the security records. You have no way of knowing how big this operation is."

"I'm aware of that." Jonathan relaxed. "Look, I know this won't be easy, but I'll see to it you won't regret it. I assure you there will be a double bonus in it for you." A smile tipped the corners of his mouth. "I'll even double your high-risk credits on this one."

"I'm not doing it for the bonus, Jon. Besides, you couldn't afford me even if I were. And as far as regret is concerned," he grimly added, "I started *regretting,* the instant I heard Garrett's voice." He fought down the mental image of Gina.

Ignoring Nick's cynicism, Jonathan continued, "Now I figure if you come back to the place with me, we can work out the details on the way. Then we can bring Tressie on back with us. Besides, I know Mary's going to want to meet you. Hell, she'll probably want to speak privately with you."

Great. Nick nearly groaned aloud "That ought to be real interesting. I just got into port, Jon. Look at me. I'm not only beat, I'm half-crocked."

Questioning his own sanity, Nick rubbed the back of his neck and tried to sort through his feelings. Having hit port three hours ago from a five-week run, he had spent the first hour and a half overseeing, as well as assisting in the unloading of cargo off his ship. He was tired, and the way he figured it, by now he should have been well on his way to getting drunk, counting his winnings and getting laid, in roughly that order.

Though past experience had taught Loring that Nick Banner was a man of his word, he looked at him for the first time since Nick had entered his office. Unshaven; worn leathers; his hair in serious need of a cut; he grimly admitted that Nick Banner looked every bit the rogue. Jonathan was certain Mary would not approve of Tressa leaving with him. In fact, he was tempted to question the wisdom of the plan himself.

Nick's eyebrow arched knowingly. "Second thoughts, Jon?"

"I haven't got time for second thoughts! I'll go on back and square things away at home. You, on the other hand, have exactly two hours to make yourself presentable. We'll meet you back at the *Victorious* at that time."

Swinging his feet down, Nick stood, crushed out his cigarette and turned for the door. "You're the *only* one I'd do this for," he said, pausing briefly at the threshold.

"Yes, I realize I've called in my markers on this one, Nick."

"Damn right you have."

www.ingramcontent.com/pod-product-compliance
Lightning Source LLC
Chambersburg PA
CBHW051428170626
46809CB00006B/2364
* 9 7 8 1 6 2 4 2 0 7 6 3 1 *